# Murder By Dental Floss

# LISBETH GLUMM

# MURDER BY DENTAL FLOSS

## WHO KILLED DR. WANG?

2008

# Murder By Dental Floss

*Dedicated To Brett And Brooke.*
*Love You, Tons And Tons, Mom*

# CHAPTER ONE
## Friends Forever

It was late August and a perfect star-filled night for the five women friends to sit back and enjoy the magnificent view of Lake Michigan. Lindsey, Julia, Heather and Traci were seated in stylish, comfortable chairs out on Lindsey's terrace talking away and enjoying the scenery when the last of their little group arrived. "Hi!" Brooke practically ran out onto the terrace of Lindsey's house.

She had let herself in, opened the doors to the terrace and headed straight to the bar to fix herself a drink. Brooke, late as usual, had a huge smile on her face as if she didn't have a care in the world. Her long brown hair was flowing and a breeze gently lifted her hair from her face, creating an illusion of a runway model on a photo shoot. Brooke was a person who drew people in like a swimming pool, or a beach on a hot 90-degree day. She had style and beauty and was also brilliant, caring, rich and determined.

Brooke was an optometrist who ran her own business; she had co-authored several books and was published in medical journals. Brooke was also the fashionista of the women's weekly 'Cheese, Crackers and Wine' evenings. Brooke had an inside track to the art of fashion; her mother was a famous model and her father ran a multi-million dollar furniture business. She was born with color samples in her right hand and a pattern in her left.

Brooke knew she looked great in the outfit she carefully picked out for this Wednesday night's get together. It was an Oscar De La Renta short and exquisite silky-white shimmering dress belted at the waist. She wore matching multi-toned white and silver pumps, accessorized with silver-chunk loop earrings and a dashing red patent leather bag purse accented with silver buckles. She knew she had exquisite taste and by now should have qualified to have her own dressing room at Nordstrom's.

Brooke was considered by most people who knew her as a great 'catch' but never had been caught. She never met anyone who she felt could keep up with her, let alone challenge her intellect, so she remained happily, and busily single.

"Glad you made it Brooke, spending more time at the office or goofing off?" Lindsey watched her friend fix a vodka tonic, and couldn't resist giving her friend some sarcastic grief.

Brooke turned to look at her friends, leaned against the outdoor bar, raised her drink and took a sip, "I'm sorry I'm late." With a look at Lindsey and a cocky half-smile Brooke continued. "You know I never goof off, Lindsey. Everything I do is out of necessity." Brooke laughed, "Would you believe I was at the spa. It took me four hours to get my hair done.....a cut, color and an eye brow wax?"

"That was the necessity? That's what made you late?" Lindsey wondered how Brooke fit everything into her schedule. "That is pure fun, and I'm jealous." Lindsey teasingly replied, shaking her head at her friend.

The Milwaukee Spa was a trendy health club overlooking Lake Michigan on the east side of Milwaukee. It was situated in an area where warehouses and run-down factories were being renovated. Several of the downtown warehouses had been renovated into stylish, swanky upscale condos. Other warehouses were renovated into dance clubs, restaurants, shopping boutiques and the Milwaukee Spa.

The views downtown were outstanding and the architecture breathtaking. Multi-million-dollar yachts lined the harbor. On many summer eighty-degree days the women enjoyed sitting outside at the restaurants or spa to take in the spectacular view and enjoy the breeze and people-watch. If they could afford the price, they would have bought a condo as a second home; it was 'the' place to live, to get out and enjoy Milwaukee's night life.

To get a session at the Milwaukee Spa without being a member you had to call and make reservations at least two months in advance, but the wait and the money were worth it. Each room consisted of its own bath and shower, sitting room and heated massage table as well as a great view of the Milwaukee River or Lake Michigan. There was also a spa and pool on the roof, something that only members were allowed to go and use.

Serenity and relaxation were guaranteed and all the women went as often as possible, even if they had to go a week without eating to afford the outrageous prices. There was nothing like it and it rejuvenated their spirit more than anything else. Brooke was a member and if any of the other women's budgets would allow them to, they would have joined in a heartbeat.

Brooke continued to enliven the group with her experience at the spa. She tossed her hair back and gave the ladies a closer look at the procedure by smoothing out her eyebrows and raising them high. "Look at my eyebrows, she did a fabulous job. It didn't hurt at all. My unibrow was taking over my face; I was starting to look like Chewbacca from *Star Wars*. I also had my legs waxed, which is always painful but afterwards I feel five pounds lighter! Have you ever had hair on your calves that

hurt? Mine is so bristly; I could sand down furniture with it."
A roaring-type laugh came out of Brooke as she joked about
her predicament. She looked down at her calves and then at the
rest of the women. Maybe she was self-absorbed but she was
happy and content and enjoyed being around her best friends.
Brooke took another sip of her drink and laughed.

Lindsey was used to Brooke's need to be the center of
attention and her exaggerated stories about herself. "Chewbacca,
from *Star Wars*? I am so sure Brooke; you never could look like
that. Now myself, I love that sleek just-shaved feeling. I feel so
clean." Lindsey lifted up her leg to give the women a peek at
her legs.

Traci declared, "Hello....Chewbacca legs! Lindsey, put
your leg down before a bird thinks it's their nest!" Traci, one of
Lindsey's best friends pointed at a bird close by.

"I know!" Lindsey exclaimed as she let out her own laugh
and pulled her pant leg down again.

Brooke turned to Lindsey, "Lindsey, go to the spa. The
pain is worth it; just get a massage afterwards like I do. Try to
get Randy; he's terrific; I could feel my tension fade away while
his hands were kneading my back. He's nothing to sneeze at
either. He looks like a young Val Kilmer in *Tombstone*,.......
before he got TB of course!"

Brooke laughed at her own joke again, and then continued
in a conspiratorial voice telling the women the rest of her story,
"As I was lying on the massage table I had a wicked dream;
Randy and I were on a deserted island and sun-bathing. I had a
strawberry daiquiri in one hand and a magazine in the other. Val
aka Randy was standing behind me massaging my shoulders. It
felt so great, I didn't want to open up my eyes, I was so relaxed.
But somehow, at the end of my massage, I managed to slowly

open my eyes. And when I saw Randy I was really disappointed. He was still cute but way too young for me, there went my dream. Poof, there's no way I could date him."

All the women were used to Brooke's pickiness in men and her non-existent love life. In her defense it was hard being single and going on endless dates that didn't work out. Dates where time stood still but you couldn't wait for the date to end.

Lindsey listened to Brooke's story and eyed her friend before letting her know how she felt, "Brooke, I don't have the luxury to go to the spa for everything I'd like to have done. But I do think you should give Randy a chance. There's always something wrong with any man you meet! You're never going to find the 'right man'; you lost your perfect guy in ninth grade."

Lindsey and Brooke had known each other since seventh grade and Brooke had been in love with the star quarterback in high school, Todd Young. They were the 'it' couple in high school. They dated for three years and then broke up during college. Sometimes Brooke would mention him but he was contentedly married and had a family.

Brooke groaned, "I can't help it, there's nobody out there!" Brooke's arm made a huge sweep as if circling the entire world. The rest of the women nodded and murmured 'yes' and 'we know', acknowledging their friend's plight. Brooke walked over and joined the rest of the women sitting around the table.

Lindsey laughed; she hadn't had much luck in the dating scene either. She had men who were friends, but it never led to anything. Lindsey looked around at her best friends and was thankful that she had them. It would be nice to be in a romantic relationship with someone but she hated dating, dinner after dinner, interview after interview, it seemed like a waste of time.

Lindsey brushed her shoulder-length, bleached blond hair off her face and tucked it behind her ear, with a smile at her friends, she said, "As a matter of fact Brooke, I was just at the Milwaukee Spa yesterday and had a steam and body wrap in the Thermal suite. It didn't do anything for my hair problem but it made me feel a couple pounds lighter. I splurged; my real estate business isn't doing too awful even in this slow market. I should have had some hair removed too, but ouch! That always hurts so much." Lindsey looked at Brooke and Brooke rolled her eyes at Lindsey.

Lindsey ignored Brooke and continued, "I love how they treat you like a queen; I could live there. But alas, my work awaits me and of course I have to take care of 'Monkey One and Monkey Two'." Lindsey pointed to the living room where her kids were hard at work watching TV. The other women nodded their heads knowing how much time and work children were.

Lindsey leaned forward in her chair and grabbed a piece of cheese from the plate situated in the middle of the table. "Anyway, back to my spa experience, it was great to escape reality for a tiny little bit at the spa. After my body wrap I ate at the new restaurant, 'The Bistro'. The restaurant is attached to the club near the south side of the building; it only opened a week ago." She swallowed the piece of cheese and then continued, "I love how they decorated it. I wouldn't choose it for my own house but it was cool to eat there. It has a French flair with swirly chairs and velvet backs. They have round café tables with attractive candles in the center and a small crystal chandelier over every table holding more candles. It's so romantic and 'old world' feeling. The surroundings made the food taste even better than it already was. I love any place that has a view too, we watched the yachts go bye while we ate. I had a light lunch with the freshest fruit and homemade bread, you could see the steam come out of the bread when you broke it, then a pat of butter on it, mmmmm I can still taste it. You can't beat the service either; I think we had the waiter all to ourselves."

"What do you mean 'we'? I thought you went by yourself?" Brooke asked coyly.

"No, I met John down there so we could talk about the kids. I would have only eaten lunch with a diet coke but John ordered a bottle of vintage Merlo, imported from northern France. I have no idea how much that set John back, I was afraid to look at the bill and I didn't ask him how much it was, but he and I did share the bottle; I can't remember the brand. I'll have to find out when I go back." Lindsey said this as an afterthought and then she shrugged her shoulders, "I'm not an expert on wine but with each sip it became more flavorful. There wasn't any of that bitter after-taste, just a smooth solid taste. That man, he only accepts the finest things in life. I guess that's why he married me and we have two perfect kids." Lindsey made a "ha ha" noise to go along with that comment.

The women chuckled with Lindsey and then Lindsey continued. "Yea, I know how that story ended. We had fun eating lunch together, even though he is my ex-husband. They also asked me for my ID. I wonder how old they thought I was? Twenty maybe?" Lindsey twirled her hair and raised her eyes up giving her an immediate face lift.

"Aren't you a little full of yourself tonight, Lindsey?" Julia commented playfully.

Lindsey leaned in and waved her hair again before replying. "This is a tough crowd. It really happened, what can I say?

I'm sure it was the lighting, but it was good for my ego." She smiled a cheerful, happy girl-next-door smile.

After a slight hesitation, she continued in a more serious tone, "It just so happened that I couldn't find my license. I hope I find it because I hate going down to the DMV. It's a loony bin down there. It's like once you walk in your transformed from a normal looking person into a side-show freak exhibit. It must be the lights, or something in the air. What bugs me even more is that when I do get up for my turn I usually don't have the right paper work or money. I hate it."

Julia jumped in with her similar experience, "I know what you mean, that happened to me at the post office. I waited in line, finally got up to the counter to get a package and the mail person wasn't back with my package! I was too early; I couldn't get it. I was so mad because that meant I would have to go down there again the next day."

As usual all the women had stories to tell on different subjects and experiences that had happened to them during the week. Sometimes they would start talking at the same time.

Brooke added her experience. She half smiled, grabbed a slice of cheese and talked while she chewed, "That's why we need the spa. There are too many un-fun things to do. When I'm at the DMV or post-office, people always talk to me when I'm in line; they think they know me or something because we're in line together for the same purpose. Or maybe they're just that bored. Oh, and halfway through the line I have to go to the bathroom. I'm miserable and I can't leave my spot."

Lindsey could relate to that, "I know! That happens to me too." Lindsey took a sip of wine and continued. "I hope my license pops up, because I don't want to apply for a new one, but more importantly it's disturbing not knowing where I could have left it. I feel like I'm going crazy, there's too much to do all the time and it's hard to keep up. With my luck, I'll have my identity stolen." The rest of the women contemplated what Lindsey was saying and they all remained silent.

*Little did Lindsey know how crazy her life was to become. Soon violence would explode on her existence, making the memory of her time with John at the Milwaukee Spa as a time when she was relaxed, happy and life was simple.*

*Soon a never ending downward spiral of fear and horror would circle Lindsey and interfere with the calm and peace she had come to expect in her life. Like the weather dropping 40 degrees in a blink of an eye so would her life change from care-free and happy to sadness and fear. She could only pray that somehow the circle of danger and fear that would soon be a part of her life would break and she could escape back to her serene life.*

The light cool breeze outside caught the wind chimes of a neighbor, making an eerie far off noise and signaling the beginning of fall. Heather, Julia, Brooke, Traci and Lindsey were sitting outside on the terrace of Lindsey's hillside villa overlooking Lake Michigan. The terrace was part of Lindsey's opulent lake front home sitting on top of a bluff with pine, maple and elm trees on either side of the yard.

The trees created a wall of privacy on each side of Lindsey's property. Lindsey's terrace was made from old-world cobblestones set in a rectangular pattern, with elegant furniture and potted plants on the outer perimeter of the terrace; it made the perfect outdoor oasis for the women.

Lindsey had added style to it with handmade wrought-iron furnishings. Each chair had orange, plush, thick-tailored cushions and matching pillows. A low wrought-iron table with a center fireplace helped to heat up the cool Wisconsin evenings and create a warm, cozy atmosphere. Two matching chase lounges completed the furniture ensemble and was used often for sun-bathing and reading a novel.

Surrounding the terrace were oversized ceramic potted plants with flowing flowers and elegant greenery. Past the potted plants was a rectangular pool and after the pool a lush green lawn leading to the edge of a bluff; the drop was 100 feet down to the water's edge. It had made Lindsey jumpy and nervous to have a steep drop so she had erected a three foot wooden picket fence at the end of the grassy lawn to deter any kids, young or old, from getting too near the bluff's edge.

The terrace, tall trees on the side of the lawn, rectangular pool, flowers, and expanse of green lawn overlooking the lake stimulated all the senses. Comfortable and elegant, it was the perfect meeting place for the five women.

From the terrace Lindsey looked into the wall of windows framing the family room where inside, Lilly and Leo were watching TV. Luckily they couldn't hear the women's conversation. The kids had grown accustomed to the women's loud laughter and screams coming from the terrace during their gab sessions. Inevitably they would put their two cents in sometime during the night, but for right now, the ladies' night and secrets were exclusively theirs and the children were happy in their own sheltered world of Disney Channel Television.

Lindsey and her two children had moved to the home after her divorce, six years ago. She and her ex-husband had invested wisely in the tech stocks of the early 90's and cashed in before the crash after 911. Lindsey promptly put her half of the money in real estate and never regretted it. It helped that Lindsey had received her real estate license and got an outstanding deal on the property. Lindsey had to do a lot of work to the fixer upper on Lake Drive, but the view was worth all the blood, sweat and bruises.

She valued the freedom she had gained after the divorce. Her life was again her own, out of the control of her domineering ex-husband. He was a vibrant, intense, and highly intelligent man. When she first met him it felt like she was flying on a balloon that took her to heights she hadn't thought she could get to.

Lindsey had reservations about her ex's self-centered personality but she discounted the bad, focused on the good and ignored her intuition. Barreling ahead she married the charismatic charmer and discovered that marriage was a one way street, with John doing all of the driving. Heaven help her if she gave any directions or questioned the wisdom of his ways. He was always right and if he wasn't right it was her fault. All the red flags that she should have listened to came back to haunt her. The echoes of those thoughts were stifled for ten years while she concentrated on the positives of her marriage and put up with the negatives.

Her marriage had been a thrill ride at times, exciting and enjoyable. However, once Leo and Lilly were born her black thoughts about John overshadowed the bright and couldn't go unnoticed. John had too many different ideologies about what was important and how to raise their children.

Lindsey's thoughts became so loud that she started confronting John on the wisdom of his choices which only made him more determined to have his own way. Lindsey felt like she was walking on a tightrope ten feet high, and couldn't get off. After going to counseling and trying to work on their marriage they decided the best thing for them and the children would be to get divorced. The very ambition, drive and aggressiveness that had first attracted Lindsey to John was the main reason why they decided to part ways and live separate lives on their own terms.

John was a successful entrepreneur, with an internet business, a thriving dental practice and several real estate holdings. Their divorce was amicable and now they enjoyed each other idiosyncrasies. They were friends and decided to put their past behind them so that they could concentrate on their future successes and the success of their two wonderful children.

As the women looked out that evening the view was tranquil and unsettling at the same time. Sailboats dotted the marina, looking tiny in the vast pool of water. Off in the distance there were pastel stripes high in the sky that looked like they were painted with water colors, in contrast was the bold solid color of the round sun. Once a week the women enjoyed sipping on wine, mixed drinks and eating from a tray of cheese and crackers. It was a welcome and relaxing part of their stress filled lives. This was their one night a week of pure solace and comfort, and fun. They relied on each other to lend an ear and their heart. They were true friends.

Traci's personality was a combination of free spiritedness with a pinch of predictability and punctuality. She was brilliant and quirky and looked at life with the eyes of a comedian. Tall and lean with sandy, brown shoulder length hair and blue eyes, Traci had a timeless, classic quality about her. Everyone enjoyed her company, laughed with her and wondered what her next move would be.

Her careers encompassed a stint as a photographer, dental hygienist, mortgage broker, lifeguard and wellness coach. Traci had a quirky smile when she talked and was too quick to tell the truth. She loved flirting with ideas as well as men. She was open to new ideas and loved not being afraid to experience whatever or whoever it was to experience.

She moved to Wisconsin her junior year in high school and quickly fit in with the four other women. They were friends since and vowed in their youth to be friends forever. The women had helped Traci recover from a messy divorce from her philandering husband. It was all five of them that went to the hospital to get the results of her AIDS test. A collective sigh of relief was emitted as the result turned out to be negative.

It was just like her ex-husband to make innuendos intended to put fear and panic into Traci's life. Traci's two sons were now 18 and 22. The boys were just as gregarious as their father and were pursuing degrees in business, intending on joining their father in his landscaping business after college. The easy conversation continued as each one shared their experiences of the past week.

Traci lamented in her usual serious but jocular way, "You feel crazy for losing your license, and I feel crazy in general. Last night I was cleaning up the dishes after Ben and John left and thoughts kept on circling in my head. I feel like I'm on a gerbil wheel. Someday I might find something to stick to longer than a year. I must have severe ADD. I can't settle on one thought, one man, one choice of an entree at a restaurant. I can't even decide if I want the chicken or the beef, or for that matter the pasta!"

We listened to Traci lament about what career to make, where to live, her boys and her romances every week. And every week she had a new crazy idea. "I'm not sure if I like my current job as a wellness coach, and I can't remember the last time I went out with a member of the male species."

Traci continued, "After Mark left me and then Scott, I'm at a standstill. None of the men I've been with want to have a loving, committed relationship. I've about had it with all of them." Traci switched gears again, "Maybe I should try party planning. I saw an ad for running your own party planning company. It sounded exciting; lately all the excitement that I've had entails eating a jar of hot Jalapenos and watching a lifetime movie."

Brooke winked, "Sounds hot!"

Traci agreed and disagreed, "It was, but not in the way I want it to be! I want hot, steamy hot, like you see in the movies. I want one relationship with a guy who treats me with respect, and is romantic too. Does anyone really have that? I saw this great guy at the park when I was walking Toto. He had a little bulldog that sniffed all over Toto. So I gave him my shoulder shrug with the 'what can we do look' and my Cheshire cat smile. You know......hoping to start up a conversation! And nothing! He looked right through me and nearly bumped me over to get to his dumb dog. Am I losing it? I've always been able to start up conversations with anyone. I felt invisible and the worst part was he wasn't even that cute."

Julia was the most level headed of the group, emitting organization and strength. Her personality matched her curly brown hair with blond highlights, sparkly brown eyes and a smile accompanied with cute dimples. Julia could whip up a dinner, keep her house clean, look put together in coordinated outfits, sit on the board of two charities, and still have time to be an extraordinary friend.

Julia and Lindsey had known each other since seventh

grade, when they both were enrolled in summer track. A passion for running the 400 made them fast friends. The competition among them was still alive and oscillated like the needle measuring earth's movement. At times there was little activity, but other times it measured 8.1 on the Richter scale. Yet their friendship was solid and the competition fueled both their desires to succeed. Julia was a social worker, helping elderly individuals get any services that they needed to stay healthy and independent.

Julia quickly chimed in and commiserated with Tracy's predicament, "Men are difficult! I was home last night doing laundry and was livid at Charlie. He can be such a dreary asshole, slumping around the house and moping. Once a month he acts like a real prick. I can't take it anymore. I think I'm better off alone and then when I'm by myself at home, doing laundry or whatever, I'm freaking out because I am alone. At this point I don't think men are even worth the effort."

"I know," Traci nodded her head and agreed. "We've got to come up with some excitement, ladies, without involving men in any way. Men are getting old....figuratively and literally, if you know what I mean." She raised her cup, "And of course, we're perfect!"

They all laughed at that and Lindsey raised her glass, "Cheers to us."

They drank more and after Julia took a sip of her drink she added, "I'm glad I didn't move in with Charlie, he leaves all his shit around my home, including clumps of hair in the drain. I can't imagine living with that 24/7. I'm this close to getting rid of him." Julia held up her fingers showing a little bit of space between her thumb and index finger.

Lindsey didn't have much respect for Charlie, he was so

generic. He might have been good looking back in the day but that day was long gone and Charlie hadn't realized it yet. He was pudgy and pale with eyes that looked perpetually glazed over. His hair was patchy at best, thin and greasy. Charlie didn't have any flare or style. He was one of those guys who existed with the belief that because he peed standing up everyone should applaud; it was such a proud moment. He lacked any ambition or drive and we couldn't figure out why Julia put up with him. He was a complete idiot who seemed to drag everyone around him down.

Charlie was a schemer and sold insurance when he felt like it. What he really liked to do was play golf and bet on each hole. We all thought he should have been a mole or a badger, and stay hidden underground. For some reason, Julia continued dating Charlie, all the while complaining how she couldn't stand him; the list was a mile long by now.

Traci couldn't resist and poked more fun at the men they had encountered, "What are we looking at? Aging bald men with big pot bellies that look like they are ready to explode, oh joy!!!"

Laughter rang out as they sipped more wine, ate more, and enjoyed the camaraderie of each others' stories. Traci couldn't resist and added, "Oh come on, men who are past forty try harder, a smile and then a shrug......at getting hard that is." They laughed again.

Traci commented, "Ok, that's a bit harsh."

Julia responded, "But it's true. That's why they have all of those nifty drugs for men." Julia always surprised everyone with her take on life. She always seemed so serious but below the surface a bit of foolery was always brewing.

Traci contemplated relationships, seriously she said, "Come

on you guys, you never know when that right guy will show up. There are a lot of men, young or old, who are very nice and caring." With a glance over at Heather and in a tipsy voice Traci added, "I think we should clone Brett."

Heather's husband was tall, had sandy blond hair and bluish grey eyes that sparkled when he grinned. He was a playful dad and made sure that everyone around him was cared for. Brett had a great sense of humor and seemed genuinely excited about everything. It didn't hurt that he was a great skier and gourmet cook too. Brett's personality made him enticingly attractive.

Heather flashed her perfect smile, "I know, how did I get so lucky? He's always listening to me, even when I ramble. We laugh all the time and our friendship keeps getting stronger and stronger. It's like every day, or every month at the very least, we learn something new about each other. It never gets boring or old. Our relationship keeps getting more comfortable and he can comfort me like I never thought anyone could."

Traci joked, "Okay, now I'm more jealous then I was before!" Traci said this as she held up her wine glass and took a large gulp. She finished the last drop and in a free-spirited, happy voice and a smile she said, "Hand over that bottle of wine, I think I could use some more."

Heather was the bookworm of the group. She was 5'6, blond, had hazel eyes and was incredibly athletic, making it easy for her to keep up with her ski-aholic husband. Working as a nursing assistant at night she took care of people all the time. If she wasn't working or taking care of her family she was reading a romance novel. Her one passion was her family. She loved to stay home with her husband and daughter, Isabella.

Isabella was only one and a dream come true for Brett and Heather. They had had a difficult time conceiving; Heather had three miscarriages and then finally after a lot of money and time, Isabella was born. It was all the women could do to pry Heather away from Isabella and Brett for their once a week get-togethers, to drink and eat, and most of all connect with each other.

Heather would never leave Waukesha, a town she called home for 39 years. The women had all gone to High School there and most of their parents still lived in Waukesha. Waukesha was home to Heather's 3 brothers and 2 sisters and both parents. If Heather and Brett were entertaining or socializing it entailed their ever growing extended family.

Heather met Brett on a lake bar in Pewaukee 20 years ago and that was that. There was a spark between them that if it was harnessed could light up a Christmas tree all winter. Brett did concrete work for the Camdon Home construction company, but chose to think of himself as a ski bum; tanned, firm, fun, but also filled with common sense. They had a remarkably happy marriage, and listened to each others' needs while maintaining their individuality.

Out through the French doors came Lilly, "Mom," Lilly yelled. "Look what I can do. I can carry things in my toes." Lilly demonstrated to the women how she could curl her toes around a water bottle cap and carry it across the terrace.

"Wow, Lilly, you are so talented. You should petition the Olympics for a new category of sport." Lindsey responded to Lilly's feat with enthusiasm in her voice.

"Really? Okay, I think I will." Lilly replied and delivered a big, toothy grin.

Lindsey asked, "Lil, could you go into the kitchen and get us some chips and salsa, we're all out of cheese and crackers."

"I thought you only ate cheese and crackers and drank

wine on the nights your friends came over." Lilly said in an all-knowing nine-year-old voice.

"Just get the snacks, Lilly." In a sidebar to the women Lindsey confided, "Kids can be so frustrating. Why can't she listen and respond exactly how I want her to? It's a simple request." And then back to Lilly, "Now tell me; Where is the capitol of Wisconsin?"

Lilly replied in an annoyed voice with her hand on her hip, "Madison mom."

"Good answer, Lil, now could you bring us the chips and salsa? I'll give you something if you do?" Lindsey winked at the women.

"Forget it mom, I know all your tricks and I don't want a pinch or a squeeze."

"Ok, suit yourself, Lil."

Lilly turned around to go back inside the French glass doors to the family room hopping on one foot with the bottle cap in her foot and screamed to Leo, "Leo, mom wants you go bring her out some chips and salsa."

The women sat in silence watching the children and enjoying the peaceful, calm night. Several minutes later, Leo came out carrying a bowl of chips with some salsa. "Thanks Leo." The women all smiled.

Leo was 11 with curly brown hair and big brown eyes. "Umm, hello everyone," he murmured politely. He grinned shyly and handed the food over, before bolting back into the family room.

The five women continued their evening, laughing and drinking. The sun had set and by the end of their night a cool breeze was coming off the lake and was getting stronger. As they finished their last sip of their drinks and wine, and the last nibble of chips and salsa, storm clouds were rolling in from the west and the first rumbling of thunder could be heard.

## CHAPTER TWO
### Lunch Date at the Mall

Lindsey hustled and bustled Leo and Lilly into her silver-grey, Lexus Hybrid SUV. Yesterday the children's summer fun ended; Leo would be starting fifth grade and Lilly would be starting fourth. It was the first day of school and both kids were bursting with excitement and anticipation to see their old friends, sit in their assigned desks and start learning the routine of their school day.

The children had been shopping for their school supplies for weeks. They wanted to pick out new backpacks, new clothes, and personalized notebooks. Lilly was fascinated with kittens and Leo wanted notebooks that were green or tan camouflage colored.

The first day of school was a beautiful, sun-drenched day. Out on the playground the children were buzzing around, playing kickball, or tossing a football around and some were hugging each other in greeting. The parents were milling about, taking pictures, catching up with each other, and observing who their children were playing with.

Lindsey was fortunate that the schools were among the best in the country, which didn't come as much of a surprise for any of the families whose children attended the public school. Among the parents were doctors, lawyers, owners of large and small businesses, political analysts and other professionals that reined in large annual incomes. As Lindsey looked around she couldn't help but feel overwhelmingly fortunate. John had been so ambitious and she had been wise in her choice of investments enabling their children to live a privileged life. She wondered if Leo and Lilly knew how fortunate they were to be surrounded with so much luxury, safety and an education at schools that were some of the best in the state.

The bell rang and masses of children ran to line up in front of their teachers, ready to begin their day. With one last look and a wave, her kids began the school year and Lindsey set off for home to begin her day as a real estate agent. She had to follow up on several leads before meeting Brooke, Julia and Traci at the mall for a quick lunch.

"Hey everyone." a big smile and Brooke was sliding into the booth with the rest of the women. "Did you all order yet? I'm sorry I'm late.....again. Sometimes the patients get super chatty. Talk,talk,talk,talk, talk...that's all they do."

Lindsey smiled at Brooke, "You should put up a sign-Optometrist/Therapist. Here, I ordered you some coffee." Lindsey pointed to the cup and carafe of coffee waiting for Brooke as she settled in to talk with the other women.

"Oh, thanks, just what I need, a volt of energy. We're actually thinking of hiring another optometrist to handle our overload of patients. My practice is getting too big and I can't keep up. That's a good sign but there's always some trepidation adding on another person to our staff. You never know how the dynamics of the office might change."

Brooke had the ability to multitask, take on a lot of responsibility and still be fun. She bounced back further into the booth talking as she grabbed the sugar for her coffee, then looked up at the other women shaking her head and lamenting on her predicament, "I need some free time too, shopping time and dancing time!" She swirled the coffee and sugar with her spoon.

The other women sat and waited for Brooke to speak. She was on a high buzz and when she was like this she needed to talk. "We might hire someone who specifically deals with children to get a leg up on the competition. There are only a few optometrists who specialize in young children and their specific needs."

Brooke took a sip of her coffee and added more sugar and cream and smiled. "At least our practice in the mall helps me with my time management; I can shop, mall-walk and eat lunch with my best friends. I thought that my practice would be successful but I never knew how much fun success is. It makes me feel like I want more!" She smiled to her friends thinking of how they were friends since seventh grade and how they were here now, friends forever.

The booth the ladies sat in at the 'Café de la Italia' was well lit by the bright windows and ambient lighting. The restaurant was attached to the sprawling upscale mall in a western suburb of Milwaukee. The restaurant provided the women with a warm and friendly atmosphere where the friends could eat leisurely on mouth-watering Italian cuisine and talk.

The women frequently ate at the restaurant so Brooke could be included in their plans and after eating it was almost always necessary to shop at the many stores included in the mall. They frequently made purchases at Nordstrom's, Macy's and Neiman Marcus, got coffee at Starbucks or browsed through Crate and Barrel and Tiffanies, just for the fun of it.

Heather couldn't make it that particular day because she was taking Isabella to the zoo with her playgroup. Lindsey looked at her best friend and was happy her practice was doing so well. Some days Brooke looked stressed out, but today she was upbeat and satisfied with her day.

Lindsey brightly said, "Isn't it great that we are all finding our niche in the workforce?" Lindsey sipped some coffee and glanced around the table at her friends.

Julia put down her menu and looked up at the women, before smiling and said, "Exactly! It's about time too. I mean, we're old."

Traci made a quick reply, "Speak for yourself, Julia. I'm only 30-something, and I still feel like I'm in my 20's."

"Yea, 30 + 10 Traci, but they do say 40 now is the same as being 30." Lindsey said congenially.

Traci replied, somewhat dejectedly, "Yeah, I know. How does time go by so fast? Doesn't it seem like we were in high school yesterday? I wish I was a bit younger." Traci added some cream to her coffee and stirred the coffee with a spoon.

Lindsey agreed, "It does seem like yesterday, and now we have so much more responsibility. Who knew back then how easy we had it?"

Lindsey wanted to share her news and added excitedly, "Speaking of responsibility, today I met with two sellers and a buyer!" Lindsey paused and then continued, "I signed up three new clients and am putting their houses on the market within the next week. Huge homes in the Whitefish Bay area. I can't wait for the commission! These homes are going to sell fast."

Whitefish Bay was a suburb North of Milwaukee with beautiful old, elegant homes set on large lots and charming streets. Lindsey added, "Pretty soon I'll need a secretary, a cleaning man, a chauffeur and errand runner. I can't keep up, and I love it!"

Brooke gave Lindsey some upbeat praise. "Way to go Lindsey, who knew you'd be selling real estate and making a fortune?"

Lindsey was feeling pretty high, "I know, it's unbelievable, and it's scary how much money you can make. I'm not a millionaire, but the income I'm receiving from the sale of homes isn't too bad. Knock on wood. I don't want my business to slow down." After that comment, they all knocked on the table top just to make sure things would remain on track.

Tracy wiped her mouth with a napkin after finishing several bites of her soft garlic bread and said, "I only wish I could one up both of you! You two have got it made. Have you been giving my card to your new patients and clients? I've got 15 clients so far but could add some more." Traci looked at all of her friends excitedly.

Brooke commented, "Only fifteen clients? You just started that business. How did you get those clients already? That's really impressive." Brooke was looking at the menu as she was asking about Traci's business.

Traci replied, "Oh, I have my ways. I put up several fliers at schools for 'bored' moms and at the local health clubs. Then I wait for the calls. As soon as they call I offer to buy the caller a coffee while we talk about what they need and what I can do for them. I've met so many people. I didn't know that this would be something I would actually enjoy. It's not too hard. I went on-line and printed a survey that helps identify a person's weaknesses and strengths. I have the clients fill it out and we talk about goal setting. I really lucked out because I had a lot of connections from the kid's school and the gym I worked at. But I know myself, and hope I don't lose interest after a few months."

Traci went back to dipping a piece of bread in olive oil and balsamic vinegar, she took a bite, finished chewing and then taking time to think about her job continued, "This job is turning out to be a real trip though, so far so good, for a job that is. I hate working but I guess I have to do something. My clients have such flamboyant personalities, sometimes it's all I can do to not get silly and laugh at their so called 'problems'."

Traci made quotation marks in the air as she said problems. "They have plenty of money, and most of them want my reassurance that they're doing everything 'right' in their lives, most need to get organized. I'm amazed at how 'messy' their lives are."

At that moment they were interrupted by a young smiling waitress who took their lunch orders. As soon as she walked away Traci continued. "Anyway, I need more clients, which means more money and the only way I'm going to do that is add to my list. So if you know anyone who might need and want some organization and help smoothing out their lives, let me know. I'm just the person to help them, to UN mass their problems, and some of their money too! Have you seen the prices on the new fall lines at Nordstrom's? I'm going to have to learn how to sew to keep up with the new trends and styles."

She raised her eyebrows and looked at Julia, "You're going to have to teach me how to sew! What kind of a wellness coach wears old, ratty, outfits from last season? It's all about 'the impression' with my job. I've got to look the part and act the part." Traci made a sweeping gesture moving her hand from the bottom of her dress to the top. "I found this outfit at Anne Taylor at 60% off."

Traci didn't have anything to worry about; she had a classic timeless look with an air of sophistication and a Reese Witherspoon cuteness about her. Traci had the ability to fit in with anyone and make them feel as if they were the most important person in her world. She livened up discussions and was confident enough to try new things.

Traci loved wearing classic dresses, low pumps and minimal jewelry. Her outfit today was an all black short-sleeved rayon dress, with a scoop neckline and a slim white stripe around the neck and hem. Her shoes were black maryjanes with a white button on the strap crossing the top of her feet; she wore a silver charm bracelet with one lone, silver pearl on it, a silver loop pendant necklace, silver octagonal earrings and a black thin strapped shoulder length handbag with a silver clasp on the front. It might not have cost a lot of money, but it looked expensive on Traci.

Lindsey commented on Traci's outfit, "That's the only way to shop. You found a great deal and that outfit makes you look very professional."

Traci accepted the praise graciously, "Thanks Lindsey. I hope so." She turned to look at Julia, "How is your job going, Julia?"

Julia, always quiet and subdued, smiled and nodded her head as she finished chewing on a piece of bread she had been enjoying......after she finished she replied, "It's going pretty well. Sometimes it can be stressful because my clients aren't happy with the services that they are receiving, but for the most part it's rewarding. I have one lady who hides from me when I try to make a home visit. She is one of my hardest cases, but my boss won't give her to anyone else, even though she's requested a new case worker. I think I'm her third case worker though. She suffers from dementia and paranoia, so I try not to take it personally. Some of the other clients are really fun and when I visit they have interesting stories to tell about their lives. It makes me feel worthwhile; lord knows I 'm not getting paid any money for all the work I do. I have to come up with 100 billable hours a month and document everything so that the state knows who to pay and how much."

Julia stopped to take a sip of water and then continued, "The paper work is such a drag, that's the worst part about the job. And speaking of the high prices of outfits, I was looking at the purses and the shoes and having an anxiety attack. I can't afford half a pair of pants, when did everything double in price?" Julia's voice rose as she asked this question.

"As a social worker, I have to dress reasonably nice but even clothes at discount stores are too expensive. I haven't bought any new fun clothes in a long time. Do I really need to take out a second mortgage on my house to get a new fall wardrobe?" Julia looked all around for added emphasis and then answered her own question, "I think I do."

Julia didn't have a lot of money but she was a whiz with a sewing machine and bought a lot of clothes and then altered them to fit her body to a t, which made the outfit look great on her. Julia was tall and thin, and always complaining how her pants were high waters and her skirts were extra miniskirts on her. She had the legs to get away with it though, so none of the friends felt sorry for her. She could make a K-mart frock look like a Vera Wang original.

At that moment the waitress returned with deliciously smelling entrees. Once all the women had their meals and the waitress left, Julia continued. "Brooke, since you're here all the time, you're going to have to canvas the stores for sales. Your office in the mall is such a great setup."

"I know, and when I do get to go out for lunch and search the stores, I'll look for sales and let you know. The only problem working at a mall is buying too much. I don't intend to, it just happens," she waved her hands.

Brooke liked to talk with her hands; fortunately she never bumped the coffee or other items off the table. Brooke was dressed to the nines today. She had on a black and gold Gucci pleated dress with black high heeled pumps, a gold, bangle, chunky bracelet, matching earrings and a Versace black clutch purse, with gold accents. Her outfit alone cost 2300. 00. We all knew she overindulged herself when it came to her clothes, but Brooke could pull it off and not act like she was a beauty queen, and she could afford it so why not? She gave all her 'old' clothes to charity, making sure she would have plenty of room to add her new finds to her closet.

The women were in the midst of eating their lunch and sipping their coffee when they were pleasantly surprised to see John and Dave. Dave was John's partner in their dental practice. The dental practice was situated half a mile from the mall in a quaint cobblestone house converted into a dental office. Other specialty medical professionals such as allergists, urologists, plastic surgeons and nose throat and ear doctors held their practices in nearby office buildings, or had offices on the second floor of the mall. John and Dave were frequent visitors at the mall for lunch and drinks.

"Hi, this is an enjoyable surprise!" John said this with plenty of earnestness and spoke to all of them with his eyes, but his gaze lingered on Lindsey's face a moment longer than the other women's. "This is going to make my job a lot easier. I'm having a party next Saturday night to celebrate my birthday. It'll be a catered event, really fun. I've invited around 250 people; it's going to be huge. I hope all of you can make it; I'll email you an e-vite."

Johnny managed to say all this in the space of two seconds, look at the women, canvass the entire restaurant and check his phone for text messages. He was the ultimate multi-tasker.

Lindsey was the first to respond, "That sounds great, John. I'm sure we'll all be there; I mean you never know if this is going to be your last birthday. We might as well celebrate until the monkeys come home." Lindsey raised her iced water and swilled some back.

John replied, "Well, thanks Lindsey. I think you mean until the cows come home? And thanks for the 'you'll live forever speech' too. You always know the right things to say to make me feel all warm and fuzzy." John grabbed his heart with his hand and grimaced at Lindsey.

Lindsey gave a slow smile, "You know I'm just teasing you John. I'd love to come to your party. And I'm sure it will be one of many more birthday celebrations. Your parties are always enormous hits and by the way, that tie makes you look even more handsome then you usually look."

"Okay, now I'm wondering what you want?" John grinned and bent down to give Lindsey a kiss on the cheek. Their movements were familiar to each other and they still enjoyed bantering back and forth.

Julia spoke up next, "Well John, I think I can make it to the big bash too. It sounds like it will be a smashing party." Julia gave John an alluring look and gave him a cunning smile. It almost looked like she was flirting but the women knew better. Julia was a consummate people pleaser. Lindsey couldn't imagine any of her friends getting it on with John.

It was taboo for any of the friends to go out with any of the other women's ex's. The friends had had more than one opportunity to have sex with the other women's boyfriends, but no man was worth destroying the bond that held their friendships together.

They had giggled about their encounters with the men in their lives, who were always flirting with them and willing to get in bed after a couple of drinks.

Traci smiled, "That sounds like fun, John. Save my favorite seat on your couch for me. I'll be at your shindig to give you a birthday spanking," Traci laughed with a mischievous gleam in her eyes.

"Well, I can't wait for that, Traci!" John kissed Traci on the cheek, ever the debonair man, smiled at her and then looked at his watch.

John was turning 46 and looked better than he had at 25. He had thick dark brown hair, enticing brown eyes and a roman nose with a smile that could melt a tray of ice in .05 seconds.

John looked happy, he looked around at all of the women, "Great, I'll look forward to seeing all of you Saturday night." The hostess appeared and was ready to take John and Dave to their table. John commented, "Our table is ready, so we'll leave your lovely company."

Dave had been drinking in the conservation and politely smiling when appropriate, nodding and laughing along with the group. Dave said, "Bye ladies, enjoy the rest of your day and I'll see you next Saturday night too. I'm looking forward to it." John and Dave left the women to finish their lunch and found a table for two by themselves.

Brooke's eyes were lit up, "How fun is that going to be? Now I have another excuse to go shopping for a party dress. Let me see, should I wear black, go off-white, wear grey, or maybe a dashing red? Regardless of what color, I'm definitely going to wear something with a plunging neckline, subtle necklace, big bangle bracelet and high, high heels."

Brooke finished her linguini and tossed her long, brown hair back and then looked at Lindsey, "What is it with you and John, Lindsey? I see the way he looks at you. He gazes at you in a most 'dearest, sexy' way. Have you two been intimate recently? And no lies, this is us, we want to know."

"What?" Lindsey choked on her vegetarian lasagna before she could reply, "You have got to be kidding. I haven't been with a man since the last star wars movie came out; the only man sleeping with me is my pet cat Merlin. John and I have a great relationship, but we are just friends! We're great parents together and we share our children equally but that's where it stops!"

Lindsey continued speaking emphatically, "We are strictly platonic friends, really good friends. I mean we have two great kids together!" A huge smile appeared on Lindsey's face. Lindsey couldn't help smiling when she thought about her kids.

Brooke looked skeptical, "He's looking really good these days." Brooke had a roll of linguini on her fork pointed in Lindsey's direction and was smiling like she knew something no one else knew.

"We're just friends." Lindsey replied again. "I already know what he's all about. He's so extreme with his business and so head strong about every aspect of his life. That, my friends, is a live and learn situation. I would have never thought that I'd end up divorced with two children and own a real estate business. I would have preferred to have stayed married, but couldn't make it with John. He's too much, too domineering." Lindsey set the record straight.

Julia didn't want to stop the nature of the conversation, always having to repeat or clarify what was being said, "John is a great catch, maybe he's mellowed out some in his old age and isn't so controlling. He's a good man. He's a great dad, if not a total family man, at least he's there for Leo and Lilly. He'd probably want to be with you Lindsey, if you let him"

Lindsey smirked, "Yeah, he's there for Lilly and Leo now, but when we were married it was a different story. He never had time for the kids or me. Now we get along great when it comes to the kids, but that's it. He would like to be with me, but he likes to be with anything that moves; you all know that." Lindsey's tone was subdued.

Lindsey looked at Julia who was starting to look as if she ate something that tasted bad. Julia's face turned pale and she crinkled her brows together and then blubbered. "I broke up with Charlie." The tears started flowing, and all the women tried to comfort Julia.

Lindsey was secretly thinking that it was about time Julia left that bottom-feeding asshole, then handed Julia a tissue and said, "It's hard to end a relationship, but Julia, he drove you crazy. He didn't do anything but irritate you. You cooked, cheered and cleaned for him, and lent him money all the time. That's just wrong. He could be such a creep."

Between sniffles Julia replied in broken words and sentences, "I...know. He was creating...sniff. so much tension.....sniff.....I couldn't stand....sniff....to look....at him....sniff.......anymore. But....sniff....I'm scared.....I'm all alone! Why do men have to be such slobs?" Julia finished with sobs and more tears.

Traci tried to comfort Julia, "Stop it, you are never alone. You have us! We love you. I know it can be lonely without someone to do things with. When Mark ran out on me I was devastated. Hang in there. Some day the right man will come along for each of us. In the meantime who cares if we aren't dating anyone, we can have fun without men. I'm glad you dropped Charlie, he could be such a jerk." Tracy didn't mince words, and then hugged Julia.

Brooke leaned closer to Julia to give her some encouraging words and handed her another tissue, "You deserve much better than him. Remember all the times he went out and didn't even bother to call you and let you know where he was, even though you told him over and over again to call so you wouldn't worry? That was so disrespectful. You'll meet someone better but in the meantime you have us. We love you and we'll keep you busy......and laughing too," Brooke gave Julia another hug.

Julia sniffled, "Thanks you guys. I knew he wasn't the 'perfect' man, but we did have a lot of fun. I've invested three years of my life with him and it's scary letting go. He knows me and I know him. It's hard to find a man who you can lay on the couch with and say nothing, talk every night to and touch with that feeling of romance and compassion."

Julia took a second to catch her breath, "I know he borrowed money all the time and didn't have many social graces; he wasn't like John." Julia looked at Lindsey. "But we had some fun; I hope I did the right thing."

Julia had stopped crying and was dabbing at her eyes. "What am I saying? I couldn't take it anymore. Do you know what he did?"

Julie's voice rose as she remembered the past night and Charlie's insistence that she lend him money. "He actually asked me for five thousand dollars! What a loser. I looked at him hoping he was joking but he wasn't. At that point I just told him to get out, get all of his things and I told him that I hoped I never saw him again. He knows I can't even afford a new pair of boots and he wanted five thousand dollars. He's such a leech. I knew he would never stop asking me for money. He knows I barely have enough to pay my own bills, and there he was asking me for my money. I just snapped and broke up with him. He probably wanted to play more golf, drink more and bet on the holes. What was I doing with him for three years?" Julia relaxed after remembering the previous night and with each sentence she seemed to look more relieved than sad.

After saying what she needed to, she ended up looking more serene and confident then she had in months. It felt good to Julia to tell her friends what was happening in her life; therapy in the form of friends. Julia had to realize how destructive her relationship with Charlie could be. Lindsey and her friends had watched Julia gain and lose 10 pounds over the past three years, a lot of it having to do with how Charlie treated her.

The women waited for Julia to calm down and compose herself. Lindsey gently said, "Julia, you sound like you know in your heart you did the right thing."

In her mind, Lindsey was doing somersaults, happy that Julia finally left that loser times three, and encouragingly she said, "Let's go shopping and get some clothes and make appointments for the Milwaukee spa. Not that it can replace a relationship, but it will be something to look forward to. Julia, we have to get you a great pair of skinny jeans for John's birthday party. I need to get something too. Full throttle ahead ladies, we're going to have fun next weekend. Now let's shop; it's September already and I've got to get past my summer wardrobe. Ti—iiiii—-mmmme is not on our side." Lindsey sang the altered line to the rolling stones tune. "This is going to be fun you guys, let's go."

Julia smiled and started tapping her fingers on the table, "Okay, Lindsey. Let's do it. I don't have any appointments this afternoon and I can do paperwork later on at my house. Let's pay up and walk the mall. I'm five thousand dollars richer and a load has been lifted from my shoulders. I can't wait to find something to wear for next weekend. I've got to get my mind off of Charlie." Julia was already smiling and digging in her purse to pay her part of the bill.

The women looked over the check, divided by four and paid the waitress. Brooke went back to her optometrist office in the mall, while Traci, Lindsey and Julia decided to see what they could find to wear to John's birthday party.

# CHAPTER THREE
## The Party

Getting ready for the party in Lindsey's case required five hours of looking in the mirror, putting make up on, taking makeup off, straightening her hair, putting different outfits on, calling people, drinking a glass of wine, putting more makeup on, straightening her hair even more, looking in the mirror every three or four minutes and then giving up.

Lindsey was in the throes of trying to look at least five years younger than she was and at least five lbs lighter. As she looked at her outfit in the mirror she wondered—-Why do I always buy outfits one size too small, hoping that in a week, I'll miraculously fit into it? This had been a shopping fiasco of Lindsey's for as long as she could remember. It was too tempting to not buy one size smaller; therefore, everything she wore was extremely tight and uncomfortable. Her closet was overflowing with size 2 outfits when she could barely fit into a size 4. Maybe one of these days she would learn.

Lindsey decided on wearing a gold-toned silk camisole with a band of gold sequins that sparkled around her neck, dark blue jeans with high heels and a bangle bracelet. Heather, Brooke, Traci and Julia were meeting at Lindsey's house for a pre-party drink of vodka and lemonade, wine, a beer or a vodka tonic with a twist of lime.

Johnny had invited two-hundred and fifty of his closest friends. Lindsey knew Johnny probably didn't even remember some of the guest's first names, and guests were allowed to bring anyone they wanted so the women were hopeful that they would meet 4 men who would sweep them off their feet. Ha, in reality they would more likely meet four men who would put them to sleep on their feet. Lindsey thought they'd be lucky to meet one man that didn't have major psychological issues, or a man that could talk in complete sentences on topics other than himself.

As Lindsey looked at her reflection in the mirror, she thought about her last date. Her client, a lawyer in West Bend, had set her up with one of her friends. He was ruggedly handsome, and had a dry, witty sense of humor. They were drinking wine and enjoying learning about each other when the waiter arrived with their food. As they continued to eat, Jerry kept talking with his mouth full of food, and Lindsey had been sprayed with flying lettuce, bread, and steak. Unfortunately, Lindsey couldn't remember half of the conversation because she was playing dodge food, which was totally gross. She didn't see a future with Jerry the food torpedo so that relationship was over before it began. Somewhere there might be a man who she clicks with.

As Lindsey looked one more time in the mirror at her hair, teeth, face, outfit and nails, the doorbell rang and the party night began. She left the mirror and walked to the door, Lindsey opened the door, "Hey, come into the kitchen, we're going to have a lot of fun tonight," Lindsey led the women into the expansive kitchen. She had the vodka and the lemonade ready, a bottle of tonic, ice cubes in the freezer and limes ready to be cut.

Each of them had dressed for an evening of excitement; hopefully they wouldn't drink too much. To her friends she said, "Okay, friends, if I start dancing call me a cab and send me home. It really is true what they say about alcohol; it makes you feel like you're good at everything." Lindsey continued, "I'm sure it will be too late by the time that happens, but if I get that drunk, I'm definitely in need of a shower and my bed!" Lindsey took a sip of her vodka with a gleam in her eye.

Julia, who was looking great in a tight, light-blue, knitted top worn with dark blue skinny jeans and simple gold slides on her feet, answered Lindsey, "Oh, please, don't dance, Lindsey. If you dance we'll all join you and then what will people think?" Julia's face was in a mock look of horror but she swayed her hips and started to dance.

Lindsey winked, "Okay we can dance, but none of us are allowed to fall all over the floor, or go home with a strange man or all of the other dumb things we do."

Traci chimed in, "Famous last words, I'm sure. Let's drink to that." Traci raised her glass. "Oh, and by the way, who is dating the birthday boy these days? Just so I know before I start telling her about him, if she asks me any intimate details." Traci and the women were always welcome at John's events and at each event he seemed to be with a new friend.

Lindsey shrugged her shoulders, "Who knows, he was with Jess for a long time and I think the kids mentioned a woman named Tara, just be careful with what you say about him to everyone. That's your safest bet. By now, John probably has a girlfriend in every state."

Lindsey knew John played around, he liked women. It never was an issue with them because his womanizing behavior started after their divorce. As long as he kept it away from their children she could have cared less.

She liked the idea of her children being innocent for as long as they could, and John's parade of women wouldn't be a model of behavior she would want her kids to replicate.

"Do I hear a hint of disdain in your voice?" Traci asked.

Lindsey tilted her head, "Are you kidding? I could care less...I know why he has a constant parade of women—He can't get over me." Lindsey and the women laughed. "John isn't serious about any of his relationships and his reputation precedes him. Those women who date him know what they're in for. John's not the only one who has that mentality, a lot of the men do."

As Lindsey was cutting up more limes to add to the beers and drinks, she cut her finger. "Shit, I can't believe I cut my finger! Excuse my language Heather. This is gross, I'll be right back." Lindsey left to clean her cut and stop the bleeding.

"Put some Neosporin on that cut," Heather called, just like a new mom to mother Lindsey too.

"Don't worry Mom I will!" Lindsey shouted back at her friend.

When Lindsey came back from the bathroom her finger was in a clear wrap band aide and the women had cleaned up the mess in the kitchen.

Looking at the clock she realized it was time to go, Lindsey danced, "It's showtime ladies, let's go and cause some trouble." Lindsey took a last quick look at the kitchen then shuffle danced, leading the rest of the women out the door to a cab that had been scheduled to come at 7:00.

Heather followed the rest of the women out and did a twirl past Lindsey. "Trouble? Oh great, that's what I'm afraid of."

Heather, in a dark blue, short dress with black trim, bare legs and blue satin ballerina shoes with silver jewelry looked terrific. None of the women wanted to drive their cars down to John's condo so they had called a cab. They got into the cab and were at John's party in less than ten minutes.

John's condo was located in one of the renovated warehouses in the third ward on Milwaukee's east side. John's condo had high ceilings with exposed beams and duct work with brick walls lending to a contemporary chic feeling. The condo had one bedroom, one bathroom and a large living room with an island separating the living space from the kitchen. The kitchen counters and the island were granite.

By 7:30 the place was starting to fill up. It looked like a festive, well-catered extravaganza. Johnny had hired a party planner. As the women walked up to the condo on the river, they were asked their names and then each signed their name in the guest book.

Women and men were walking around with champagne, wine, beer and mixed drinks. A bar had been set up in Johnny's condo and the condo that was next to his. Johnny knew Ron well, and Ron had agreed to open his house up for the party too. Lindsey and the women started mingling, and every so often would meet up to chat about the men they were chatting up.

Lindsey took the surroundings in. It was a warm fall night with the smell of past autumn seasons, trees swayed full of colorful leaves, squirrels ducked around searching for food waiting for the winter to arrive. John had invited a blend of couples and singles that included women and men of all different ages and generations who new Johnny from his dental practice, previous parties, business dealings, high school, or a friend of a friend who knew Johnny.

There was a tidal wave of people mingling, meeting, laughing, eyes meeting across the room, drinks clanking, giggles, sauntering cat walks and hands and arms around friends. People were filling up on martinis and cocktails, wine, champagne and the standard Milwaukeean favorite- beer.

The condo was immaculate and some of the furniture had been removed to accommodate the guests. White tulips in crystal vases and tea light candles were scattered throughout the condos keeping the atmosphere elegant and festive. The rooms inside flowed to the patios outside, where people milled around, going from inside to outside and then between the two condos. Light, energetic, contemporary music played from the speakers as a back drop to the purring conversation.

The women and men were dressed from casual jeans and stylish tops to gorgeous party dresses, with equally impressive jewelry and most importantly, glamorous shoes. Looking around, Lindsey tried to figure out who everyone was. Some women she recognized from John's office, some men from past parties, but there were also a lot of people she didn't know, which made the party much more interesting.

John was busy taking care of his guests, leading people to the bar and introducing them to other people. He had a definite knack for putting people at ease, welcoming them and introducing them to each other. His generosity always amazed Lindsey as well as his energy.

As Lindsey was gazing around and sipping her drink she saw Heather and Traci deep in conversation with two men who she didn't recognize. One looked like a toothpick and the other looked liked a bowling pin. Lindsey went over to introduce herself and find out who the two men were. She knew instinctively that they were probably talking about their careers, their kids and the war in Iraq: the never ending topic of the single world.

She burst out with, "Hi, I'm Lindsey, how are you guys?"

The men looked at each other and then back at her, before the toothpick responded. "I'm Greg" and then the bowling pin,

"I'm Rod," Lindsey thought, Hmmmm, what kind of a rod, lightning or fishing?

Lindsey asked in a bubbly fun voice, "What do you all think of this party? It's fun, hey?" Lindsey started this thread of conversation without finding out what they had been talking about. She wasn't trying to be rude; she was only looking at starting up a conversation. Heather and Traci looked relieved that she had entered the circle before the conversation grew stale.

Rod smiled, "It is fun, and there are so many people to look at. Who do you know here?" Rod was a serious sort of man, and seemed nervous when he spoke.

"I'm John's ex-wife." Lindsey saw the startled reaction from Rod and quickly added, "We've remained good friends."

At that moment another man with a sleek, muscular body came over and joined the conversation. He seemed to have a purpose as he butted in on the conversation, "You're John's ex-wife? And you're good friends? That's a nice twist. Are you two friends with benefits?" And then he extended his hand to Lindsey, Heather and Traci, "Hi, I'm Tom." They made their introductions. Tom was a George Clooney lookalike, with a cute wickedly, sexy smile, a thick head of hair and a body meant to be touched. It was hard and thick.

Lindsey sassily replied to Tom's insinuation, "No benefits. Is everything always about sex with you guys?" Lindsey's eyes checked Tom over, looking him over, up and down. As she answered her eyes were sparkling at him and she was smiling, challenging the sexy intruder.

"No." He smiled and gave Lindsey the once over, appraising her. "Really, I'm here like everyone, just trying to get out of my house for a while and meet some new people." He quickly added and asked Lindsey, "Are you dating anyone?"

Tom looked at Lindsey and then at the other two women while waiting for a reply.

He was direct with everyone he met, and didn't fancy a lot of idle conversation. Tom thought Lindsey was the sexiest women at the party. Lindsey looked at Tom with an air of confidence and a bit of an attitude. She didn't trust too many men that she met at John's parties or out at the bars.

Tom liked the attitude and the confidence Lindsey seemed to have. He realized she looked intelligent and cute and when he talked with her his assumptions proved correct. Tom had met women who seemed to be desperate to please him, which was fine but he wasn't sure if they were being honest about who they were or what they wanted.

It was a delicate dance getting to know someone well. It was difficult to understand anyone, let alone have a relationship. He tried to steer away from relationships because he liked being alone, but at the same time was lonely for someone to care about.

Lindsey looked at Tom skeptically before responding, and then she resignedly said, "There's no one to date. Once in a while I'll go out on a date with someone that my friends set me up with, but that's about it. I have two great kids and work full time. There isn't much of me left over." Lindsey tilted her head and took a sip of her drink as she looked up at Tom.

Tom smiled reassuringly at Lindsey, "Oh, I know what you mean. I have two kids too. They keep me busy, in a good way."

A family man, maybe Tom would turn out to be half-way normal. Let the small talk continue, thought Lindsey. "How old are your kids?"

"Twelve and fourteen. They're good kids. So far they haven't given me any trouble. I've had to cart them around to soccer practices and diving lessons, but I'll take that over them not being involved in anything. I wanted them to play some sport or play an instrument. It seems like they get a lot of confidence from learning how to be on a team and practice. They say being in sports or music helps children understand patterns and do better academically. I think it's fun watching them too. Kids have an interesting take on things." He smiled at Lindsey.

He seemed genuine enough about being in his children's life and Lindsey was impressed that he knew something about child development. Maybe he had a brain. So many of the men she met were extremely arrogant and thought their main goal was to drink and socialize and brag about themselves. Tom didn't seem like that at all. His eyes lit up when he talked about his kids, his mouth curled up at the ends in a smile like he couldn't stop it from happening even if he wanted to.

"That's cool." Lindsey decided to flirt with Tom but got stuck with not knowing what to say next.

Tom continued, "I love being a dad, divorce sucks though; I have my kids every other week. I wasn't sure how it was going to work out for their lives, having two homes, but they seem to handle it well, better than I thought. I hope they do anyway. Their mother is somewhat sane. She's not that good at homework though. I guess we all have our good and bad points."

Did she detect any anger or irrational views on dating? Not so far…., so far so good. It was something she had grown accustomed to, men and women who were too bitter to start a new relationship. But she tried to enjoy the banter and meeting people despite the personal baggage she and others brought into a relationship. Tom seemed open-minded and seemed to enjoy his life. She thought she would ask him a bit more about his days.

"So what else do you do besides cart your kids around?"

"I'm a detective in Milwaukee. I investigate crime scenes, murders and theft mostly. Theft mostly, but I have been on some murder investigations. It's gruesome, but I believe in justice, especially for the victim. Can you imagine killing someone?"

"Yes, I mean no. Of course not! I mean I agree with you, I don't believe in murder or capital punishment, and I feel sorry for the victims." With that said it was Tom's turn to ask the questions.

He looked interested as he said, "What exactly do you do?"

Lindsey was ready to talk about herself and said, "I'm a realtor. I started out as a teacher but when I had my two children I took off. After my divorce I decided to go and get my realtor's license because it allowed me more flexibility with my schedule. I like to go into my children's school and help my kids or go on fieldtrips, especially the ones to the theatre."

"Oh, cool. You like the theatre?" Tom also liked the theatre and thought it would be fun to ask Lindsey if she would like to go.

Lindsey thought maybe Tom was leading up to asking her on a date so she quickly did a 180 and ended the discussion, not wanting to get herself involved with anyone at the party; she still wanted to scout about and meet more people while she had the chance. She replied, "Well, listen it was nice meeting you. I'm going to go mingle some more and drink a little more too. I've got some friends that I want to catch up with. I haven't seen some of them in months. You know how it is."

Tom wasn't offended, he smiled, "Well, it was nice talking to you." Tom handed her his card at the same time, "call me if you want to have a coffee."

Lindsey took the card and smiled "Okay. Nice meeting you."

Not bad. Lindsey liked the case cracking cowboy. At least she thought he looked like a cowboy and George Clooney. Close cropped thick hair and a flashy smile with dimples. He had thick muscular legs and his shoulders were taut and large. She thought she'd feel safe and sound surrounded in those arms.

Snap out of it Lindsey! The man probably had a girlfriend stashed away somewhere. She went up to the bar and ordered another vodka tonic. Wow, this night was turning out to be better then she thought. Another man caught her eye; A blond cutie with a suit on. She decided he looked lonely and went over to strike up a conversation.

*Look at him so smug and happy. He deserved to die. He is so full of hypocrisy and deceit. And he is a success at it, so intelligent but full of conniving cunning and a life full of seduction and evil. It wouldn't take much to see that he got what he really deserved. He had power and used it to horde possessions. He is sinful, breaking all commandments and he needs to be stopped. It will be a brutal execution to match his uncivilized ways. How disgusting he is, eating lavishly and dining and drinking with his vulgar women and men friends.*
*He is the perpetuator of the growing stain of chaos and suffering. Every relationship he touched was scarred and doomed to end with distrust and jealousy. He is going to feel every bit of pain and suffering that I feel. It won't be hard to lure him away with the promise of sexual treats,*

*visual enticements and illegal ecstasy. He is such a sucker for that type of life. He deserves to die and tonight would do wonderfully. The emotional pain inside of me will cease once his heart has stopped beating. The rivalry will be no more and what was out of place will once again be in order. People will be happy, they will breathe again. Their lives will be able to move forward, ending the stagnation he kept them in.*

*It will be a violent death, the only type he deserves. The wait was over. Tonight is the night he will be destroyed, and everyone can start breathing again.*

The blond cutie was nice enough, but Lindsey got tired of the chit chat fast and decided to sit at one of the bar stools in the condo. Overall, it was a very fun evening. She noticed that Heather had left, but Traci, Brooke and Julia were still going strong. Julia kept looking at her phone, probably expecting Charlie to call. Some people are hard to get past, and that was the case for Julia.

Since she had broken up with Charlie she and Brooke had gone out several times, looking at the relics that were still available. Knowing that there wasn't much of a selection to pick from Lindsey was content to worry about other matters. But Julia was all alone; she had no children and relied heavily on Charlie for entertainment. Lindsey worried she would get back with him for lack of anything better out there, which really wasn't a reason to date someone, especially because Charlie seized every opportunity to belittle Julia and make her more dependent on him and was determined to undermine any self-confidence she possessed.

Lindsey's house was always open for any of the women to come and stay overnight. She hoped that Julia would feel free to come over any night and hang out with her and her kids so that she didn't feel lonely. As Lindsey sat observing the guests and thinking about relationships, Tom was thinking about Lindsey and wondering what was beneath her cool and calm exterior. What was hidden behind those dark eyes?

Tom watched Lindsey sipping from her tumbler and the ease with which she managed to sit there all alone and look completely comfortable. He was taken with the eyes that promised mischievousness when least expected. He thought it would be a challenge to get to know this guarded, intelligent and vibrant woman. He knew he would see her again.

Julia, Traci and Brooke descended on Lindsey's perch with stories of the evening. After whispering and confiding in each other about their night they decided to take a cab back to Lindsey's. The women found John, wished him a happy birthday again and thanked him for a great evening.

John looked like he had had an excellent time. His face was in a perpetual smile as he chummed with his friends from high school and the old and new friends he had made throughout his life. The women headed out and into a cab that brought them back to Lindsey's house. It was already 2:00am. The night had been a hit.

Traci and Brooke departed, driving home in their own cars as soon as they got to Lindsey's house, but Julia decided to stay and have some food and water with Lindsey. At 2:45am Julia decided she was exhausted and decided to drive to her house, which was in Brookfield, not far from Milwaukee. Lindsey went up to take a hot shower and get under her warm comforter. The weather had started to turn a bit cooler and the comforter enveloped Lindsey in calm and peace. The last peaceful night she would have in a long time.

At 6:00am her phone rang, startling her out of a serene dream and into a real life nightmare.

# CHAPTER FOUR
## The News of the Murder

Lindsey was startled out of a calm and cozy dream to the blaring blong of the doorbell. What is going on, she thought. Immediately she was concerned and her heart was racing. The doorbell ringing at 6:00am on a Sunday could only mean one thing; *Trouble.*

*It was a horrific site. The body was lying in a pool of blood, the corpse was almost unrecognizable. Handcuffs had been used to secure the body to the steering wheel of the once immaculate black jaguar. What was once posh tan leather seats now took on the appearance of dark red- stained, saturated blood-soaked rags. Blood was everywhere, spattered on the mirror and the windows, smudged on the steering wheel and dash. It was a blood bath. Johnny had been positioned sitting in the driver's seat with his hands cuffed to the wheel.*

*His body was slumped forward but his head was tilted off kilter to the left; a knife was sticking out the side of his gashed neck. His neck was cut so far down that his head was dangling by a thread and was resting on his left shoulder.*

*Dental floss circled his throat at least 10 times and cut deeper and deeper into his fleshy neck. The dental floss twirled around his neck making thick indentations, slicing right below his Adams apple and above his collar bone.*

*John had been left completely naked and the dental floss had been used to not only strangle him but it looked as if several teeth had been pulled out too and strung up as trophies hanging from dental floss on the rear view mirror.*

*The seatbelt had been placed around John, used to confine John in a death trap. His shoes had been left on as well as his socks, but the shoelaces had been tied together as a child would do to another child when playing a practical joke.*

*The whole thing was surreal. It almost looked like John was a manikin, so unreal were the crime scene and the caricature of the cold, white person sitting in the driver's seat with open dead eyes staring into nothingness.*

Lindsey was wide awake in less than a millisecond. She grabbed her robe and rushed down the carpeted hall to the front door. A little hesitant she looked out the window. Outside was a squad car with lights circling on top and at her door was Tom. Immediately she shivered. Either he was insane and wanted to see her really bad, or something dreadful had happened.

Lindsey opened the door, "What's going on?" Her eyes were wide and her voice was a shaky whisper. Tom took a little step back and asked if he could come in. Lindsey tried to look into his eyes to discover what was going on but Tom had on a poker face. In the early morning he showed no signs of what he had just witnessed. Lindsey let Tom in and showed him to the kitchen where they sat down at the island.

Lindsey asked, "Would you like a glass of water?"

Lindsey still didn't have a clue what Tom was doing there; she was grabbing a glass out of the cabinet for some water when Tom started to tell her what had happened. "Lindsey, I have some bad news."

Lindsey was bringing the water over to Tom. She turned and immediately thought the worst, "My god. Is it my children?" Lindsey dropped the glass on the floor, her whole body started shaking and she was unable to stand. She sat down on one of the stools at the island.

Tom quickly replied, "No, your children are fine. There is no easy way to say this." Tom paused and then said, "Last night someone murdered John."

He looked for her reaction. Lindsey looked at him, not comprehending what he had was saying to her. "What do you mean?" were the only words she could whisper. She couldn't catch her breath, she couldn't hear anything and her body had gone numb. It couldn't be. It had to be someone else. She thought about John, he was the father of her children, her friend, a confidant and someone she still cared about. How could he be dead?

She spoke to no one but herself, "Oh no, that's impossible. He was so alive; he was having so much fun. I just saw him. Everyone was there." Her mind could not register what Tom was telling her. She didn't feel, she didn't cry, she just went dead. Her mind had stopped working.

Tom led her to the couch in the living room and went to get a new glass of water. He quickly cleaned up the spilled water and put the cup in the sink, luckily it hadn't shattered. He bought Lindsey the glass of water.

Lindsey looked up at Tom as he handed her the glass of water, thankful for the water she drank a couple of sips before setting it down on the coffee table. She caught her breath but still couldn't really talk. Tom waited for Lindsey to say something before he had to ask her where she was last night between the hours of 2am and 4am, when the murder had taken place.

When and why, who, was all she could think about, she finally collected herself enough to ask, "Tom, when did the murder happen? He had so many people over. How could he have been murdered? Are you sure it's him? I just can't believe it?"

And then she thought of Leo and Lilly and tears started to fall. It was one thing to get divorced but to have John gone, she couldn't even grasp it. Leo and Lilly would miss out on his love, his energy and miss the times that they would have spent together doing activities. It wasn't possible but here was Tom, telling her John was dead, and murdered at that.

In a serious but caring voice Tom told Lindsey what he could, "Lindsey, I can't tell you everything but the murder happened around 3:30 with the police getting a call around 5:00 this morning. A woman who lived in the condominium complex was walking in the parking garage to her car and noticed John's Jaguar had blood stains on the window. She thought she saw a person in the driver's seat too and immediately called the police." He continued in a calm voice, "We found John's body around 5:10 this morning, in his car in the parking garage attached to his condo. The crime scene investigators are there right now doing all they can to get as much evidence from the area as possible. So far we have no witnesses except the lady who called in on her suspicion that something was wrong. I'm sorry." Tom said this as a matter of fact, as professional as he could.

Lindsey looked at him but couldn't think of anything to say. Nothing could be said at the time. Tom knew she was suffering from shock and he showed empathy, professionalism and had the decency to wait for her to steady herself so that he could listen to whatever she needed to say. She felt he was there for her and somehow had a calming effect on her. She sat, looking stone-faced at Tom and then finally her brain started grasping the facts.

She softly spoke, "I don't know what to do about my children. I don't know what to tell them. I guess the best thing to do is tell them the truth as soon as possible." She looked up to Tom as if he should tell her what to do, even though she knew that it was all up to her.

Tom knew it would take time for Lindsey to absorb the information. He waited while she gathered herself, then he finally spoke. "I know John's death is going to be very difficult for you and the children to deal with. The police are going to do all they can to find the murderer of John and to help you and your children as much as possible. I will have to ask you all sorts of questions about John and his life. This is so we can help find the murderer. Usually the killer is someone close to the victim." He said this last line with as much sensitivity as he could; he knew Lindsey wasn't in a state of mind to answer questions about the previous night.

He wanted her to calm down and again, spoke gently to her, "Lindsey, can you call someone to come over and stay with you? I don't want to leave you all alone."

Lindsey looked at him and the words fell heavy....all alone. She felt very alone at the moment. She knew she had to call her mom and have her bring the kids back home. She needed them more than ever right now and she knew she had to let them know about John as soon as possible.

She abruptly got off the couch, "Of course, I'll call my mom and she can bring the kids over here. I've got to tell them right away." Lindsey went to the kitchen and retrieved her cell phone from the charger. She called her mom and tried to control the quivering in her voice as she asked her mom to bring the kids home right away. Her mom was quick to catch on that something was wrong but didn't ask questions. She knew whatever it was could wait until she saw Lindsey in person.

Tom decided to wait to question Lindsey about her whereabouts last night after she had time to recuperate from the news of John's death. He left as soon as she had called her mom and he knew that they were on their way to Lindsey's house. Within 15 minutes the kids were home and Lindsey had to break the news to them too.

It was only 10:00 but already it seemed like weeks had passed since the party last night and John's murder. She had told Lilly and Leo of John's death and they had cried together. The children and Lindsey decided to go to church to keep their minds off of their father's death and possibly get some comfort from the sermon. Lindsey was proud of them for being so brave, knowing that the recovery would take a long time.

Hovering above the priest were stained glass portraits of angels and prophets. Lindsey looked at the wonderful windows and breathed calmly but didn't hear a word of the service. The glass seemed to speak to her, that everything was there to see, if she could figure out the way to see it. Wasn't life always like that, you could see everything but understanding it and making sense out of experiences was a lot harder.

As soon as they were back from church Leo and Lilly were asked to go out to lunch with Lindsey's parents and stay with them for the afternoon. The children were used to Sunday get-togethers at her parents and because they both felt like going, Lindsey let them. She had already discussed the death with Brooke, Traci, Heather and Julia, calling them in the morning before heading out to church. The women decided to meet at Lindsey's after Lindsey returned from church around 1:00.

There were grey clouds hovering over the lake that morning, making the day appear gloomy, fitting Lindsey's state of mind. The temperature was warm but was accompanied with a cool breeze, stirring the trees and making some of the leaves fall in a tailspin down to the cold dewy grass.

The day was so typical of a fall day, unpredictable and erratic. Lindsey and the women decided to sit outside on the terrace and try to piece together the events of last night. Brooke made coffee, Julia brought out the cream and sugar and Heather had brought over some fresh chocolate and vanilla biscotti. Julia put the biscotti on a serving plate and placed it on the table to share. Although it was a warm day for September there was a chill running through the breeze that morning that felt like a frosty hand on Lindsey's shoulder. Lindsey started the gas fireplace in the center of the table to shake off the goose bumps that she felt and take the chill out of the air.

Lindsey confessed to her friends, "I'm in shock. John's mother and father went to the medical examiners to identify the body and then called me. It was definitely John, although they said he had suffered a violent death and something had been done to his face to make it hard to recognize him. They couldn't go into details, and honestly I'd like to remember him as he was last night. He was so full of life, and so happy. Who would want to kill him?"

The question lingered out there as each of the women thought their own private thoughts. The fact was, John was bigger than life and with a personality like that was the target of men and women's jealousy and envy. There were always rumors circulating about his business dealings, his many women, and his staff. John liked to live large; he enjoyed his position as a prominent cosmetic dentist. If Lindsey and the women had to, they could think of many women and men that John, inadvertently, had offended.

The question still lingered in everyone's mind until Traci broke through the silence. "We all knew he liked women, it could have been a shunned ex-lover." The dam broke and they all had a say in who else would have a motive or a reason to kill John.

Among the list of possible suspects were ex-lovers, business partners, boyfriends or husbands of John's ex-lovers, irritated staff or patients and lastly disgruntled tenants. The women found themselves talking about the possible murderer and thus were born the beginning of their new purpose—to find out who killed Johnny Wang.

They reviewed who they thought might possibly have a motive to kill Johnny. They unofficially started lists and they vowed to investigate, hunt for clues, interview and collect their own evidence so that Johnny's murderer would be caught. They knew the police were going to do all they could do, and they would help out any way they could. But they also knew that the police were understaffed and underfinanced. The women were determined to do all they could to help out Lindsey.

Julia sparked some debate, "Okay, we're definitely forced into the roles of investigative sleuths. *Charlie's angels* watch out. We're going to catch whoever did this." Julia wanted to make certain the women were motivated to actually proceed with their plans. "Let's come up with a name for ourselves like *Charlie's angels* or something. It will be our business name, if we're ever asked by anyone who we're working for."

Traci wasn't sure about finding a name and never one to stay quiet she voiced her opinion, "Do you honestly think that's a good idea? We're not grade school kids putting together a club, Julia. We're going to be investigating a murder of someone we all knew and loved. I don't think we should trivialize the situation." Traci was taken aback with Julia's idea..

Julia reasoned with Traci, "I'm not trying to trivialize this, Traci. I'm trying to keep us motivated so that we actually do what we said we would. Besides, this could be the beginning of a new career for all of us. We should come up with a name. When we do our investigation and people ask who we're working for we can tell them. It will help establish trust between us and them, it's purely for psychological reasons, but it works."

Julia wasn't mad, she was always calm and matter of fact. She continued, "I know we're not kids and I know we're not starting a business, yet; but we do have to help Lindsey with this horrific situation."

Julia had made several valid points and it was inspiring to the rest of the women to think of themselves working together on the murder mystery. Julia and the rest of the women thought the name would provide an attachment between them and the course of action they took. They also felt it would be safer to be connected by a business name in case the investigation turned dangerous. Nothing was trivial about murder and as the women looked around they knew that the situation was serious. It didn't stop them from living and proceeding forward. That's what they did together, and so they started to establish different names for their group.

Traci smiled at Julia, "Okay, I guess I can see your side. It would be fun, and we should still have fun. It also would be good to use a business name." Traci looked at her friends, crossed her legs and sat back in her chair, shifting her weight trying to get comfortable. The women began contemplating their options.

Brooke was listening and commented, "Well, I think it's a fun idea. We are in this together and a name bonds us together.

We could call ourselves the 001 through 005 agents for code names. Who says we have to be grown up all the time? Let's think up some sassy names. I like the idea of having a name to tell people if they ask who we're working for. It sounds more authoritative. Then we don't have to say Lindsey's name, it will be a company name."

Brooke paused and looked around the table, "Hmmmm, I mean we are going to be delving into the investigative business. We should call our group something like, secret sleuths, or PI's and spies, or 'Gotcha now', or 'mystery solvers'," Brooke went on and on.

Lindsey giggled at Brooke despite the situation, "Okay you guys, now you're making me laugh and poor John is dead on a slab. Yuck,"

Lindsey took one chocolate biscotti and dipped it in her coffee. She couldn't believe they were sitting around talking about names for a murder solving club. But the idea did put some sparkle back in her eyes. Wasn't it just last week they were all so content with their lives and jobs. How had this happened?

Heather sat back in her chair and wrapped her sweater around her a little tighter, and then got into the spirit of naming the club. "How about II, for Intelligent Investigators?"

"I like it Heather." Lindsey said enthusiastically.

"Or how about 'Home and Heart Investigators'? After all we love our homes and we have big hearts." Heather continued thinking of a name that reminded her of her family.

Lindsey wasn't sure, "Yeah, I like that but it's kind of long and not that catchy. Why don't we put on hold the name thing and really think about the investigation. After all, we don't even know anything about investigating. We haven't even thought up a plan, or how we are going to execute the plan. None of us really knows anything about being an investigator, or finding clues." Lindsey wanted to move on to the heart of why the women were sitting around her table on a chilly fall day.

Brooke responded, "How hard can it be? We'll develop a plan, we'll do interviews of the people at the party, and we'll search John's home and look at his computer and cell phone records. We'll go through his business files and look into who would profit the most from John's death. We'll also have to see what the forensic evidence is, which I'm not sure how we can find that out. That is something we'll have to learn about. Come on you guys, we can do this."

Traci was nodding her head agreeing with Brooke. "We can solve this. After all, the police are going to be looking at Lindsey as one of their prime suspects. They always look at the spouse first." Traci was being practical and all the women knew she was right.

By the end of the afternoon the women had set a tentative plan in motion, and Lindsey, although still sad, had a new focus and felt that with the help of her friends she was going to get through this. The women left to complete some of their 'real life' tasks and decided to meet back at Lindsey's that evening to review and formalize their plans.

As soon as all the women were gone, Lindsey took a shower and decided to follow her children's example and get back to her normal routine. Although nothing was normal, she didn't know what else she should do. She knew that she would be the prime suspect in John's murder, but she didn't have any clue as to whom, how or why he was murdered.

Lindsey's mind was racing a mile a minute. She had had only three hours of sleep but every cell was buzzing with adrenalin. What would happen to her if she were arrested and somehow found guilty by association? What would happen to her life, her freedoms, and her children? The thought was so devastating to her; she couldn't think about it. She shut that thought pattern down before it drove her insane.

She thought about her kids and John's parents and what needed to be arranged for the funeral. John was an only child and most of his extended family lived in California. She knew a lot of the details of John's wake and funeral would rest in her hands. The funeral would have to wait until after the medical examiner was through determining the cause of death and released John's body.

Lindsey had already talked extensively to John's parents and commiserated with them. Lindsey thought John's parents were handling the news as best as they could. However, he was their only child and their loss was incomprehensible, the worst fear of a parent to have their child die before their time. Lindsey had to keep her thoughts together for John's parents' sake as well as her children.

Lindsey decided to clean up the dishes in her sink. It was mindless work and it helped to soothe her nerves. As she was drying the dishes she thought of the perfect name for her and her murder solving friends; the 'case crackers and wine' club, but they'd say they were the 'case crackers investigations team' when asked by other people what their business name was. With that problem out of the way she went into the family room to catch up on paying bills.

She sat down with the pile of bills in her lap. Sitting there the quiet of the house was starting to feel oppressive. Normally she loved the seclusion and quiet, but today it felt like she was in an eerie spook house. She needed to get out and see people who were moving, breathing and busy living.

She went to her closet, put on a pair of jeans and a comfortable t-shirt. She was going to her office to look over some papers, talk with her realtor partners, and try to get her mind on something besides John. As soon as she was ready and started walking out the door, ready to escape to her office, the phone rang.

# CHAPTER FIVE
## The Interrogation

Lindsey contemplated not answering the phone, having a premonition that whoever it was and whatever they wanted wasn't anything she cared to know about. Her hand hovered on the front door knob leading out to her car but before she turned the knob her curiosity ruled her need to escape and she ran back inside to the kitchen to pick up the phone. "Hello."

"Hello, am I speaking to Lindsey Wang?" By the impersonal and authoritative sound of the man on the other end Lindsey regretted answering the phone.

"This is she, who's calling?" She replied in her best confident-sounding voice.

"This is detective Riley from the Milwaukee police, homicide division. I know this is a trying time for you and your family but part of our job is interviewing those who were closest to the victim. As his ex-wife, we need to ask you several questions. Could you come to the station on 6th street at 4:00 and help us piece together John's last night alive and inform us of any other information that you think might help us in solving his murder?"

Lindsey understood what the question was and the officer did a commendable job not talking to her like she was a child, or a suspect for that matter. She thought she might have had more time to collect her thoughts and mourn, but on the other hand was grateful that the police were acting in such a timely manner. In a pleasant voice she replied, "Of course I'll be there. I'll do all I can to help you find out who murdered John. You said 4:00 at the station on 6th street?"

"Yes, thank you for coming down. We're going to do all we can to solve this as fast as possible." The officer was all business and Lindsey could visualize him sitting at his desk with an old Styrofoam cup of weak coffee and tapping his pen as he talked with her on the phone.

"I'll see you at 4:00 then, Good Bye." Lindsey waited for the polite officer to respond.

"Thank you, Ma'am, Good Bye," and that was it. She hung up the phone and turned to look around at her surroundings.

Every sound seemed to be magnified, she heard the ticking of the clock; it sounded like a time bomb. She heard the whirl of the refrigerator, it sounded like a train. The lights which always seemed to be calm and serene while illuminating the kitchen seemed to act like a spotlight, hot and blinding on her eyes. One phone call and the reality of John's death, once again, came crashing down on her psyche.

Having been through a divorce and living all alone felt quiet but peaceful before John's death., but now that he was gone and the task of raising Leo and Lilly without the voice of John created a stillness, a fog. The thought of finding out who murdered John seemed an impossible task, and a depressing one. Lindsey was feeling like she was stuck in a muddy swamp of dirt, and thick sand that she would have to dredge through before she got to the clean water, and then back on to safe land.

Lindsey's motivation to go to work waned as she sat, virtually frozen in time. She realized she hadn't moved in five minutes, or for that matter even blinked her eyes. Her hand was still hanging on to the phone receiver, her thoughts dangling with anxiety and confusion, and she didn't really know what to make of the police and what they would want from her.

With no motivation to go to work, she went back to her bedroom. It was only 2:30, but she was tired and decided to lay down on the bed and rest. The next time she opened her eyes it was 3:45 and she bolted up out of bed like an arrow off of a bow, ran down the hall, grabbed her coat and set off to the police station.

The drive down to the police station was filled with near misses as she swerved out of the way from an oncoming cars loose turn; the car barely missed her. She hoped this wasn't a precursor to swerving out of untold accusations at the police station.

With the sense that this wasn't going to be a friendly encounter, she thought back to the night of the party and wondered if anything unusual had happened. She wanted to give something to the police, some form of a clue from that night. However, she couldn't focus and her mind was filled with buzzing and nothingness. The next thing she knew her car was parked at the police station and she was standing at a window talking to the policeman behind the security counter.

Lindsey gave her name to the officer behind the counter, "Hi, I'm here to see detective Riley. My name is Lindsey Wang."

The plump officer gave her a once over as he leaned on the counter and chewed his gum. He pointed to a sign-in sheet and in a gruff voice said, "Sign your name and we'll call you when we're ready for you." He tipped his head and then went back to reading a report on his desk.

This wasn't a friendly hotel receptionist. He barely looked at her with his loopy eyes. Lindsey signed her name and then sat down on the wooden bench to wait for someone to escort her through the metal detector and into the lion's den. As she sat she watched several people come up to the desk and pay traffic tickets, get a permit for parking and ask minor police questions. Then she reprimanded herself and again tried to focus on the night of the party.

Nothing was sounding off any alarms from that night and again her mind drifted. She thought, 'how long were they going to make her wait on this bench?' It was a form of torture, even worse than waiting at the doctor's office. She glanced at her watch and realized it was 4:15. She had been waiting for 15 minutes, but it seemed like 15 hours. When were they going to come and get her?

Lindsey had to get Leo and Lilly from her parents at 6:15, so she needed to leave the police station at 6:00. Should she be here with a lawyer, or would that be stupid? She knew she wasn't guilty, but sitting at the station, waiting, made her feel like a criminal. She thought she better stop with that type of thinking before she started to confess to something she didn't do, and then her thoughts were interrupted by a nice looking police man in dark brown slacks and a blue dress shirt. "Ms. Lindsey Wang, I'm detective Riley. Won't you come this way?"

'What if I don't want to go that way', she thought. Lindsey followed detective Riley through the metal detector without sounding the alarm. 'Oh good, one test passed', she thought. Why was she so nervous? The detective was walking her through a series of hallways and doors then down the stairs to the basement.

For some reason Lindsey had thought she would be in a big, crowded, loud room with a lot of police officers sitting at their desks, some talking on the phone with their feet up, some drinking coffee, and some eating donuts while they talked with suspects and took down information on tablets. She didn't think she'd be led through a maze and down some stairs which got colder and colder with each descending step.

Finally Detective Riley stopped in front of a green metal door and led her inside, where she was asked to have a seat across the table from a middle aged woman dressed in a blue suit and no-nonsense, sensible blue buckled shoes. Her hair was pulled back and held by a barrette.

The chair that Lindsey was asked to sit in had a standard, plastic blue seat with silver metal legs. The table was metal with wood laminate on the top, and after Lindsey sat down across from the woman at the table, Detective Riley took a seat over in the corner of the room to her left. The anxiety and uncomfortable feeling Lindsey felt increased and led Lindsey to wish she hadn't volunteered to come down to the station at all.

The woman officer began, "I'm Officer Stevenson, and you've been introduced to Detective Riley," she pointed to Detective Riley. "Thank you for coming down here to talk about the events of your ex-husbands death. I'm sorry for your loss."

Officer Stevenson paused so Lindsey nodded her head up and down in acknowledgment, not knowing what else to do and seemingly too hoarse to say anything.

Officer Stevenson continued, "It is a tragedy when life is ended so abruptly and so violently. Don't you think?"

Again Lindsey couldn't seem to find her voice and nodded.

"We're here today to ask you simple questions, we will remind you that you're not forced to answer any questions and if you want legal counsel at any time that is your right."

Hmmm, Lindsey felt like she was being arrested, but nodded anyway. She looked around and as she did Detective Riley gave her an encouraging smile. Maybe this was their good cop, bad cop routine. Lindsey continued to look at Officer Stevenson, but still didn't say anything.

Officer Stevenson continued talking in a serious tone, "You were married to John Wang for 10 years?"

Finally Lindsey found her voice; "yes" a simple answer was all she could get out.

"John was 46 years old?"

Again she answered simply "Yes."

"You and he have two children?"

"Yes."

"You and John divorced 6 years ago?" Lindsey was getting tired of the questions, but knew that it was part of helping the police get a picture of John. Lindsey nodded her head up and down.

"And you divorced John because he was a terrible husband?"

Okay, now this was weird. Lindsey was automatically getting ready to say yes, but the detective's demeanor and tone changed from fact finding to an accusatory tone in her voice and a glare in her eyes.

"No, he wasn't a terrible husband. What is your point? I thought you brought me down here to find out about the events on the night of John's death?" Lindsey was irritated; she looked at Detective Riley as she spoke.

Detective Riley stood up and looked at Officer Stevenson as if he thought she was being a bit overzealous and wasn't on the 'right' track and responded, "Officer Stevenson, Ms. Wang came down here to help us with the events, particularly Mr. Wang's birthday party on the night of his death. Please stick to questions about that night; she's not being interrogated like a suspect at this moment."

He smiled and tilted his head apologetically at Lindsey. Now the role of the 'good cop' was firmly established. Lindsey didn't trust either of them. Of course she knew she was a suspect in John's murder, she was the ex-wife. How stupid did these cops think she was?

"Oh yes, you're right, Riley." Officer Stevenson replied between clenched teeth; she didn't look up and jotted something on her notebook before she continued asking questions.

When she looked up she had an irritated expression on her face as if Lindsey was wasting her precious time. "Ms Wang, tell us about the night of Mr. Wang's death. Did you notice anything strange that evening? Did you see or hear anything that didn't sit well with you?"

Lindsey looked directly at the 'bad cop' and tried to think of something to say, but her mind was too tired to go back in time and rehash that night especially in front of 'good cop' and 'bad cop'. She wished she had something useful to say but without any type of useful information simply said, "No."

Both the cops looked at each other as if to say "she's guilty". Lindsey could feel the unspoken 'guilty as sin' telecommunications going on between the two officers. Lindsey decided the best thing for her to do was get the hell out of there.

With a quick look at her watch, she grabbed her purse and looked directly at the two cops, "I'm sorry I can't think back to that night right now. I really have to be going; I've got to pick up my kids from my parents. If I think of anything I'll call you." Lindsey stood up and started towards the door.

Detective Riley opened the door to let her out. "Just one moment Ms.Wang," Officer Stevenson caught her before she was out the door, "Don't plan on going anywhere for a while."

Lindsey thought she did a really good *'Colombo'* imitation and responded, "I'm not planning on it."

She followed Detective Riley out the door and up the stairs. Detective Riley didn't say a thing, he kept quiet and the only noise that could be heard was the echoing of their feet on the cold steel stairs. This time as she took each step, she felt warmer and the light seemed to refresh her spirit as she climbed higher and higher out of the police station's pit.

She couldn't wait to get to her car and lock the door to keep out the outside world and especially the interrogating police. As soon as she got to her car Lindsey breathed again, turned on the radio and drove speedily in the direction of her parents' house.

*No one would ever know who really murdered Dr. Wang. The clues that were scattered about all pointed to Lindsey. She didn't even realize how big of a hole she was in. Poor Lindsey, it wasn't her fault that she fell for John, the dumb-assed bastard. Watching Lindsey leave the station as if being chased by a bee was quite sad, but unavoidable.*

*The media was all over John's death, swarmed his condo like red ants on a piece of chewed up gum. It was because of his murder; the murder of a f___ing well-liked business professional. Well, no one knew that he was really an asshole who deserved to die. And if Lindsey had to be the fall guy, well, that was the way it had to be.*

*The media made it seem like John was a saint; society was so pathetic, believing everything they read. Maybe the tables would have to be turned on some more of these idiots. Maybe more people would be spared hurt and discomfort if a few more lying, cheating friggen bastards died.*

Tom had grabbed a hot coffee in a standard Styrofoam cup and stood behind the mirror. He was tired from having no rest after last night's murder. He had gone home for a quick shower and shave before heading downtown to the station. Working on pure adrenalin, Tom watched Lindsey from behind the glass. He couldn't pretend that he didn't have any romantic feelings for the wild, free-spirited woman that sat there at the table, looking frustrated and scared but defiant at the same time. Tom hoped she wasn't involved in any way with the gruesome crime that he had witnessed and was determined to solve.

Could Lindsey be someone who was psychologically crazy? What was lurking behind her intelligent, beautiful, caring exterior? He had thought she was mysterious, but not insane. The forensic lab had collected all the DNA samples from the car and bagged all the physical evidence. The knife, the dental floss, the handcuffs, were all being analyzed for fingerprints and blood, hair and any other microscopic evidence that might be useful. Tom hoped that they would find their murderer and that the evidence would not point to Lindsey.

# CHAPTER SIX
## Case Crackers, Meeting One, Plan One

It felt like a ton of bricks had descended on Lindsey's head and shoulders. After picking up the kids they drove home in a dead silence. Leo and Lilly weren't talking or singing and she was too tired to ask how their time with her parents went. As thoughts of the media swirled in her head she approached her house with apprehension. One news van was stationed at the end of her drive, white, impersonal and out to get what dirt they could on Lindsey and her two children.

Too many times Lindsey thought that the media had no conscience and thrived on sensationalism, making up facts and embellishing the truth to suit their ratings. Out of disgust for the news hound dogs, she revved her tires until dirt blew up, hoping the news van would get lost. The gate was open to her drive so she gunned the car and sped into the drive. The gate closed behind her and hopefully the rest of the world would be a little less able to intrude into her and the kids' thoughts and lives. She drove into the garage and both kids ran out of the car, through the door and right into the kitchen.

Some things never changed and she was happy that both children were eager to find something to snack on before she made dinner. Already the time was 6:40; she had better hurry with dinner before her best friends arrived; they had planned on coming at 7:30 to discuss their plan to implement their secret sleuthing techniques.

Visions of old fashioned cameras, hairpins used to pick locks, magnifying glasses, trench coats and fedora hats came into focus in Lindsey's mind as she surveyed the contents of her almost empty refrigerator. Her mind drifted to old, murder mystery movies again. Then she quickly refocused and looked in her refrigerator.

A package of American cheese slices caught her eye along with a half loaf of bread. The decision had been made, one dinner of grilled cheese sandwiches, with a side of chicken noodle soup would be the order of the night. She looked in the pantry and with relief got out a can of soup.

Lindsey loved her kitchen with all its space to spread out her dinner ingredients. She appreciated the island to prepare food on, as well as sit around and talk and eat. She had renovated the kitchen with off-white counters that had specks of brown and tan sprinkled throughout the granite. She had bought brand new energy-efficient, stainless-steel appliances and put in dark walnut flooring that contrasted nicely with her cream colored cabinets. And she had painted the walls a deep shade of peach. The stools in the kitchen were comfortably upholstered in the same shade of color as the walls, with wooden legs and wrought iron backs.

She loved her kitchen, and remembered that Tom was sitting at the stool closest to the sink when he told her the devastating news of John's murder. She could see Tom there, looking at her with concern, as if to question what she was thinking, like he really cared about her and hated telling her the news. She thought he was handsomer now then when she first met him at John's party. His helping her to the couch and getting a glass of water was true manners, and he stayed put to make sure she wasn't alone. He had an air of confidence about him but with humanity interspersed for good measure.

But what if he thought she was the murderess? They would become cat and mouse with him chasing her, but not for the right reason. With that thought in her mind she quickly turned the grilled-cheese sandwiches making sure the side was crispy golden brown and then stirred the soup with a wooden spoon. It had taken five minutes to put the dinner together, but she knew the kids would enjoy the light dinner just as much as if she had been cooking for five hours. They loved simple meals, thank goodness for that too.

"Leo, Lilly, dinners ready!" She yelled down the hall to Lilly, who had been in her room probably writing a story, and Leo, who was on the computer in the family room. Both children's footsteps could be heard pounding their way to the kitchen.

Leo observed what was in the pan, "Grilled cheese? Looks good Mom. Do I have to eat the soup?"

Leo rarely ate vegetables and when he did he became a contortionist with quite the shriveled up face and gagged as if he had a wad of Kleenex in his throat that he couldn't get rid of.

Lindsey gently said, "Try a little soup, Leo. It's good for you. It will warm you up and keep you from getting sick."

Lilly spritely said, "Can I have his soup? I love soup." Lilly always liked soup and vegetables, and loved to trump Leo with her eating repertoire. Lindsey filled two bowls of soup and put the sandwiches on a plate before giving the kids their meal.

Lilly asked, "Aren't you going to eat any, Mom? You never eat." Lilly complained to Lindsey.

Lindsey smiled at Lilly, "Yes, I do. I just wait until you two have had your fill. My friends are coming over tonight to talk about what happened with your Dad. I'm going to be munching on cheese and crackers while we talk and catch up with each other."

Leo cautiously said, "That's all you ever eat Mom, is cheese and crackers," he said this with a mouth full of sandwich.

Lindsey nodded her head, "I know, just wait until you're old, you'll be eating a lot of cheese and crackers too." With that said Lindsey went upstairs to brush her teeth and get ready for the evening.

After a quick picking up and straightening out of the family room, living room and bathrooms she headed back to the kitchen to see how Lilly and Leo were doing.

Lilly teased, "Mom, Leo didn't finish his soup." Lilly pointed at Leo's bowl.

Leo looked exasperated at Lilly. "Be quiet Lilly, I took a couple of spoonfuls mom. Do I have to finish the soup?"

"Try eating three more bites, and then give the rest to Lilly." Lindsey couldn't stand to watch Leo suffer over soup, maybe when he was older he would acquire a taste for vegetables.

Lilly's face looked questioningly up at Lindsey, "Why are you having your friends over Mom? What are you going to do about Dads death? I thought when a person was dead they were just dead and that they floated around as ghosts. Can you bring Dad back? Is that what you mean you and your friends are going to talk about?"

Lilly, in true nine-year-old fashion was inquisitive and matter-of-fact about John's death. Lindsey thought about how to respond, she patiently said, "Lilly, nothing will bring your dad back to life. He died and he might be floating around our house right now, keeping watch over you and Leo. Your dad's death was completely unexpected and he didn't die naturally. Unfortunately someone took your dad's life, and my friends and I are going to figure out why and who it was."

Leo looked contemplatively at Lindsey, "Oh wow, why would someone want to hurt dad? He was so nice to everyone." Leo's expression was so sad; Lindsey didn't know how to respond without choking up.

Lindsey's voice was shaky, but she tried to sound strong, "I know. People who hurt other people are mentally ill. No one deserves to be hurt, Leo. It was nothing your dad did. He was a great man. The person who killed him is very ill and needs help. My friends and I are going to help the police find out who murdered your dad so that they don't do it again and the person will go to prison."

Leo was concerned, "Mom, I don't want you to get hurt. What if the bad person goes after you?" Leo had put more thought into this situation then Lindsey gave him credit for.

"Don't worry about me, I will be very careful. Nothing will happen to me, you guys. I'm just going to be looking at computers and filing things away, no danger whatsoever." Lindsey was sorry she said anything at all about investigating John's death to her kids. The last thing she wanted was for them to worry, but she had always been honest with them about everything and her feelings.

She wanted to protect them from everything, but she also wanted them to be aware of the world so they would be strong. Just then the doorbell rang. Lilly got up to put her plate and bowl in the sink, and was off to play in her room. Leo finished up his milk and emptied the soup into the disposal, put his plate and bowl in the sink and went back to the family room.

Lindsey went to the front door and opened it, she smiled, "Hi Brooke. Come on in."

"Hi Lindsey, how are you?" Brooke gave Lindsey a quick hug.

As they walked into the kitchen Lindsey said, "Thanks for coming over tonight. You'll never believe what happened to me today. I'm sure this is only the beginning of a long and arduous ordeal with Milwaukee's best." Lindsey was referring to the police department.

Lindsey and Brooke walked into the kitchen. Off in a corner of the kitchen was a breakfast nook with an oval, wooden, dark chocolate brown table. It was surrounded by six matching dark brown chairs and lit by a metal chandelier with six candle bulbs.

Brooke went to sit down at the table, while Lindsey brought out a plate of cheese and crackers, several bottles of red wine, and glasses. "Here Brooke, you look like you need this just as badly as I do." Lindsey handed Brooke a bottle of wine.

As Brooke poured the wine she said, "I am so tired. But my day can't compare to what your day must have been like. How are you even still standing? And here you are waiting on me. Plus, you've had to take care of Leo and Lilly. Lindsey, how are you coping with John's death?" Brooke thought Lindsey was handling everything too calmly, she was concerned for her friend.

Lindsey shook her head and answered, "I can only tell you that I'm on pure adrenalin and not thinking clearly. If I think too much about it, I'll lose it. I'm staying focused on who did this, and John's death is so unreal to me right now. It's going to take a while to sink in, and then I'll have to adjust my life to live without him in it. That will take forever. I'll probably never quite get used to not seeing him around anymore. It's so sad. Who would actually murder him?" Lindsey poured a cup of wine for herself and then the doorbell rang again.

"Lindsey, sit down and drink your wine. I'll get the door." Brooke got up to get the door. "Hi Traci, Hi Julia, Lindsey's in the kitchen, we've already started on the wine."

"How is she doing?" Julia asked.

"So far so good, but something happened today and she was a bit shaken up by it. I think it has something to do with the police." Brooke answered in a hushed tone.

Julia replied, "Wow, how scary. I can't imagine what she's going through." The women walked into the kitchen and hugged Lindsey. "How are you?" They both said in unison.

Lindsey looked up at her friends and asked, "I'm okay. Is Heather coming?"

"Of course, she's running a little late, but she'll be here," said Julia. Just then the doorbell rang; Heather let herself in and met the other women in the kitchen.

"Hi" she gave Lindsey a hug, "I'm so sorry I'm late. How are you doing?"

"I'm okay," Lindsey poured Heather a glass of wine. The women were all present and sat at the table sipping their wine. "I can't believe John is dead, and murdered. We're going to have to find out who did it. You'll never believe what happened to me today."

Lindsey explained to her friends how she had been 'interrogated' at the police station. All the women's attention was held steadfast as Lindsey relayed the details of the meeting, including the description of the detective and officer.

When she was done the women were more determined than ever to come up with a list of possible suspects. Things were real and Lindsey's life was changed forever, but at least she was free; the women knew it could all be taken from her if the meeting at the police station was any indication of what the police were planning.

Brooke's mind was eager to begin and with concern in her voice for her friend she said, "Well, the police are focusing on Lindsey. As usual, they always look for the person who will profit the most or who they think has the biggest motive. We've got to come up with whom and why fast. The police won't give Lindsey any rest without having another strong suspect to focus their energies on."

Brooke got up and got a pen and notepad from Lindsey's desk drawer. Brooke had a theory, "I think we should look at Tom's business. Maybe Dave wanted the insurance money and wanted to run the office his own way. He's quiet. You know what they say about those quiet ones, they're always the least to be suspected and sometimes the worst delinquents out there."

Julia agreed, "Yeah, all the serial killers were quiet and kept to themselves, never causing any problems except a couple murders here and there." Julia met Brooke's eyes, lifted her eyebrows and nodded her head up and down. Julia continued, "Okay, let's get busy!"

Julia's organization skills came into play and she advised Brooke, "Ok, put down on the paper, Case Crackers, meeting one. Possible suspects: Number one, Dave. His motive, to get insurance money from loss of profits since John is dead and also to run the practice as he chooses without John's input. They probably had a huge falling out and couldn't agree on how to run things." Julia was creating the motive and Brooke was writing down notes as she was speaking.

Heather chimed in, "Good, so we have one other suspect who might or might not be a serial killer because he's quiet. But are we letting our imaginations get the better of us?" Heather, who was very reflective, asked.

Traci added her input, "No, I think he makes a great suspect. He has motive, he was at the party, who knows? I think he makes a terrific suspect. We should also check out the practice. There could be patients who got unusually attached to John and then John rejected him or her; or it could be a patient that was upset and angry at him, or owed him a lot of money."

Brooke wrote down under John's office and under Dave's name: patients of John's who were infatuated with him, or owed him money, or were dissatisfied with their procedure. Brooke said, "Those are all great ideas, I've got that all written down. Now let's focus on John's social life." She looked up at the women.

Brooke looked back down at the paper and began writing. She wrote heading number two, John's social life. "Who comes to mind as a possible suspect?" Brooke's pen was poised, ready to write down more names that the women came up with.

Lindsey started with the obvious; "John's current girlfriend and John's past girlfriends, he could be a jerk about breaking up with them. Sometimes the women didn't know that he was dating someone new until they heard about it from one of their friends."

Heather asked, "Who was John seeing in the past?" They all looked at Lindsey who knew from her children that John had a long standing relationship with a woman named Jess.

Lindsey told the women in a matter-of-fact tone, "Most of you know that John dated a woman named Jess for at least a year and then she found out he was also sleeping with Tara, his current girlfriend. Jess went ballistic. I didn't think much of it at the time, but now I'm wondering. She could have been angry enough about it to murder him. She could have been waiting and plotting for the right time to kill John. We know this murder had to be by someone who knew that he was having a party that night. It had to be someone close to him." Brooke wrote Jess and Tara under social life. Then she wrote down ex-girlfriends, ex-girlfriend's boyfriends.

Lindsey's eyes shown bright, she started to feel hope, "This is great you guys. Not that I want it to be any of those people, but it wasn't me and that is all the police are focusing in on. This at least puts the suspicion on different people. Any other ideas?"

Traci had another idea. "How about the group of guys he works on the inventions with? Maybe they came up with something spectacular, and one of them wants all of the glory."

Brooke interrupted, "Yeah, like a supersonic hydro electric flying car run on water and dog energy, or a telephone that can pinpoint the place the person is that you're calling, or a cheeseburger with 20 calories, or tomatoes that don't go bad after a week."

Lindsey stopped her friend from going on, "Okay Brooke, we get the idea, put down under another heading, 'group of inventers'." Brooke wrote down under heading three: inventors.

"What about friends and acquaintances?" Heather added.

Lindsey answered, "Put that down under heading four, but I can't think of one reason why a friend of John's would want him dead. What would be the motive?"

Heather answered, "I don't know, but if we're assuming that it is someone that he knew then we should add them to our list."

Lindsey thought about it, "Okay, that's a good point. We have our suspects now, how should we go about investigating?"

Brooke was always full of information and got the women thinking about a plan. She tapped the pen on the paper as she thought out loud. "Yes. How should we go about investigating? Let's see, someone has to go to John's office and search through his records, including all the business papers. Lindsey you should do that, and get into Dave's desk too. Find out all you can on how much insurance money Dave gets in case of John's death. Then go through the files and see if there are any patients who owe John a lot of money or were dissatisfied."

Lindsey listened to Brooke's suggestion and agreed, "Okay, I'll go to his office and search his records. I'm not sure how I'm going to get into Dave's office, but maybe Lori, John's office assistant, can help me out. She practically runs the show, I mean, not the actual procedures, but the business end. Hopefully she'll help me out, she and I always got along really well."

Brooke wrote more notes on the paper, "Lindsey and I will go to the office. It's better to work in pairs. Julia and Traci can 'by chance' run into Jess, buy her a drink and see what she has to say about John. You two should also interview Tara, and John's neighbors at the condo. They always seemed to know what John was doing and have a good idea who's been coming and going lately at John's condo."

Traci and Julia nodded in agreement, Traci said, "Sure we can do that, sounds like a great plan."

Brooke continued, "Heather, you said that Brett knew someone on the police force. Try to get in contact with him and find out all you can on the autopsy and forensic evidence. Even though he's in Waukesha, usually in these cases the cops from surrounding areas know what's going on; they are bigger gossips then a group of reporters at a local pub."

Heather knew she could get a lot of information because her husband's friend was her first cousin and they had grown up together in Waukesha. They had also gone to the same middle school and high school and spent all of the major holidays together growing up. It helped to have someone on the police force. "I'll get all the information you want, but it can't leave this room. My cousin trusts me explicitly and he would do all he can to help me and my friends but I can't jeopardize his job. He loves his job and his family." Heather talked in a hushed serious voice.

Brooke spoke for everyone present, "Of course, anything we uncover is to be kept among us, the ghosts and the walls. We've got to help John and we've got to help Lindsey. After her day with the police and the media we've got to move; things will just snowball after today. The media is ruthless and the police want to make sure they've got a key suspect."

Heather leaned in and folded her hands, "I'll get the forensic information and that will help us narrow down the suspect list."

The room fell quiet for several seconds before Brooke broke it, "Let's recap, we've got John's office covered, his ex girlfriend, his current girlfriend and any other acquaintances covered, the condo neighbors and the forensic/autopsy angle, oh yea, and the inventors. We still have to look at John's computer and cell phone records and go through his stuff at his house in Brookfield and the condo. That is going to be work, but it will be worth it, for Lindsey's sake and for Johns."

Lindsey got back to planning, in a somber voice she said, "I can get his computers and cell phone records and bring them here. John left me and the kids everything in his will. Brooke, you'll have to help me go through John's house in Brookfield. Knowing John he has everything in perfect order, even the dust bunnies will probably be in order from biggest to smallest. He was meticulous about everything in his life; and when I say meticulous, I'm being nice.... a nice way of saying, very anal."

"At least it will be easy to sort through his stuff; that should help us out a lot." Brooke replied in an optimistic voice.

Traci was upbeat too, "Well, we have got a ton of work to do." Traci held up her wine glass, "We can do this you guys. Case Crackers and a little bit of Wine united in finding out who in the world murdered John. Unbelievable, it's still hard to comprehend."

They toasted John, and with the warm glow of the chandelier and in her heated, cozy house, Lindsey felt comforted and had hope that with the help of her friends the killer would be found.

As if on cue, two of the bulbs in the chandelier went out and Lindsey's calm feeling took a turn to an uneasy, menacing feeling, like she was in danger and being warned of a threat. Something wasn't right but she couldn't put her finger on it, maybe someone was looking at her through the window. It felt like someone was watching her; could the police already have someone tailing her?

As Lindsey pondered her state of uneasiness the rest of the women drank a little more wine and chatted briefly about their lives. Lindsey took the lull in the case to put Leo and Lilly to bed and tuck them in their cozy rooms. She joined the rest of the women for some more wine before they headed out the door and back to their homes. Traci was the last to leave and then the house became deathly quiet again.

Lindsey turned on the TV, turned on all the lights and went to her bedroom to shower. She had never felt like she had ever been in much danger before. Could it be that she was next? Was someone targeting John and her? She told herself to not be silly and create unnecessary drama, she was only being silly. The facts were that someone had killed John but they weren't after her. Someone out there was the murderer, but whom?

Lindsey walked aimlessly through the house and then checked in on Leo and Lilly. They looked so peaceful sleeping and bundled up under the covers; she had to smile when she saw them, kissed them on the cheek and continued pacing the house.

At one o'clock, with all the lights still on in the house, and the TV blinking, Lindsey finally closed her eyes and fell asleep, tossing and turning with unsettling dreams. She slept until Leo woke her up at 7:00 the next morning.

# CHAPTER SEVEN
## John's Office

**W**ake up mom." Leo was the official alarm clock in the family. Ever since he was one he was waking up at 5 or 6 in the morning, ready for business, a true early bird. He always made sure that he woke Lindsey up at 7:00 so she could get them and herself ready for school and work.

Lindsey woke from a hazy dream; she was picking up men's underwear from along side of the road and putting them in a laundry basket. They were all different styles of men's briefs; polka dotted ones, solid colored ones, ones with diamonds on them, some with stripes. She was in her car snatching them up as she drove down the highway. What a strange dream, no use trying to figure out that one, although she thought some weirdo psychologist might have a field day with it.

"I'm up," she called to Leo. Lindsey put her robe on, staggered to the bathroom and looked at herself in the mirror. A quick wash of her face, an even quicker brushing of her teeth and she was ready to get dressed. What does a Case Cracker wear, black seems to be the color of anonymity. She chose some dark blue jeans, black boots, and a black long sleeved shirt. After inspecting herself in the mirror, she put her contacts in, a little eye liner, some powder, a hint of lipstick and she was ready. Lindsey felt pretty good considering her dreams weren't the most relaxing and she got to bed late last night.

Leo and Lindsey had already made themselves a bowl of cereal and had their backpacks ready for school. Lindsey prepared her children for school, "Now before you go be prepared for kids to ask you questions about your dad's death. There also might be some media vans. Your dad was a loved business man in this city and the news enjoys making stories up about people. Don't talk to them, and try to ignore them."

"Will we be on TV?" Lilly asked hoping she would be on TV.

Rather irritated Lindsey replied, "It doesn't matter Lilly, you've got to ignore them, that's the most important thing. They try to get information from people and then they make insinuations about other people based on what they want to hear. It's unfortunate, but some of the media might try to get you to say something or try to take your picture. I want you to be strong and not say anything. Your teachers at school will help you. The kids at school will probably be curious too, but they'll probably want to make you feel better. Don't you think?"

Lilly answered, "I think they'll try to make us feel better. I hate that dad is dead but I know he's still around. I can feel him. I keep telling Leo he's really not gone and that he's watching us all the time."

Leo gave Lilly a look, "Lilly! I just miss seeing Dad. He won't be coming over or taking us to the movies, or coming to our games anymore. He's gone!"

Lilly replied heatedly, "No he's not; he's just a ghost now."

Calmly Leo said, "Okay, so he's a ghost, but he can't take us to the movies!"

Haughtily Lilly said, "But he'll be there with us when we go with mom or our friends."

Not wanting to fight with his little sister Leo gave in, "I suppose so. I just miss him already. He used to call every night to see how I was doing in school. I guess I'll have to settle for him watching me like a ghost now."

Lindsey raised her voice a notch, "Okay, you two, stop arguing. You're giving me a headache. Your dad is watching over you and he loves you very much. He'll always be taking care of you even in the spirit world. His love is strong for you, okay?"

"Okay." Leo said quietly.

"Okay." Lilly softly spoke her reply too.

Lindsey might have been overdoing the need to talk about the media and what they might do, but she couldn't help it. "Now what did I say about the media?"

Lilly spoke with a hint of disdain and worry. Her mouth sounded unusually dry as she begrudgingly replied, "Don't talk to them, and walk away." Thank goodness her kids were smart and listened to her with open ears.

Lindsey's sad eyes turned away from her children so they wouldn't suspect that she was having a hard time with their dad's death. Lindsey's hoarse quiet voice replied, "Very good."

The kids sat quietly pondering over the circumstances of their life. They finished their bowls of cereal, placed them in the sink and picked up their backpacks. The backpacks seemed to weigh down her children adding to the emotional weight of their dad's death.

In a fake cheerful voice Lindsey said, "Let's go! It's time to have a great day at school." Lindsey shut the door behind them to the garage and they piled into the SUV and drove to school. She was relieved to not see any media vans; maybe they would leave her and her children alone.

After dropping off the kids, she headed back home to call Brooke. Today they were going to John's office. It was the perfect morning to do some sleuthing. Dave and John didn't open until 12:00 on Mondays because they had office hours on Saturday from 9:00 until 12:00; they gave everyone Monday mornings off.

Brooke would be meeting Lindsey and Lori at 9:30 to go over the files in John's office as well as Dave's business files. Lori agreed to help out as much as she could; she had been a dear friend of John's since the beginning of his dental practice. She didn't think Dave could have killed John, but she professed that she didn't know Dave that well; he was a quiet man who kept to himself.

Dave was a slight man with black horn-rimmed glasses that could have been worn by men in the 1950's. He wasn't married and she didn't know what he did on his days off. As far as she could tell he was nice, loved working and was a bookworm. He never spoke too much, even to the patients. When Dave spoke it was always in a calm, controlled and quiet voice. Lori had never heard him raise his voice or laugh loudly. Even when Dave laughed it was controlled and quiet, more like a chuckle than a laugh. Nobody could fault Dave for his quiet demeanor since he was polite and congenial even when he disagreed with whomever he was speaking too.

Dave had joined the practice two years ago after receiving his dentistry degree from Marquette University. John had interviewed a lot of dentists. He had found out that Dave was one of the top in his class to graduate and thought he would be the perfect candidate to help him with his busy practice. John had a patient base of 11,000 patients, which was five times the amount that 'normal' practicing dentists have.

At 9:30 the three women met at a church parking lot across the street from the dental practice. They didn't want their cars parked in front of John's practice alerting the killer, if it was Dave, or one of his patients. John's office was a converted lannon stone home built in the 30's. Its arched wooden door was green and an old fashioned dark steel metal door knob and a matching metal door knocker placed in the center of the door made the office look like something from a fairy tale.

Once you walked in you were treated to a center foyer with three beautiful stucco arches leading to different areas of the practice. As you entered the foyer, one arch was straight to the front of the building, one led off to the right and one led off to the left.

Through the right archway was a waiting room and directly across from the entrance was the office reception desk. The receptionist's counter was bar height and was made out of marble. To the left of the receptionist's desk on the far wall was a magnificent fireplace also with an arch inlaid on the top like the walls. The fireplace was made out of stucco blending in with the walls. Across from the receptionist's desk on the near wall was a flat screen TV for the patients and the patients' family to watch while they waited. Patients could look at books and magazines while they waited and could sit in any of the overstuffed comfortable couches and chairs. Paper cups were provided for water or coffee which was always freshly made. The floor was carpeted in traditional green, flat pile carpet with a diamond pattern.

Through the arch that was straight ahead you would be walking again on the flat pile green rug until you entered through a door where the dentist chairs were. It was a bright sunny room with 6 chairs set up for the dentist and dental hygienists to work. The chairs looked out the windows and on the opposite wall were the counters and sinks and supplies. Off to the corner of the sunny room was a small room with an x-ray machine set up to take pictures. It was very clean and the room was bright and warm and cozy. The last arch to the left led to John and Dave's offices.

The women went left and ended up in John's mahogany paneled office that looked like a well maintained old fashioned library. Everything was in its place. Lindsey, Brooke and Lori looked around at the neat office and noticed that some files were lying out on John's desk and that his computer had been removed.

"The police must have taken John's computer, great." Lindsey said sarcastically. "Well, let's start looking through the files. What's his system Lori?"

Lori was knowledgeable and talked with authority, "Well, you know John, he has everything color coordinated. The red files are patients who for whatever reason are behind in their payments. The yellow folders are for patients who have had procedures and everything is up to date; they've paid and they won't be due for another visit for six months. The green folders are also patients that have everything done, but I need to send out reminders of teeth cleaning and pull the files when they make appointments. The black folders are for patients who have major teeth issues or are unsatisfied with their procedure and need follow up care. Of course this is all on the computer but the folders will do just as well."

Lori continued explaining, "Several patients come to mind of John's who have recently called and complained. Usually John let the patients come back for more work if they weren't satisfied with the initial procedure. A lot of times they were confused and needed an in-depth explanation. Once that was complete, John was satisfied and so were his patients. I wouldn't put too much hope in finding a murder suspect from the patient list, but we should look at them anyway. The other 'problem' patients were people who didn't have insurance and owed a large sum of money. John was never after them for their money though, so I doubt they would murder him over the payment."

Lori opened up a drawer in John's desk, "In this drawer with the brown folders is all the information about the business, insurance papers, taxes, employee files, and misc. expenses. We should make copies of these and have a lawyer look over the insurance papers and the taxes. That will give us a much better idea of why Dave would murder John. Maybe the business was in some sort of financial trouble, but it's more likely that Dave would murder John for total control of the business."

Lindsey raised her eyebrows at Lori, "Wow, Lori, you sound like you think Dave did it?" Lindsey thought Lori was ready to convict Dave.

Lori hesitantly replied, "I like him. He's never been rude. I'm basing this on my gut feeling. I don't know him. After two years I don't know anything about him. I didn't think that was strange until now. Now I don't trust him, if that's what you mean. I wonder about him. He's okay, but he has his own way of doing things. He's extremely quiet, and ultra secretive, if you ask me. I haven't been paying attention to him but now my eyes and ears are going to be like watchdogs, watching his every move." Lori put her hand up to her eyes and pointed around the room.

Brooke chuckled, "Lori you're a riot. Let's start making copies." The women took the brown folders and started copying them. They also took several of the red and black folders. With Lori's help the copying didn't take long. They put everything back as close to how they found it.

Lori was reaching in to the drawer to put a file away and lying at the bottom of the desk drawer was John's cell phone. "Hello, what is this doing here?" Lori held up a small square object. "John always carried his cell phone; this must be a second back up phone." Lori held the phone up and opened it up.

"Bingo, you guys, we can look at the calls!" Lindsey said excitedly.

Brooke was excited, "That's great, it might give us some clues, put it in your purse Lindsey; you'll probably be able to recognize the calls better than anyone else." Lori gave the phone to Lindsey.

Lindsey held the phone, "Cool, they'll probably be some text messages too." Lindsey eyed the phone quickly and then put it in her purse. After a hurried last look at John's office they walked over to Dave's office to take a peak around.

Dave's office was across from John's, smaller, less neat and not as grand. It also had mahogany paneling and a nice wooden desk with a desk lamp. When they got to Dave's door and turned the handle they realized it was locked. The only people who had the keys to the office were Dave and John. Lori had a hair pin keeping some of her raven black hair in place, and just like in the old movies she used it and tried to pick the lock.

Lindsey could hear the wicked witch's music in her head as they waited for Lori to open up the door. Don da da da, da da, Don da da da da da. And on it went in Lindsey's mind. Lindsey looked around hoping that Dave wouldn't be charging through the front door, finding them intruding in his private space. She knew it was wrong to be snooping in his office but if they would find something that implicated him it would be worth it. If they didn't find anything that gave him a reason to kill John they would have to look elsewhere and hope Dave never found out they were sneaking around in his office.

The hair pin wasn't working at all; I guess that only worked in the movies. Lori decided to look in John's office again for a set of master keys. They headed back to John's office. Lindsey was feeling panic. Maybe sleuthing wasn't the profession she would excel at.

The women looked in all of John's drawers and rifled through his closet. In the back of the closet was a tennis racquet, a pair of gym shoes and a gym bag. John must have taken up tennis which didn't seem like John at all. The other items in his closet were a sweater and three jackets lined up on wooden hangers. It could double as *Mr. Roger's* closet from the old children's show. On one of the hooks at the side of the closet were a set of four keys. Voila, they were found and Lori took the keys, they walked down to Dave's office and tried them on his door.

Lindsey anxiously said, "Let's go, I'm getting nervous, it's already 11:00." The key slid in and the door knob turned easily. The women entered Dave's office and were surprised to see a pair of women's sandals with a three inch wedge heel next to his desk.

Lindsey commented on the shoes, "Maybe Dave likes to dress up."

Brooke gave Dave the benefit of the doubt. "You guys, it's probably his girlfriends."

Lori piped in, "I would know if he had a girlfriend."

"Maybe he brings her here after hours," replied Lindsey. The women were standing by Dave's desk, assessing the office. Lindsey was ready to begin the search, "Okay, that's enough speculation, let's look around."

Dave's office was not as neat as John's. The women shuffled through the items on the top of his desk. Nothing much stood out as a red flag; there were some stickers, a full can of coca cola, a calculator, a stapler, a bin with a ruler, scissors, some educational DVDs and a cup with pencil, pens and markers. On the left side of his desk was his computer. Lori tried to get into the computer and after three attempts she got lucky. She typed in DDS1 and it worked. Lori knew Dave had put that same title on his car vanity license plate.

"You're really good." Lindsey was happy Lori was there with them.

"Not really," Lori replied. "It's just lucky that men are so predictable." She flashed a smile at Lindsey and Brooke, who were looking at the screen with her.

As soon as the files were opened Lori said her favorite word, "Voila!" The business file was opened and as fast as she could Lori sent it to the printer.

As the printer whirled into action the phone rang. Lindsey was so startled she screamed "Ahhhhh Hurry up!" She wasn't used to being a sleuth and uneasiness filled her body. Her hands and face were sweaty and hot. Her heart was skipping around, playing hopscotch inside her body.

Although Lindsey was scared she couldn't resist and asked Lori, "Go to his mail too." Lori clicked on his mail and scanned the in-box. Nothing really popped out at her. She opened up the mail that looked as if it contained correspondence letters to John and started making copies of those letters first.

Some of the mail was from John, other items were from people she didn't recognize but she opened them up and sent them to the printer too. The clock hands were turning, and fast. Whirrrrrr, the printer couldn't go quickly enough for Lindsey.

While Lori was sending documents to the printer Brooke and Lindsey peeked into Dave's closet. They both looked at each other when they found a blond, long haired wig, a short brown wig, three dresses and two different sets of women's shoes.

"Is Dave a transvestite?" Lindsey asked.

"Could be, he has all of these women's clothes. It's very strange, not like *Mr. Roger's* closet......or is it?" Brooke smirked. "It doesn't mean he's a killer, but it is weird."

Brooke and Lindsey moved away from the closet and shut the door. Nothing else in Dave's office sparked their interest.

After what seemed like ten hours, the final paper flipped out of the printer and the women closed down the computer, grabbed all of the paper and locked Dave's door. It was 11:45 and it wasn't a minute too soon.

They were running out the door hoping no one would see them. They crossed the street determined to get out of there without being discovered. In the parking lot Lindsey took the papers and said goodbye to Lori and Brooke.

"Thanks so much you guys. Lori, we couldn't have done this without you. I know you were a great friend to John and he always said such wonderful things about you. I know we're going to find out who did this to John. And I'm glad you trust me."

The sudden death of John bonded the women together in a joint adventure. Lori had listened to John talk about his kids and Lindsey and knew that Lindsey could never have committed any crime, especially murder.

Lori smiled warmly at Lindsey, understanding how Lindsey felt, "John only had good things to say about you too. I'm sure you didn't do it, Lindsey, and I want to find out why someone would murder John. He was my friend. I'll do all I can." With a final wave of their hands the women left each other. Lori had to go back to the office to resume her office duties, Brooke went to her practice at the mall and Lindsey headed home to do some heavy reading.

The women had taken and copied six patient files, copied four of John's files from his business folder, copied Dave's business folder from his computer and several emails. The task seemed daunting to Lindsey; it was the proverbial finding a needle in a haystack, but she would do it.

Staring at the folders she decided to procrastinate. Lindsey could use some coffee to keep her alert and her eyes open. Before she went home Lindsey decided to get some coffee and call Julia and Traci to see what they had uncovered.

Tom had been watching Lindsey with interest. What was Lindsey up to? He had appointed himself as Lindsey's surveillance detective, which was common police detective work and wasn't normally done by the detective in charge of the case. However, he was taking a more personal approach to this case and wanted to see for himself where and what Lindsey was up to.

His heart and head had been twisted as he watched what seemed to be evidence piling up as big as a mountain against Lindsey. He couldn't let his feelings for her distract him from the forensic evidence, but he had to admit that she had gotten under his skin. He watched as she came out of her house, looking spectacular with her hair pulled back behind her head and caught in a ponytail holder. She had on dark glasses but they couldn't hide her beauty.

He trailed her in his unobtrusive Volkswagen Pissat, making sure he stayed a couple of cars behind. Where was she going? After a twenty-five -minute drive he found his answer. Of course, he thought, she's doing her own sleuthing. Tom watched her from the car. He had his binoculars and soon saw

John's office assistant and Lindsey's friend meet at the church parking lot. He would have to wait there until they were done. Maybe she was innocent, maybe she was hoping to find out who murdered John because she didn't do it.

At 9:30 the three women went into the office where John's practice was; he waited for the women to emerge. His seat hurt from sitting so long and arrows attacked his spine. He sat there staring at nothing and drinking from a water bottle. Finally at 11:45 he saw Lindsey with a stack of papers, and the two other women exit the building. They quickly crossed the street to the church parking lot and said their goodbyes.

Tom's instinct would have been to intercept Lindsey and confiscate the papers reminding her that she was interfering with a police investigation. But he knew that his officers had already gotten a search warrant and went through the office, taking the computer. It was always hard for him to delegate and when he saw Lindsey walk away from the office with a stack of papers he wondered if his officers had really done a thorough job last night or had just taken the computer and called it a night so that they could get home. In some ways he wouldn't have blamed them; it was a long night, and he had told them to get the computer from John's office and his home in Brookfield. Time would tell what the investigation would uncover.

Right now his thoughts focused on Lindsey. He wanted to know what she was aiming to find, what she had found, and what kind of investigating she was going to embark on. But instead of confronting her, he waited patiently and followed her to see where she would go. Already, he was making exceptions for her, but she had to be innocent, didn't she?

# CHAPTER EIGHT
## Coffee with Detective Tom

Lindsey's heart was beating a mile a minute as she rushed away from John's office. As she was leaving, out of the corner of her eye, she saw Dave's white Beamer pass her on the street. Instinctively she ducked and hoped he hadn't seen her. On the other hand, why couldn't he see her? She had a right to be on the road and if she needed to go to John's office that wasn't breaking any rules.

Her guilty conscience was bothering her; breaking into Dave's office wasn't something she relished. He could be innocent, which left her feeling guilty of invading Dave's privacy. Why did he have those high heel shoes by his desk and those women's wigs and clothes in his closet? Maybe he was gay.

Lindsey tried to focus on driving but her thoughts were wandering and with a wary eye she looked at the stack of papers lying next to her on the driver's seat. And how long would it take to look through all these documents? What did she really know about the business end of John's office, her thoughts chased each other, her mind doing battle with each idea at hand.

Somehow she drove and found her way to the nearest Starbucks. She hadn't had enough coffee yet today and needed the comfort of a warm cup of jo. She took out one folder from the pile labeled 'insurance' and walked into the Starbucks.

At 12:00 o'clock there was a lunch crowd. People were lined up to place orders; women in business suits, men in slacks and ties and groups of two or three women dressed in casual jeans and sweaters talking about their children. Lindsey envied them, knowing that her life until a few days ago resembled the rest of the clientele at Starbucks. Now her ex-husband was dead, she was a suspect in his death and she was running to get to the truth of John's murder before she was handcuffed and put in the slammer. Way to be dramatic Lindsey, she thought.

After standing in line for five minutes she placed her order and went to put cream and two packets of equal in her coffee. The coffee smelled great and warmed up her cold hands. She took the coffee and went to a corner table to sit down and enjoy the coffee and glance at the contents of the insurance folder. Unfortunately her adrenalin was keeping her from actually concentrating on the folder; she took a sip and looked around before putting the folder down on the table next to her.

She stared mindlessly out the big window looking at the parking lot, until she spotted Tom. What was he doing here? He must be following her. She grabbed the folder from the table and put it in her purse. He saw that she spotted him and she waved. He waved back and then before she knew what she was doing, she was signaling with her hands for him to come and join her. How about that? She was going to be drinking coffee with the enemy, drinking with someone who was spying on her and trying to convict her of a crime. . . . . but he was really cute.

He had driven a couple of car lengths behind her and ended up parking in the Starbucks parking lot, wishing he could go in too and have a big cup of coffee to keep him going. He noticed that as Lindsey got out of her car she was carrying one of the folders. Well, he was stuck in the parking lot bored to tears. He sat for around 10 minutes before he saw her again through the window. Wow, she was gorgeous.

His thoughts went back to her house the morning of her ex-husband's death. He had wanted badly to encircle her with his arms and make her feel safe and warm, and to calm her down. He breathed heavily as he remembered her quiet, shaken demeanor and the hurt in her eyes. He wished he could fix everything for her, and yet here he was, tailing her because she was the prime suspect in her ex-husbands murder. Damn it all to hell. Just then he looked up and their eyes met, she waved. What could he do? He waved back; caught in the act.

Lindsey was too smart for her own good; he could tell that from the moment he met her. She was signaling him to come join her. Without thinking twice about it and with some anticipation he wandered out of his car and joined Lindsey in the coffee house.

As he approached the table where she was sitting she said in a light, half humorous and half serious voice, "Are you following me? I mean, what brings you to this part of town?" She smiled up at him.

Tom thought about the question before replying. Would Lindsey believe him if he told her it was a coincidence. She probably wouldn't believe him, but he said it anyway in true cat and mouse play. "Oh I was out here on a different case and needed some coffee to keep me going. There's no rest for a cop, we're working 24/7, non-stop." He smiled and crossed his arms.

"Oh, really?" Lindsey said in a teasing, light voice. "You're out here on another case? What case would that be?" Lindsey knew he was following her and was having fun putting Tom on the spot.

"Ummm, only police work; nothing I can share with you. It's too dangerous and highly confidential."

She thought about that statement as she crinkled her nose at him. Oh great, he'd always have the excuse of 'confidential police work' making his life even more secretive then most peoples' life. Lindsey shrugged her shoulders and took a sip of coffee before replying, "Oh, well, I don't really want to know. I was only trying to be polite. I'm sure it's a bore compared to real estate." She knew she was flirting with him.

Tom replied glibly, "Really, what's so exciting about real estate?"

"The sale of a home, of course, and meeting different people, their life styles, what they're looking for and where they want to live. It's really fun. The rush you get when you've sold the home, the commission. I've been working with a client all morning." She said the last sentence looking directly into his eyes. She looked for his reaction. Nothing, a complete poker face, he was so good at not letting on what he knew through his expressions. And Lindsey loved all his expressions.

He smiled as he said, "Okay, if you say so. I'm going to go and get a coffee, I'll be right back." He got up to stand in line.

Lindsey watched him as he walked away. He had an agile, muscular body. There wasn't an ounce of fat on it and she wanted to touch his broad shoulders. While she waited for Tom to return she couldn't help but think about him.

When she talked to Tom he had a twinkle in his eyes, like he enjoyed life and could see people for the good they possessed. She thought he was playful too, and quick, a perfect combination. Ok, back to reality, she just lied to him and he had just lied to her. There was no chance for the two of them, but she sensed that he was attracted to her and she was definitely attracted to him.

Even with John's death so new in her mind, here she was becoming all dreamy about Tom. Something was definitely wrong with her. The timing stunk; here he was, following her, as if she could really murder someone. But that's what Tom and his companions thought.

Lindsey wondered what type of evidence the police where basing their assumptions on. Was it merely a case of suspecting the ex-wife, knowing that she would profit the most from John's death and collect on his life insurance policy or did they have more? She couldn't imagine that they had any evidence pointing to her; she knew she hadn't done it.

Tom came back with his coffee and sat down next to Lindsey. His close proximity to her was making her hot. He opened up the next conversation asking her how she was doing. "How is everything with you and your family? Are you coping alright?"

Lindsey thought that was a fair question. She wanted to answer truthfully, but she also wanted to get some information from Tom. She looked up at him and answered, "Honestly, I haven't had time to get used to the idea of John not being around. I know he's dead, I can feel it, but it hasn't sunk in and for some reason the police seem to have me on their suspect list."

Tom felt her intense stare as she got straight to the point. He replied just as matter of fact as she was, "Lindsey, we're doing everything we can to find the murderer and we have to look at those closest to John as suspects. You would have a lot to gain from John's death. He did have a hefty amount of life insurance to his name and you are the beneficiary."

Lindsey looked straight at Tom. She knew he was doing his job, seeing how she would react, giving her the piece of information she was all too well aware of. She agreed with him, "I know you have to look at me as a suspect, but the only possible reason you could have me on your list of suspects is because of the life insurance policy. There couldn't be any other physical evidence linking me to that crime. I didn't do it." Lindsey took a sip of coffee waiting to see what Tom would say. How could he say anything but that they didn't really suspect her, she was someone that they had to check-out. They were making sure to follow police procedure.

She fully thought he would say so but instead he slowly replied, looking her straight in the eye. With inquisitive and intense eyes he asked, "You didn't do it?"

Lindsey's eyes opened twice the size they normally were, "Of course I didn't do it!"

She almost spilled the beans about investigating John's death on her own and looking at Dave and the others as suspects but she held her tongue. She didn't know if she could trust Tom just yet, especially with his latest accusation.

Tom replied in a sincere and concerned voice, "I'll be honest with you; there is some physical evidence that points to you." Tom didn't want to shake Lindsey up or cause her to worry but he did want to see how she would react.

He knew that she would be interrogated again and that she would find out that he was in charge of the case. He also knew that there were several items from the crime scene with her fingerprints on it. It would be only a matter of time before she would be taken down to the police station and booked on suspicion of murder, with search warrants in place for her house on Lake Drive and her vehicle.

"How could there be evidence against me? I didn't do it! You've got to believe me; you know I couldn't do it." Lindsey couldn't believe what she had heard. As she talked she used her hands, waving them around, her voice had risen and was too loud. After she stopped talking she sat back to calm herself down and crossed her legs.

Tom, she realized, was only being honest with her, and she was thankful for that, but she sure felt like 'shooting the messenger.' "Are you on my case?" Her voice had a crisp edge to it, without her even realizing it.

Tom was too honest to lie to her again, he gently told her the truth, "I'm the lead detective on the case Lindsey. I'm investigating all different possibilities, including other suspects besides you. It just so happens that there is some evidence that ties you to the crime scene."

He watched her as she stared intensely into his eyes, a penetrating stare, trying to get more information from him. He sensed she didn't do it, but he also knew that the best psychopaths were extremely adept at deception and that her exterior expressions could be an act.

She replied slowly and made sure she kept her voice soft and calm, "Well, I didn't do it. I hope you are seriously looking at other suspects and not pigeon-holing me as the only suspect. I've been in John's car many times; it's only natural that my fingerprints would be there." She tried this out on him and he nodded in agreement.

"I know, there's more then fingerprints and hair. We will be talking with you more." He handed Lindsey his card. "Stay around here Lindsey. I've got to get back to work even though I've enjoyed our meeting." He knew it wasn't what she wanted to hear. He saw her body language change, her eyes had started to throw fire his way, her arms were crossed in front of her. He expected that to happen.

Lindsey felt like a school girl getting reprimanded by the principal. What did he mean by her staying around here, of course she was going to stay around. What a jerk. A very cute jerk, but still, how could he suspect her?

She composed herself, he was only doing his job. She replied, "Of course I'm staying around, I've done nothing wrong and will help in the investigation 100%. Have a great day. I'm sure I'll be seeing you around soon." She had a sarcastic edge to her sentences even though she tried to stifle her tone and appear calm, cool and collected.

He smiled seeing right through her, "I'll see you soon. Take care of yourself and your family." With a closed-mouthed grin, and a tilt of his head he got up and walked back out to the car.

Lindsey made a quick call to Julia and then to Traci before she sipped more on her coffee and contemplated Detective Tom's words. What could they possibly have on her?

Lindsey had asked Traci and Julia to meet her for a yoga class at 4:00. Traci and Julia hadn't had any time to conduct interviews of the party goers or the tenants at the condo. Lindsey decided to go back home and look at the folders before she would have to pick up Leo and Lilly.

She sipped some more coffee, got up, put the empty cup in the trash and went out to get in her car, got in and drove back home to start compiling a list of the suspects. It would help her calm her nerves if she got started right away on her investigation. She decided that the best thing to do as soon as she got home would be to start writing notes about the suspect's motives and their personal information so she would know how to contact them.

How had it come to this? What did the police have on her? She drove home in a cloud of wonder and worry. Before she realized it she was parked in her garage and taking the folders to her office to read. What she found out was almost incomprehensible.

# CHAPTER 9
## The Folders

Lindsey managed to drive home and fortunately not get into an accident, which was surprising because Lindsey was thinking about the crime and solving the case instead of concentrating on the road or the drivers around her.

Her head was buzzing with thoughts of the murder as she got out of her SUV and went straight into her office to sit at her desk. The desk had been a gift from her mother, handed down from several generations; it was an antique oak desk with a center drawer and an old fashioned key slot. It had stylish curved legs with a drawer on the right side for files and a drawer above the file for other office materials. Her laptop was on the desk, a country wooden lamp, a set of three candles, and Leo and Lilly's school picture. She loved the rich look of the desk and had the matching big seated, high-backed formal but comfortable chair upholstered in her favorite rich green, chenille material. The contrast of dark wood and the soft green fabric made the room feel cozy and warm and happy.

Lindsey had decorated the walls with portraits of her family and flowered prints. Also, on a side table in her office was a vase of fresh lilies; she spoiled herself with fresh flowers in her office hoping that it would lift her spirits when she was working on selling homes.

The view out her office windows was of the side yard, with a view of beautiful pine trees and bushes. On either side of the window were two solid matching oak book shelves, filled with her favorite reading books, candles and more pictures of her family. She loved her cozy office, the one place she kept organized and clean, and clutter free.

Lindsey looked at the insurance papers pertaining to John's and Dave's business first, assuming that Dave would have the biggest motive and that the patients would most likely turn out to be false leads. She opened the insurance folder at her desk and tried to decipher the contract. The insurance papers had two beneficiaries. The first beneficiary was none other than herself; her signature was written on the document.

Lindsey knew that the signature was a forgery because she had never signed the papers, let alone even looked at the papers. Who would go to all the trouble to forge her name on these documents and put her name as the beneficiary? Did John know about the insurance? How could he sign it without her there? Her heart skipped a beat, was this the proof she needed? Or did this incriminate her even more?

Someone was impersonating her; someone close to John who would know when he would need the paper's signed. Was it Lori? She has a handle on all of the business transactions. She could have had John sign and notarized it, then sign for Lindsey, give it to Dave, notarize all three signatures and taken it to the lawyer. She felt sick, hopefully that wasn't the case.

Maybe Lori and Dave were working together and wanted John out. Lori could be lying about her feelings for Dave. Or was it Dave? He could have signed his name, taken it to a different notary wearing a wig and dress and heels and had the papers signed in her behalf. Then again, maybe it was John and he didn't want to bother her so he signed her name, gave it to Lori to notarize and sent it to their lawyer. She looked at the other signatures, one was John's and the other was Dave's.

She would have to talk to the lawyer who drew up the papers to find out if there was a procedure for witnessing insurance paper signatures.

Lindsey felt like she struck gold, but this type of gold left her feeling cold and frightened. According to the insurance papers she would own John's half of the business which was estimated at a value of three million dollars. John and Dave had stipulated that in case of one or the other's death, the partner would recoup a set amount of that partners earning potential for one year. Lindsey and Dave would share equally in the insurance money delegated for one year of business profit and Dave would continue to run his end of the business, which would make his earnings double.

The two business owners had separate accounts and financial management services that divided earning made as if there were two separate businesses. Dave's motive became even more substantial, which made Lindsey excited. The only problem with the business insurance money was she would also profit substantially and the papers incriminated her even more.

Still, if she were to die or to be otherwise incapacitated, as in incarcerated, then Dave would be the sole beneficiary of the business insurance money and would have enough to buy John's end of the business. Maybe he had set her up? Detective Tom had said there was DNA of hers. Dave could get her DNA when he cleaned her teeth and he knew her fingerprints would be found in John's car. Lindsey was a patient of Dave's on several occasions when John was too busy to see her.

Dave was always so quiet and sneaky according to Lori. And why did he have women's clothes in his closet and the wigs. That alone was incriminating. What was the possibility of him being a transvestite? He probably used those items when he wanted to impersonate her. She put his name in her notebook and wrote down notes about the insurance money. She wrote down the date of the party. She put down interview Dave, his whereabouts on September 15th. Then she put down motive as the business insurance money, jealousy and resentment of John and his life, arguments over spending money and procedures. She also wrote down that there might be the possibility that Dave was setting her up to take the blame for the murder so he could be the sole owner of the dental practice.

It had taken Lindsey 2 hours to go through that one folder and try to decipher the fine print. Her eyes were tired and the print on the paper started to blur. She put the folder down, rolled her neck down to the right and left before looking up and noticing that it was already 3:15.

It was time to get Leo and Lindsey from school and drop them off at orchestra and gymnastics while she made her way downtown to join Traci and Julia at the Milwaukee Spa for yoga and a tea afterwards. She couldn't wait to do her yoga and release the tension in her back and neck. John's death and the murder investigation were making her shoulders rise to her ears and made her constantly clench her teeth, hurting her jaw and making her feel dizzy.

She picked up John's cell phone and placed it in her purse. She hadn't had time to go through John's cell phone thoroughly, but had taken several minutes looking at the list of numbers stored in his phone. Looking at the phone again reminded her of her initial reaction to one number in John's cell phone. It immediately caught her attention and activated something in her long term memory.

John's phone had a multitude of numbers stored and one number kept flashing in her mind. The number was repeatedly displayed in the "missed calls" category of his phone memory.

Lindsey looked in the "recent calls" numbers to see if there was a name associated with the number, but according to his cell phone, John had not returned the call.

She knew that number from somewhere but couldn't put her finger on it at the moment. Time was ticking so she decided to think about the mystery phone number later. She took the folders and carefully put them in her desk and locked the drawer. Lindsey got up and stretched her hands over her head. She was tired from reading the folder and the stretch helped. She grabbed her coat and purse, found her keys and went to get her kids.

The children's school was near Lindsey's house. As Lindsey approached the all brick elementary school, she noted that a media van was positioned across the street. Oh brother, thought Lindsey, the circus is about to begin. She quickly put a scarf around her head, put her sunglasses on and braved the walk up to the school to collect Leo and Lilly, hoping she'd get there before the van realized who she was. Once inside she saw Leo and Lilly standing by Lilly's teacher, Mrs. Doutty. Lilly was clutching her hand.

Lindsey quickly gave an appreciative glance at Mrs. Doutty and greeted her children, "Hi, how was your day?"

Both kids looked tired, and subdued. Lilly answered, "It was fine, mom, but everyone knows that our dad is dead. They've been whispering all day about it. And Sally asked me if dad was murdered."

Lindsey gave Mrs. Doutty a glance, making eye contact in the form of a question trying to learn more about the kids' day. Lindsey calmly said, "I think we need to talk about that when we get home. Let's get going, okay guys?" and to Mrs. Doutty she said, "Mrs. Doutty, thanks for waiting with Leo and Lilly, could you call me later tonight?"

Mrs. Doutty smiled, "Of course, I think we'll be able to help make Leo and Lilly's day here better if we talk about what we can do to help." Mrs. Doutty was a well-liked, caring, rather plump teacher with soft, short, sandy blond hair in her mid forties. She was one of those teachers that you hoped your kids had. She was caring and motivated, organized and planned exciting lessons.

Lindsey mouthed a silent 'Thank You', certain that Mrs. Doutty would call later that night.

Lindsey again donned the scarf and glasses and said to the kids, "We'll have to get to our truck fast; I'll tell you why when we get home."

Lindsey put one arm around each of the kids and whisked them to the car. The media personnel were descending on Lindsey and the kids, bombarding them with questions. Lindsey kept walking until they were safely in the car, locked the doors and practically ran over one of the reporters.

"Wow, mom, way to floor the gas!" Leo thought that the reckless driving brought on by the need to get away from the media was pretty cool.

Lindsey grinned at Leo, "Don't get any ideas, Leo; you know mom usually drives with a steady hand, and within the speed limit."

"Boring!" Both kids sang in unison.

Other than having a lot of questions about their dad and his death, Lindsey was amazed at the composure and grit her children had displayed. They had weathered the first day without their father alive. Lindsey hoped they would keep up their good spirits; she had to find out who murdered their dad.

Lindsey drove them to their respective practices; it would probably help them to unwind too. She arrived at the Milwaukee

Spa, wanting to do anything except think about the murder case; she hoped the class would give her the mental break she needed. Unfortunately, like an aching tooth that couldn't be ignored, the murder continued to haunt her.

# CHAPTER 10
## The Spa

"Hi Traci. Hi Julia." Lindsey caught up with the women in the swanky women's locker room. Scented candles warmed up the surroundings and baskets of shampoo, cream rinse, perfumes and lotions were placed throughout the room.

Lindsey was all wound up; she explained in a quick breathless voice, "I am so stressed out. Brooke and I were at John and Dave's office all morning scouring the place for clues. I felt like a real *Charlie's Angel*, but I'm not sure if I'm cut out for sleuthing, my heart was racing like a thoroughbred at the Kentucky Derby. Afterwards, to recollect my thoughts and calm down, I went to grab a quick coffee and guess who I saw?" She looked at Traci and Julia.

Julia quickly said, "Who?"

Lindsey answered, continuing to tell the women the events of her day, "You'll never guess. Tom, the detective on John's case; I'm sure he was following me! He got out of his car after I waved him in and we had some coffee together. I am their number one suspect. Can you believe it? He even told me he found some fingerprints of mine at the crime scene. I'm not nervous yet because I didn't do it. But innocent people have been locked up before and I don't want to be one of them. Have you two had any luck finding and interviewing any of John's old girlfriends or the people around his condo?"

The women had been changing out of their business clothes into their yoga pants, tank tops and sweatshirts. No shoes were needed for yoga so the ladies donned their flip flops. With a toss of their hair, a quick finger comb and a look in the mirror the women headed out to the yoga room.

Traci answered Lindsey's question as they walked out of the locker room and to the yoga studio, "No, we haven't interviewed anyone yet. It would be interesting to hear what Jess has to say. I remember seeing her at John's birthday party; she had the off-white strapless dress with diamond gems stitched around the top of her dress and white high stilettos. She looked ready to kill John when he was busy talking and kissing the other women at his party. Her face was strained in a smile but it looked more like a grimace. She's not a good actress. I don't think Jess can stand being 'just friends' with John."

They walked into the door of the yoga studio. It was located on the third floor of the spa. It had 14-foot ceilings with mirrors on two sides of the room and a view of the river out of the wall of windows on the opposite wall from the door. A fountain was hung on one of the walls and the drizzling ripple of the water helped to transform the room into a yoga retreat, high baskets filled with bamboo also helped create a room for relaxing and meditating.

Lindsey spoke in a whisper, afraid that other's around them might hear her, "I noticed Jess at the party too. She did look upset; she looked like she was trying to have a good time, but wasn't succeeding. I don't know if she has enough hatred towards John that she would have killed him though. She loved him tremendously."

Julia whispered back, "It's happened before; jealousy is a strong emotion and the perfect motive. She could have planned it, she's certainly strong enough and John would have followed her out to his car if she asked him too. Have you ever seen the arms on her; you could ski down her biceps." Julia pumped up her own arm.

"You're right," laughed Lindsey; the visual made her chuckle. The women found a spot to roll out their mats.

Marci, the yoga instructor was already in the front of the room. "Welcome everyone, grab your blocks, mats and straps and find a spot." Marci smiled. The music was soft and comforting; the lights in the room had been dimmed creating a peaceful, relaxing atmosphere. Marci led the yoga instruction for 60 minutes.

Lindsey's mind concentrated on the stretches and the muscles involved in holding the yoga stances. For 60 minutes her mind was filled with nothing but peace and stillness. After 50 minutes of stretching and strength poses Marci led the ladies through the relaxation portion of the hour long yoga session. "Breath in, let your lungs expand. As you breathe, inhale, taking in the good air, and on the exhale, get rid of the bad air and all your bad thoughts. Breathe in, take in the good air, breathe out and as you exhale let out the bad air. Relax as you exhale, feel your body sink into the floor; your shoulders, your back, your hips your thighs, your calves and your feet are heavy and relaxed. Let your body relax as you release tension and feel your body sink slowly into the floor. Release tension around your eyes; release the muscles in the back of the head. Your muscles are relaxed, let them float away from your neck and loosen up. Your shoulders are relaxed, your arms are relaxed, and each finger is light and tingly as you feel the ground below you. You are centered and calm."

Lindsey was breathing, completely intent on relaxing her mind and body. At the end of the session she felt like a new person. Her body felt completely relaxed and she no longer had her headache and muscle pains. The women left the yoga room and headed back to the locker room to change. They decided to head to the attached café after they changed for some tea and to talk some more about the investigation.

Julia smiled, "Wow, what a great workout. I think I grew an inch from stretching, although I might have popped one of my hamstrings. She always says to let gravity take you down when we're stretching, but I can't help to force myself further. Someday I would like to do a waist bend and plant both of my hands on the floor!" Julia stopped in the hall, held up her hands and tried to place them on the floor as she bent from the waist. She wasn't quite there before she stood up again.

Traci laughed, "I know we'll get there, we just have to come here more often," Traci looked at her friends and then yawned. "I don't know about you guys but the relaxation portion puts me right to sleep. One day they're going to have to poke me and wake me up. It's so tranquil."

Lindsey agreed, "Wouldn't it be great if we felt like that all the time?"

Traci smiled, "That would be a trick," The women were almost back to the dressing room again. As soon as they were there they changed from their yoga clothes into their street clothes.

"I am so cold. I hope the tea room has the fire going. I want to sit right next to it." Lindsey was always cold no matter how many clothes she layered on her body.

"Okay Lindsey, why don't you gain some weight? Then you won't be so cold." Traci eyed Lindsey and gave her some free wellness advice.

Lindsey was putting on her jacket and commented, "Traci, if I get fat, I'll still be just as cold, and then I'll be miserable too."

Julia looked at her friends and coolly said, "Let's just go to the tea room and sit by the fire." Julia grabbed her bag and started for the door.

Lindsey looked at Julia, "Sounds good, we have a lot to talk about."

Lindsey and Traci grabbed their bags and the three women headed up to the café to warm up and drink some hot tea. A roaring fire was beckoning the women. They walked over and sat in the cushy chairs by the fire. The waitress came over immediately with a porcelain teapot filled with soothing English tea and three teacups. Scones were brought out on a porcelain plate to accompany the tea.

As soon as the waitress left, Lindsey pulled out John's cell phone from her bag and held it up. She brightly said, "Look you guys, everything we need to know, right on this little cell phone. There are text messages and phone numbers. We found it in John's desk drawer. The police must have the other cell phone, which is too bad since that cell phone probably had more information in it than this one. It was probably on John when he died. John never left home without his cell phone. I haven't had time to search through this cell phone yet but I thought we could start scrolling down the numbers together and see if we recognize any of the people."

"Did you find anything else at his office?" Traci leaned toward Lindsey to hear more about the office search and get a better look at John's cell phone.

"Yeah, Lori helped me find some folders and I started to look through the business papers and the insurance papers. I've put down Dave as a prime suspect; he would be sole owner of the business if something were to happen to me. We went into his office and found a pair of women's chunky wedge shoes and some dresses and wigs in his closet. Whatever that means?

Lori thinks he might be gay and dresses up in women's clothes, which would be different but doesn't prove anything. She also thinks that he's one of those secretly psycho serial-killer guys, like Jeffrey Dahmer."

Traci rolled her eyes. "We're not looking for a serial killer. Would he want John dead?" Traci asked.

"Yes, he has a huge motive. He stands to benefit financially due to the loss of wages to the business that John generated; He'll get the insurance money. He also would be the sole dentist and have more control without John around. Lori had read some of the emails sent back and forth to him and John and they weren't all cozy-friendly. There was some rivalry there and John usually won out, since he owned the business."

"Dave could have resented John, or even had a crush on John." Julia added her psychological profile of Dave and John's relationship. "It could have been a crush." Julia took a sip of her tea and looked at Lindsey.

Lindsey shrugged, "I don't know. I don't think John would ever encourage Dave in that way, but I can't be 100% sure." Lindsey was pretty certain John wasn't bisexual, but you never know. She continued talking, "Even if John didn't encourage Dave, Dave could have been hurt if John rejected him. It would have been another source of tension between them."

Traci took a sip of tea and added to the conversation. "Wow, you've come up with a lot of possibilities today. You've got a motive for Dave, and I bet they'll be some indication in those texts that implicates Jess and maybe Tara, or someone that we haven't thought of. "

Lindsey nodded her head up and down and held John's cell phone in her hand. "I know. I'm glad with what I've found out already. If the police have done their job, they'll also be checking out Dave and get off my back. Hopefully the files that I have at home and this cell phone will give us some more leads."

"Let's start scrolling through the numbers," Julia said. Lindsey turned John's cell phone on and they started reading the texts and looking at the list of names saved to his phone. They decided that there were several possible names on the cell phone that they would need to call and interview. The names were familiar enough and repeated enough to find out more about them, like where they were the night of John's death or if they knew anything that would help the women solve the murder.

Lindsey had Traci and Julia look at the number that was causing her problems. "Look at this number. Who does this number belong to? There's no name attached to the number but I know that I've seen this number before. And look how many times they've called. I've looked at the dates and not once had John returned the call. I can only speculate that it was someone who wanted desperately to make contact with John and he was ignoring them. It's not Jess, or Tara's either, their name and numbers are sprinkled throughout the phone and John was still calling and texting both of them. It's unusual, don't you think? Especially because I think that this number has appeared on my phone before."

Lindsey handed the phone over to Traci and Julia to take a closer look. "Call it up and see who answers," Traci gave the phone back to Lindsey.

"Oh that's a good idea, why didn't I think of that?" Lindsey took her cell phone out and dialed the mystery number. She held her breath as she waited for whoever it was to answer but she was immensely disappointed when she heard the operator, "We're sorry this number is no longer in service, please hang up and try your number again."

"Oh great, the number is no longer in service. Nothing can be simple. There's always a snag." Lindsey said with frustration. "There has to be a way to find out who it belonged to, isn't there?" Lindsey asked.

Julia answered, "I don't know but I've got to get going. I'm meeting Charlie out tonight. I know he's a loser; I'm not getting back with him. We're just going to talk and remain friends." No one believed Julia so no one said anything, only Lindsey smirked and thought friends....right!

Lindsey had written down on a pad of paper she kept in her purse several names and numbers from John's cell phone and handed them to Julia.

Julia took the paper and looked at the five numbers. "I'll take these numbers and call them tonight if I have time or tomorrow for sure. If I think I need more information then what they give me over the phone, I'll make appointments to meet them. Wish me luck," and Julia got up to leave.

Lindsey eyed her friend, "Be careful Julia, let me know what you find and who and where you're meeting them. And thanks! I'm so scared that I'm going to be arrested for John's murder before we find out who really did it."

"Don't worry Lindsey, we'll find out who it was. And we all know it wasn't you." Julia locked eyes with Lindsey, "Take care you guys, see you Wednesday night Lindsey, 7:00?"

Lindsey responded, "Yes, we'll go over everything we've found out so far and take it from there. Bye." Lindsey watched as Julia took off. She said to Traci, "I hope she doesn't get back with that scum bucket."

The fire was keeping Lindsey warm. She looked at Traci who was sipping her tea with a cool glint in her eye. After her sip she calmly spoke. "All *men* are scummy, you just have to pick one and make the best of it." Lindsey looked at Traci's unsmiling face and sad eyes.

Lindsey responded, "Oh yuck, Traci, that's not a pleasant thought."

Traci murmured back, "I know, but that's how I feel right now. I met a man out for a lunch date today and it was so depressing. I couldn't wait to eat and get back to work."

Lindsey could empathize with Traci's experience, "I know what you mean; bad dates are depressing. I had a date too, but an unexpected date. Tom was following me and we ended up having coffee together. Even though he suspects me in John's murder, I'm secretly attracted to him. There's something caring in his demeanor and he has a cute, boyish quality about him. It gets me. Not only that but he has a great body, which is fun to look at."

Traci's eyes suddenly looked up, searching Lindsey's face to see if she was joking or serious. Then she leaned in before saying, "Lindsey, he's trying to find evidence to put you in jail."

Lindsey was ready for Traci's reaction "I know," she shrugged her shoulders. "There's always something." Lindsey grinned half apologetically. "I can't help it. When I see him I'm excited."

Traci hesitated then decided to give up on Lindsey's illogical attraction for Tom. She looked at Lindsey and stood up, "You're crazy Lindsey. I've got to get going too. I'll call these numbers and report back with you Wednesday night. Have a relaxing night Lindsey. And try to get your mind off of Tom!" Traci smiled and shook her head.

Lindsey said, "Okay, Traci. Take care and be careful. If you're going to meet anyone on the list, let me know."

Traci replied, "I know, I will. Bye"

"Talk to you later." Traci left and Lindsey sat staring at the fire thinking about Tom.

The fire crackled and Lindsey suddenly had an uneasy feeling, like someone was watching her at the spa. She looked around at the other people in the tea room, resting her eyes on each person for a split second. The other costumers seemed to belong, no one seemed out of place and they weren't paying any attention to Lindsey. Still....she felt that something wasn't right, it felt to Lindsey like someone was following her. Maybe it was Tom; she looked around for him or anyone else that seemed to be watching her.

She sat there for a couple of minutes before the waitress came around. She wanted to ask the waitress if all the patrons were members but then thought better of it. How would the waitress know? She had to ask though, thinking that it couldn't hurt and remembering she was an investigator now. She needed to pry into John's life.

The waitress walked over to Lindsey's table, "Can I get you anything else today?" The young waitress smiled politely and waited.

Lindsey smiled up at the waitress, "Yes, I was curious about something. How long have you waitressed here?"

"I've been here for a year. I'm a student at UW-Milwaukee and work here on the days and nights I don't have class. Why?" She held her pen and tablet in her hands, down by her sides, and looked inquisitively at Lindsey.

Lindsey explained and then continued to question her, "I'm wondering about the murder of John Wang, I'm asking some questions about his life before his death. I hope you can help me. Is there a regular crowd that gathers here or is it different every day?"

The waitress eyes traveled around the room, "Like any place there are some regulars and then some people who for whatever reason feel like coming in for the day and I never see them again."

Lindsey continued to ask questions, "What about today; are there any new people that you've never seen before?"

The waitress looked around at the patrons closely, after a minute of looking she answered. "Most of the people here are regulars. I see them at the club quite frequently. Those two women over there I've never seen before," she pointed in the direction of two women sitting at a table by the window.

Lindsey asked, "Thanks, do you know who they are?"

The waitress looked apprehensively at Lindsey, "I don't know their names; I haven't seen them before. Are you John's ex-wife?" The waitress was putting two and two together.

Lindsey shook her head up and down, "Yes, are you familiar with my ex-husband?"

The waitress talked slowly, quietly, "I didn't know him personally but he came in here quite frequently. He told me he was training for a ½ marathon and was learning how to play tennis. We talked here, little bits of chit chat; I didn't know him that well. He was a great tipper and always seemed happy."

Lindsey smiled, "Was he here frequently with his girlfriend?" Lindsey tried to sound friendly and congenial.

The waitress looked at Lindsey and thought about how to answer. After what seemed like a minute she hesitantly replied and tried to smooth her words over for Lindsey, "He came in here with women. A lot of women, I couldn't even tell you how many because I couldn't remember all of their names. I'm sorry; I hope this isn't causing you more pain."

Lindsey liked this waitress immediately. "No, you're not telling me anything new. We had been divorced for six years, don't worry about it. What I need to know is if there was any one woman that he spent more time with, someone you noticed him with more than the others."

Looking again at the other customers she said, "Let me get back to you. I'd like to help you but I've got to go fill my tea pot and refill some of the guests' teacups." She went back to the kitchen, came out and circled the tables with fresh tea and scones.

Lindsey watched the other guests at the tables. Two men were sitting by a book shelf having an animated conversation. One had a computer and the other man would look to see what was on the computer every other minute. They looked like they were working on a project. There were also several solo people reading a newspaper, a magazine or talking on their cell phone. Which one looked suspicious? Lindsey could have guessed, but they all looked like they were busy with their own lives and not paying any attention to her. She looked over at the two women seated by the window. They were talking and laughing, they didn't look suspicious. What was it that was causing her to feel uneasy? Lindsey tried to focus on the warmth of the crackling fire place and the scent of the delicious tea.

The waitress returned with a scone and more jam; she also filled up Lindsey's tea cup. She smiled friendly and said, "Here you go, it's on the house."

Lindsey smiled up at her, "Thank you. Can you sit down and talk for a minute? I would really like to hear about John. I'm trying to come to terms with his death and trying to find out all I can about his life. It might help solve his murder."

The waitress sat down next to Lindsey and quickly told what she knew. She didn't have much time, but thought Lindsey looked like she needed a friend, and so she decided to talk. "John used to come in here every Wednesday morning, at 8:00, like clockwork. He was always with one woman at 8:00, a long blond haired woman. They would stay for approximately half an hour talking, giggling and fondling each other. On other days I'd see him with other woman. I don't know how many women but it was quite a few. He'd carry on with these other woman too, just like he did with the blond on Wednesday morning. It was entertaining for me but I wouldn't want to be one of his girlfriends, he was playing them all."

"Did you ever get the name of the blond haired woman?" Lindsey said with some hope in her voice.

The waitress looked around the room and then back at Lindsey. "No, I didn't pay close attention to their names. I knew John because he came in here often, and we were introduced."

"Thanks for the information. I didn't realize John was with that many women. Learning about his routine might help me solve his murder. What's your name?"

"Colleen," she smiled and extended her hand.

"Thanks for your time, I appreciate it," Lindsey smiled and they shook hands.

Colleen placed the remainder of the bill on the table. "Have a great day. I hope you find out who did it. Your ex seemed like a nice man, he always had a smile on his face." She smiled then left to help the other people at the cafe.

Lindsey paid up, grabbed her purse and bag and left to pick up Leo and Lilly from their practices and spend a quiet evening at home alone. She still couldn't quite shake the feeling that someone was watching her and following her every move. Maybe it was Tom.

# CHAPTER 11
## Who did it?

After feeding Leo and Lilly dinner and giving them showers and kisses goodnight, Lindsey decided to take a warm and relaxing shower herself. She was exhausted but wanted to look over the information in the other folders before going to bed.

Had it only been one day after John's death? So much had taken place, the interrogation, snooping at John's office, Tom and the coffee house, afternoon yoga and the numbers from John's cell phone. That one particular phone number that had been repeatedly called on John's cell phone was constantly on her mind. Who did it belong to?

She thought about calling Tom and asking for help but didn't know if that would be appropriate. He wanted to help her, she was sure of that, but he did say that physical evidence was pointing to her as the murderer. How crazy, if there was something that pointed to her she was sure it had to be planted by someone who wanted her to take the blame for John's death.

Lindsey reached her hand into the shower to make sure it was the perfect temperature and then stepped in. The beating water on her face felt soothing; she closed her eyes and rubbed her face, trying to make sense of the list of names she and her friends had compiled. As she was taking her shower, she could have sworn she heard a door creak open and then shut again. Don't be so paranoid, no one could get in and why would they want to? Then she heard another squeaking noise and the beeping of her phone as if it were off the hook. Her heart jumped with fear, she grabbed her towel, wrapped it around herself, dried off, put her robe on and tiptoed out to her bedroom, eyes darting from right to left trying to see everything at once.

Next to her bed, on the side table she saw that her old-fashioned dial-style phone's handle had been bumped off the receiver. She went over to the phone, listened to see if she had a dial tone, realized she did and put it back on the receiver. Then with her head up looking all around her she reached under her bed and grabbed the baseball bat she kept there. Searching the room with the baseball bat in her hands she went to inspect her walk-in closet. She opened the closet door; turned on the light and heard "meow" it was Merlin, their cat.

Lindsey picked up Merlin after setting the baseball bat down. Talk about being jumpy, thought Lindsey. "Merlin, you silly goose, why are you scaring me? Did you knock the phone off the receiver?"

Merlin's only reply was to purr and look at her with his big fluffy face and bright green eyes. As she turned to go out of the closet, the closet door was slammed closed and Lindsey screamed, "Who's out there?" She dropped Merlin and grabbed the bat again; hesitantly she opened up the door and went tentatively out of the closet.

She held the bat up looking around ready to hit anyone who got in her way. She didn't see anyone but the door leading out to her bedroom patio was wide open. She slowly walked over to the door, looked out but saw only a foggy black darkness. She quickly closed the French door and locked it.

With her bat in her hand she ran down to look in on Leo and Lilly. They were resting peacefully under covers and hopefully dreaming about chocolate candy bars and playing with friends. She ran back to her bedroom, dug in her purse, grabbed Tom's card and quickly called him. She didn't care if he thought that she was the killer, she needed help and her intuition told her that he was trustworthy and would believe her. She had to rely on someone so she dialed the number.

After the third ring Tom answered in a groggy-sounding voice, "Hello."

Lindsey's words tumbled from her mouth as she spoke, "Tom, its Lindsey. Someone just broke into my house. I was in the shower and I heard a creaking noise. Of course, I thought I was just imagining it but then I went to investigate. My receiver to my phone sounded like it was off the hook and I felt there was something amiss, that there was something strange going on. I got out of the shower and grabbed my robe. I cautiously stepped out of the bathroom, checked the phone, grabbed my bat which I keep under my bed and went to check out my closet. Then I....."

Tom cut her off. "Okay, have you searched the rest of your house?"

"No." How rude; she was telling him her story and he cut her off.

It sounded like he stifled a yawn before slowly saying, "I'll send a car over, and some crime scene investigators to look for prints and other evidence." He wasn't coming over himself? What kind of detective was he?

"Aren't you coming over too?" Lindsey should have bit her tongue and not ask but she couldn't help it.

"Yes, I'll be there too." Lindsey stifled a sigh of relief; a lot of detectives in her home that she didn't know didn't appeal to her. At least having Tom with her would alleviate some of her stress.

Hearing that he was soon going to be with her transformed her anxiety into comfort and excitement; not that she hadn't had her fair share of excitement lately, but with Tom it was partly romantic excitement. Ok Lindsey, someone just broke into your house and all you care about is seeing Tom. Get a clue. Maybe the police would get a clue tonight; that would be something.

Lindsey replied in friendly voice, "Okay, good. I can't believe someone broke into my house."

Tom was all business, "I've got a car on route and I'll be there as soon as I can. Sit tight and stay on the phone until one of my officers gets there." Within another minute someone was knocking on Lindsey's front door.

"They're already here," she told Tom.

"Okay, let them in. Bye."

"Bye." Lindsey replied.

Tom cursed himself after he hung up the phone. Why hadn't he had someone in place watching Lindsey's house. She might be the next target of the dental floss murderer, or she could be making the whole thing up trying to steer the investigation in a different direction. He would have positioned someone to watch her all night but budget cuts were making 24 hour surveillance almost impossible. He cursed again and put on his shoes and jacket before getting in his car.

It was only 10:00pm, but the sky was black and the air chilly, he didn't want to venture out again. Then he thought of Lindsey and her voice and warmed up a little on the inside. Don't even think about going there, he thought, after all, she could be a heartless murderer.

Tom pulled up to Lindsey's house and noticed that a squad car and lab van was at the scene. Thank god, he thought; then he wouldn't be tempted to do anything inappropriate or tell Lindsey too many details about the case. He felt like he could trust her, he was leaning in that direction the more he talked with her, but he needed more time with her and more time for the case to take its course. That was the great thing about his job, like pieces of a puzzle one by one the picture became clearer until the view was finished, the crime was solved, and all the clues fit together. She just had to be innocent but time would tell.

Lindsey was watching the crime scene investigators with one eye and the drive leading up to her house with her other eye. Finally, his car approached, her heart started to beat a little faster as she went to answer her door. "Hi, looks like we're going to be seeing a lot of each other," Lindsey looked up at Tom and smiled, secretly she thought—coffee, tea or me? Why couldn't they have been together tonight for different reasons? Get back to realty, Lindsey.

"Hi Lindsey," He looked intensely into her eyes. "Are you okay? Tell me everything that happened?" Tom tried to maintain a tone of professionalism and compassion. If he weren't there on professional police business he would have wanted to take her in his arms, and kiss her lips, caress her neck, her shoulders and her back.

"I'm fine," Lindsey looked at the soft-hearted man standing before her and gave him a small close-lipped, shy smile. She led Tom into her kitchen and they sat opposite each other at the center island. Before Lindsey sat down she grabbed bottled water from the refrigerator and handed one to Tom and placed one on the island for herself.

With a sigh she sat down and began to tell Tom her account of the break in. "I was in the shower and heard a creaking noise. At first I thought I was being paranoid, but then my phone started making a beeping noise which wasn't normal. I got out of the shower and started to search my bedroom. I went into my closet and found Merlin, our cat, so I assumed it was the cat that knocked the receiver off the phone. I was petting Merlin and someone slammed the door to my closet shut. I dropped Merlin, grabbed my bat and opened up the closet door. When I looked out I noticed the door leading out to my patio off my bedroom was open. I then walked over to the door and looked out, but I couldn't see a thing. There was someone though, the lingering smell of whoever was in my room stayed; someone was definitely in my room." Lindsey's eyes flashed dark as she was adamantly talking about the details of the break-in.

Lindsey continued, "I can't imagine why anyone would break in and it doesn't look like anything was taken. In fact everything, except the phone being off the hook, looks exactly as I left it. I don't think whoever was in my bedroom went past my room. It looked like they came in through my bedroom door and left the same way. I don't know where they were hiding when I came out of the shower. Maybe they were hiding behind a drape? I didn't see anyone. It spooks me out that they were there while I was in the shower. Why would they want to get into my room? I'm beginning to feel like whoever murdered John, wants something from me too. It's creepy, what do they want from me? What if they want me murdered?"

Lindsey's stomach did a couple of upside-down flips as she thought about John's phone and files locked up in the study. Maybe someone wanted the files, or cell phone, but no one knew she had those so she quickly discounted that thought and wondered about her safety and the kids' safety.

Tom looked at her and in a calm, serious voice said, "You are going to have to be extra careful with your keys and checking your doors and windows to make sure that they are locked. Better yet, I'm going to send someone over tomorrow to change your locks on your doors. It seems that someone, possible someone close to you or close to John, has a duplicate of your key. Or did you have your door unlocked?"

He said the last sentence in an accusatory tone, as if she didn't know how to take care of herself. She thought about the door to the bedroom and wasn't sure if it was locked, but she wasn't going to tell him that; she replied defensively, "Of course it was locked."

Tom was all business, "It's better to be safe than sorry. Whoever did this to John is extremely unstable. They're acting on emotions that are real to them and have the capability of planning and acting out their crimes because they believe they're doing the right thing." Tom didn't know if he should be sharing this information with Lindsey but he wanted to keep her safe and he was adamant that she take precautions to protect herself.

Her sweet voice and caring eyes got to him and he continued telling her more about John's murderer. "We've had our criminal psychologist profile the crime scene, and whoever murdered John did it in an exceptionally personal way. It wasn't a random serial crime, it was someone who wanted to make sure that we knew he or she knew John. The murderer used dental floss to strangle John. By using dental floss it was someone who was connected to him and associated with him at his practice. And by the violence it was someone who was furious with him for some act or wrong he inflicted on this person. Someone viewed him as source of constant pain; it might have been that every time she/he saw John, they became more and more upset until they snapped and planned the murder to release their agony, having no other means to cope."

The words were dark and the kitchen felt suddenly cold. Lindsey answered off-handedly, "Wow, what kind of a person does that? Why would someone feel tortured by John?" Lindsey hadn't known about the use of the dental floss.

Tom spoke gently, "Whoever killed John enjoyed killing him, wanted to see him suffer and felt like it was the only thing that they could do to restore some sanity back into their life. The only problem with this type of murderer is that once they commit the crime, it becomes an even easier option the next time they are unhappy with someone or someone is perceived to be in their way. It's like that with any crime. The first crime that is committed is the hardest, the next time it becomes a little easier, and it becomes easier each time until the person is caught." He paused and took a sip of water. He looked at Lindsey and wanted to take her away from all of the turmoil and the problems that were walking all over her life. Instead he said, "Why don't you call one of your friends to stay with you tonight?"

Lindsey's listened and pondered the idea for a second before responding, "No, I couldn't ask anyone to do that. I'll be fine." If Tom wanted to stay with her she'd start getting the pillow and bedspread out, but he didn't offer. Lindsey was confident that Tom didn't think she committed the crime. Something had happened in the case between the time she saw him for coffee and tonight. She didn't know what it was, but she could tell he was kinder tonight and more giving.

In response to her he said, "If you're not going to call anyone to stay with you I'll assign someone to watch over your house tonight and get someone to come over tomorrow and change the locks."

"Thank you. I'm sure I'll be fine." Then she added, "You know I didn't do it?" Her eyes locked eyes with his and she couldn't help but to touch his arm as she inquired, "You do believe me don't you?"

Tom didn't know what to think, he wanted to believe her and so he reassured Lindsey, hoping he could keep his conviction. He gave her the answer that she wanted, "I don't think you're capable of murder." His voice was serious and solid. Lindsey was relieved.

Then Tom stood up from the kitchen stool, "I'm going to have to talk to the head crime scene investigator to find out what they've uncovered. I'll be back soon." He left her sitting on the stool, drinking her water.

Tom went to ask questions. He found out the detectives had lifted some partial prints from the door and shoe prints on the carpet that led out the bedroom door. The forensic experts would let Tom know if they had any matches once they put the prints through Interpol and the prints that they had developed from a list of people at John's party.

Tom watched as the forensic experts packed up their suitcases and then he walked them out Lindsey's front door. Tom said, "Thanks, I'll talk with you tomorrow about the case." He closed the door and went back in the kitchen to see how Lindsey was doing.

She had made some tea and was sipping it, sitting on a chair at the breakfast nook and staring out the window. As he approached she turned to look at him and she smiled. "Thank you for coming over, Tom. I know you're only doing your job but I feel a lot safer with you on this case." She didn't tell him about John's cell phone or the files she had been looking at; she wasn't ready to divulge that information yet.

"It's no problem whatsoever. I wish I could stay with you and make sure you and your children were safe. Try to get some sleep tonight. I've posted a man outside and I'll be in touch with you tomorrow. The forensic team has left and my guy is outside. I've got your statements written down for my report so I guess it's time for me to go." She wished he would stay and curl up on the couch with her, watch an old movie, wrap her up in his arms and make her feel protected.

Lindsey got up and walked Tom to the door, "Okay, thanks again for coming over. I'm glad you've posted someone outside. I feel safer."

He turned and said, "Try to get some sleep."

"Okay, good night." She closed the door and locked it.

Tom drew his breath in as he walked to his car; she was stunning, even at night without any make up on. He wanted to stay over and touch her, feel her lying next to him, her heartbeat and her warmth.

As he was thinking warm thoughts about Lindsey, he also remembered the manila envelope staring at him with the cold hard facts, waiting for him to contemplate at the office the next day. The reality of the bitter, cruel forensic facts had made his stomach wrench, turn around in somersaults and made him feel queasy. What was he missing? Who did it?

*Lindsey you are in trouble. John had to be murdered and you're the most likely suspect. They'll find the same dental floss used in the crime against John in your bathroom. Nothing can stop me now from getting what I need, from getting what I deserve. It's been a long wait but soon I won't be alone. It's all going to work out just like I planned.*

# CHAPTER 12
## More Suspects

"Hey Mom, wake up." Leo knocked on the bedroom door.

"I'm up; thanks Leo," Lindsey replied in a hoarse voice with one eye open and one eye closed.

Leo was up, as usual, and at 7:00 pounded on the door. He only woke her up one time, and then went back to watching cartoons or playing on the computer. Today 7:00 seemed to come much too early for Lindsey. Stretching, she yawned and closed both eyes again; maybe she could lay there for five more minutes. Merlin, their cat, was at her side snuggled in a ball right next to her head. He stretched and extended a paw to tap her face a couple of times to wake her up. Lindsey knew from past experience that Merlin didn't have any food in his dish and this was his way of letting her know. "Okay Merlin, I'm getting up." She scratched Merlin behind his ears and then slowly sat up.

She sat up and looked around her bedroom; everything seemed in place as if nothing had happened the previous night. Half awake she thought how life always kept moving forward regardless of the past. She dragged her feet into the bathroom, put her robe on, put her contacts in, brushed her teeth, flossed and went to wake up Lilly.

Lilly was the opposite of Leo, she loved to stay up late and sleep in late. Her children were polar opposites in a lot of ways, but similar and liked to do familiar activities together. As Lindsey walked down the hall to Lilly's room she stopped, something felt different when she was using the dental floss in her bathroom. She went back to the bathroom and opened the drawer that held her dental floss. In the drawer she noted the dental floss was the same brand, maybe it was all-in-her-head. She looked closer at the two containers of floss and compared the labels.

She was surprised to find out that the thickness of the dental floss was different. Who knew dental floss came in different sizes? When did she buy that? She probably hadn't even noticed at the grocery store that dental floss came in different widths, picked the same brand and thought nothing of it. Many times Lindsey would grab an item at the store and not realize that it was the wrong item. Brooke loved three cheese macaroni but she'd mistakenly pick up the spiral macaroni instead. The coloring on the box was the same and usually when she was shopping she was rushing to get it over with. Choosing the wrong item happened to her all the time.

Lindsey chalked the dental floss incident up to another case of 'close but no cigar' and put the two packages back in her vanity drawer. The mistake wasn't a big deal; she could use both sizes to fill up the different gaps in her teeth, sometimes those mistakes proved to be advantageous. Lindsey put the dental floss back in the drawer, checked her teeth out in the mirror and went to wake up Lilly.

Lindsey opened Lilly's door and turned on the light, "Wake up, Lilly."

"UMmmm" was the first sound out of Lilly's mouth, and then "What time is it?" Lilly's voice was tiny and slow in the morning.

Lindsey loudly said, "7:15, time to get up."

Lilly replied, "Okay, I'm awake." Lindsey closed the door, knowing that once Lilly was awake she didn't need to worry about her getting ready. Lilly was independent and strong. She knew what she wanted to wear every morning and was organized enough to put all her papers and supplies in her backpack. Leo was the same way and had probably already fixed himself some breakfast and got all his supplies ready for school. Lindsey was in desperate need of coffee so she went to the kitchen to fix a pot, got it started, and went back to her bathroom to get ready for the day.

At 8:15 she and the kids were in the car and she drove them to school. The media vans had quit obsessing about her and the kids. When she did put on the news, if the story of John's murder was being covered, it was always reported at the site of his condo or the reporters were reading off their sheets on the set. With other news stories to report, John's murder was no longer a 'top of the news' story. Lindsey figured that once there was an arrest the media frenzy would multiply 3x's and follow the court room dramatics, but right now there was a lull as people waited and anticipated who would be arrested for John's murder.

The speculation was that she was a suspect, but the police had done a good job keeping the murder details contained and also were quiet about who they were targeting as their prime suspect(s) in John's murder.

Lindsey dropped the kids off and headed straight back to her home. She wanted to continue to look at the folders, have more coffee, make necessary phone calls and look at the texts from John's cell phone. Even though she had accomplished a respectable amount the day before she felt like time was speeding by and she'd never finish everything she wanted to get done during the day. She spent valuable time taking care of Leo and Lilly and taking care of herself. For the meantime she had stopped making contacts with her business partners so that she could concentrate on the investigation.

Once back home, Lindsey got another cup of coffee and started reading the folders. As soon as she was settled in her chair in her cozy office the phone rang. Lindsey had probably only read one sentence in the first folder before the interruption. Oh well, being used to interruptions, she answered the phone, "Hello."

"Hi, it's Lori."

Lindsey told Lori what she had been doing, "Hi Lori, I was just starting to search through more of the folders that we copied from John's and Dave's offices. I've only been able to look at the insurance and business folders so far. It took me two hours to look and read through them and try to understand what everything meant in the business folders. I'm all for solving this murder, but I wish we had more time!"

Lori agreed, "I know what you mean, and I'm calling because I have more information about Dave. I've been in charge of calling all of John's patients and signing them up with Dave. Dave's practice has grown already twice its size. He has been benefiting tremendously from John's death."

"Do you think he really did it?" Lindsey was programmed to think the best of people that she knew.

Lori continued talking excitedly, "He's been buying new equipment already with the promise of the insurance money. I'm in charge of every aspect of ordering items for his business now, just like I was for John. I'm not saying he's been rude to me or acting too strange but he's very eager to charge new items and change the layout of the office. I haven't learned any more details about his private life. He keeps it hidden, but if I snoop maybe I'll find out that he's been buying some big ticket items for himself." She paused, took a breath and then continued, "He has a strong motive and he's making decisions fast, now that he's the only dentist at the office."

Lindsey was nodding her head up and down as she listened on the phone to Lori, "Yeah; that is true. He has a huge motive. Could you take him out to lunch and get to know where he was that night? Find out what he says, how he acts. He might be the one," Lindsey said shuddering at the thought.

Lori whispered back, "Listen, I'll take him out to ask him about the business, and I'll weave the conversation back around to what he did at the party, what time he left and see what he has to say. And I'll try to find something out about his private life. He's so secretive; it makes him seem more suspicious." Lori was keyed up and was talking fast, but kept her voice low.

Lindsey's reply was enthusiastic and serious, "Great. That sounds perfect. You've got to be careful. If he is the murderer he'll feel no remorse murdering someone else. He might even enjoy it because he got away with it once.

Lindsey continued, "I'm going to spend the day looking over the folders you gave me and calling the patients that were dissatisfied with John or owed him money. I'll try to find out where they were that night and see if any of them sound like they have a motive or act suspicious. Hopefully my 6th sense will boot up." Lindsey thought her intuition was on target a lot of times and hoped it would help her solve John's murder.

Lindsey continued talking to Lori about her plans, "Later on during the afternoon I'm going to spend some time searching John's house and his condo. I'm not sure if I'll have time to get to the condo. Making phone calls can eat up the entire day. I never knew how hard it was to investigate. I couldn't do it without you guys!"

Lori replied, "No problem, I'll ask Dave to go out to lunch with me today, or tomorrow, depending on the schedule. Now that John's not here we've cancelled his appointments and rescheduled them for Dave. I'll have to look at a block of time when he can get away and leave. The dental hygienists should be able to handle the cleanings while we're eating. It shouldn't be a problem but I'm not sure I'll be able to convince him to go today."

Lindsey replied, "Don't worry about that, just do it when it's most convenient."

Lori was looking at her calendar and Dave's schedule as she talked to Lindsey. Slowly she said, "I'll probably ask him to go to lunch tomorrow, that would work better then today. We are just swamped." Lori was anxious to get Dave talking.

Lindsey could tell Lori was doing all she could to help Lindsey, she said, "Thanks for the call and all your help. I'll talk to you some more tomorrow. If you want, I'm having my friends over tomorrow and I'd love it if you could make it too. They're also helping me with this murder investigation. They'll be over at 7:00 and it would be great if you could join us. We'll be talking about what we've discovered, motives, and alibis, anything else that has to do with John's murder."

Lindsey waited for Lori's response and in a matter of seconds she said, "Of course I'll come. I'd like to help and maybe I can shed some more light on what you and your friends have already discovered."

"Great, I'll look forward to hearing from you tomorrow or seeing you at 7:00. We usually have cheese, crackers and wine every Wednesday night and talk about what's going on in our lives. Now we've changed to case crackers and wine nights, focusing on finding out who murdered John. Once we're done with solving John's murder we'll be right back to our previous cheese, crackers and wine sessions. Hopefully, we won't be looking to solve any other murder cases any time soon." Lindsey was smiling as she was talking on the phone to Lori.

"That's for sure. Let's get this one solved first. I'm going to get going now, have a great day and be careful. There's a murderer out there somewhere, and he/she is probably someone we know." That sent goose bumps up and down Lindsey's spine and her smile faded.

"Don't I know it."

"Bye." Both the women clicked their receivers to end the conversation. The break-in last night receded to the back edge of Lindsey's mind. Her focus turned to what Lori had told her about Dave. It seemed he had a motive and opportunity. Still, something wasn't quite right. She refocused her efforts to find other suspects besides Dave.

Lindsey went back to the folders of John's patients. Nothing seemed to jump out at her but she called several of the patients anyway. None of them said they were angry at John. They told Lindsey that John had communicated to them that their dental problems could and would be able to be fixed at no charge to them. The patients had seemed relieved to have a call from Lindsey and each had expressed their condolences. Lindsey would run the names past Lori on Wednesday, just in case she had a different opinion of the patients.

Lindsey also called the patients who owed him money. All the patients from the red folders said that they had no problem with John and that John had been overly accommodating. They were quite pleased with the payment options that Lori and John had set up for them. Most of the patients were paying their bill in monthly installments. They also had expressed condolences and some had commented on John's unique ability to put them at ease while in the office and reminisced about how he told funny jokes to them while working on their teeth.

Lindsey couldn't see any real potential suspects with any of the folders she looked at, or with any of the patients that she called. She worked all morning on the folders and by 11:30 was in need of a break. As she started to get up and leave the office her phone rang again. "Hello."

Brooke was on the line and in a cheerful voice said, "Hi Lindsey, it's Brooke. I'm on a break and thought I'd call to see how you were doing. I've got some free time this afternoon if you want me to go over to John's house with you." Brooke knew Lindsey needed someone to go with her and Lindsey was glad she had offered.

"Thanks Brooke, I have a company coming over this afternoon to change all the locks on my doors and check to see if my windows are secure. Last night someone broke into my house. Tom came over and he arranged for this company to come over and help me. They'll be here around 1:00; I'm not sure how long they'll take. I can't imagine it taking longer than an hour." Lindsey continued, "I've been dreading going to John's house but it would be best to get it over with. I'll have my mom pick up the kids today from school and take them to her house. Let's meet at John's around 3:00. I'll call you when I leave my house; it takes me about 20 minutes to get to John's house in Brookfield. I really wanted to get to his condo too but that will have to wait until a different day."

Brooke gasped into the phone and said, "Lindsey, you've got to be kidding. Someone broke into your house? That's terrible. How did you sleep last night?" Brooke was astonished that Lindsey was taking everything so calmly.

Lindsey's voice was steady and clear, "I slept great. Tom had someone watch the house last night. The break in makes me more determined than ever to catch whoever it was that killed John. Tom was here last night and we talked. The police have been delving into the possibility of other suspects and Tom thinks I'm innocent." Lindsey took the phone and was walking around her office, grabbed a towel and started dusting.

"He told you that. Don't put all your trust in him Lindsey. He might be trying to get you to say something he can use against you. Did he tell you anything else about the murder? Have you found out anything more about John's murder?" Brooke asked insistently. Lindsey knew her friends were only trying to look out for her but she was a bit perturbed by Brooke's rushed, all-knowing tone.

She explained calmly to Brooke, "He was helpful and meant well. He told me what the papers said and gave me information about the type of suspect he's looking for. He's a good person, I can tell, but you're right. I need to be careful. The fact is he might end up hurting me and accusing me of John's murder." Brooke was silent on the other end.

Lindsey changed the subject, "I got a call from Lori, Dave's assistant. She's been helping me sort through John's business papers. We've got a motive for Dave but no crucial evidence. This is going to take some time. It seems impossible." Lindsey had been worrying all morning if it was possible for the women to get real evidence, not just speculation and circumstantial evidence.

Brooke relaxed and heard the tense feeling behind Lindsey's words. She tried to cheer her up. "I know, but we've only just begun. There'll be something, somehow that will lead us in the right direction." Brooke spoke optimistically about the investigation and knew there was a light at the end of any dark tunnel.

Lindsey cautiously said, "I hope you're right, Brooke. I get the feeling that the police know something. I'll tell you more about it this afternoon."

Brooke wanted Lindsey to be careful, she said, "Lindsey, make sure you guard yourself and hang in there. Maybe we'll find something at John's house."

Lindsey replied gravely, "I know, and that alone scares me."

Brooke was distracted by one of her assistants, "I've got to go now, talk to you later."

"Okay, bye." Lindsey clicked the phone down and went to the kitchen. She had an hour to kill before the locksmith was to arrive.

After fixing herself some lunch and calling her mom to make arrangements for Leo and Lilly she sat down on a stool by the kitchen island and called Julia. Julia had told her yesterday that she would be meeting John's ex-girlfriend, Jess, out for lunch and Lindsey wanted to hear if she was still planning on meeting. She still hadn't read any texts from John's phone. There was so much to do; it was exciting and overwhelming, tiring and energizing all at the same time. Lindsey dialed and waited for Julia to answer.

"Hello." Julia finally picked up after the 5th ring.

"Hey Julia, it's Lindsey, how is your day going?"

Julia cried in the phone, "Hi. I hate my job. I have so much paper work to do. I'm behind in documenting my billable hours this month, so I've been trying to get caught up and have been stuck in my office all day." She ended talking with a sigh.

"Oh, that doesn't' sound like fun. Are you still planning on meeting with Jess about John's murder?"

"Lindsey, I'm so sorry. I should have called you earlier but the morning flew bye. I talked to her on the phone and she couldn't make it for lunch today, we'll be meeting on Wednesday instead of today. Do you think you can make it? Jess is right on the verge of taking anyone's head off if they tell her something she doesn't want to hear."

Lindsey replied, "Really?"

Emphatically Julia continued, "She has the personality of an angry bull, charging towards anyone who gets in her way. I think she thought I was accusing her of John's murder. At first she was short with me. I tried not to take it personally but when I asked if she would meet with me she practically slammed the phone down. She said the police already talked to her and that she didn't know anything. I thought that I had better approach her in a different way so I asked her to help us compile a list of different women that she knew John had been with. That approach worked like magic. Her attitude changed from combative to cooperative. She couldn't wait to tell me the long list of women that have been with John. I'm way to busy today to meet her for lunch today, so I thought tomorrow would work. Jess was okay with that too. Are you going to be able to make it tomorrow around 1:30?"

Lindsey knew from Julia's tone that she wanted Lindsey to be there and wouldn't want to talk to Jess alone. "Of course I can make it, Wednesday. That's tomorrow right? Did you tell her I would be coming?"

"No, I'll send her a text to let her know that you're coming. She'll probably love that you are, it will be more of an audience for her and who better to vent to then John's ex-wife."

"Good, I'll put down lunch for tomorrow. What time?"

"1:30 at Previews on Grand Avenue, downtown Milwaukee."

Lindsey wrote it down on her calendar, "Super, and thanks for calling her and setting up the lunch date."

"I'll catch up with you later. I've got to get back to this paper work," Julia was aggravated from working hard but good natured and wanted to help Lindsey. She took everything in stride.

Lindsey said, "Good luck finishing up your work, Bye."

"Bye."

Lindsey hung up the phone and was going to get a diet coke from the refrigerator when the doorbell rang. It was already 1:00? Lindsey answered the door.

A nice looking man with sandy brown hair and a crooked nose was at the door in overalls and a dark blue work jacket that had the company logo 'Sure Lock Homes' embroidered on his jacket pocket. The friendly man smiled and introduced himself, "Hi, I'm from 'Sure Lock Homes', I've come to change your locks."

Lindsey grinned while reading the name; she was a big fan of Sherlock Holmes, the mystery sleuth. "Great, come on in. I have French doors in the kitchen, the family room and my bedroom that lead out to various parts of my yard. I'll show you where they are, follow me."

Lindsey led the man around to the various doors and then left him alone to do his job. She sat down in front of the TV in the family room with John's cell phone, a diet coke and a bag of chips. While the locks were getting changed Lindsey scrolled through the text messages. Very interesting and disturbing texts were written from Jess. Some were threatening, some were violent and some were disgusting. There were threats and accusations of John sleeping around with various women, insinuating that he'll sleep with anyone and was always ready and willing. The texts led her to believe that maybe it was Jess.

The texts were recent; Jess was not letting John get on with his life without her in it. Lindsey never knew anyone could be so dark and think such vicious thoughts. The hair on the back of her neck stood up after reading a particularly scathing text from Jess to John. Jess seemed vindictive and threatened to hurt John where it hurt, so he would feel the same pain he inflicted on her. She was glad she was going to be with Julia when they talked with Jess.

Maybe it was Jess who had broken in last night, looking for John's cell phone. Talk about incriminating evidence; John's cell phone held a lot. She might have John's other cell phone and she would know he kept one as a backup. Maybe the police weren't aware of the texts to John that she had sent. On the other hand the police talked with Jess already and were probably quite aware of how angry she was. And who knows what was written on John's email? Maybe the answers would come after she and Brooke went rummaging through John's house.

"Ms. Wang?" The locksmith came into the family room to let Lindsey know he had finished. After Lindsey inspected his work and paid him, she grabbed her coat and headed out.

She called Brooke, "Hey Brooke, I'm on my way to John's house, I just left my house."

"I'll meet you there, see you in twenty minutes." Brooke hung up the phone. Lindsey backed out of her driveway and headed for John's house to face the mountainous task of scaling through John's personal belongings. Her palms were sweaty as she handled the steering wheel; nervousness was descending upon her and steadily increasing with every mile she drove closer to John's house. What would they find?

# CHAPTER 13
## John's house Tuesday

**W**as it only two days ago that she was with John at his Condo celebrating, dancing and flirting with Tom? I guess that is death, one minute you're breathing the next minute, well…..who knows? She was almost at John's house in Brookfield wondering what she would find.

She knew quite well that the police had already been there, they had gone through John's house and had taken whatever they wanted. John's parents had already been there too. Out of respect for his parents' feelings, she had called and asked them if she could go through John's things for any hints as to the reason why he was murdered. They had readily agreed, reassuring her that she could take whatever she needed.

John's parents had taken the garbage out, took the food out of the cabinets and straightened up after the police had shuffled around John's items, but other than that the house remained the same as a week ago when John was alive. Lindsey figured that everything would be neat and orderly, spotless and shiny, just the way John liked everything in his life. However, at some point his personal life must have slipped and had become messy. Lindsey needed to clean it up, for John's sake and her own. Her freedom was at stake.

She drove up to the cul-de-sac, with houses restfully looking at her from all sides. They didn't know that life had stopped for one of their neighbors. In this neighborhood nothing ever shocking happened; kids went to practices, did their homework and played basketball, hockey or skateboarded in the road. It was safe and friendly. The houses were modern huge palaces, fit for families of 8 or 9, but in today's society smaller families of 3 or 4 resided in the vaulted ceilinged, rich, brick homes with 15 foot windows that were warmed by crystal chandeliers and elegant fireplaces.

Lindsey pulled up to the drive and finally took a breath; she hadn't breathed for ten blocks and was feeling light-headed. Thank god that Brooke was already waiting for her in the drive.

"Hi Brooke. I'm so glad you could get some time off today and help me look through John's house. What are we going to find?" Lindsey's eyes were worried as she approached Brooke's Mercedes S600.

Brooke saw the worried expression on Lindsey's face, "Hi Lindsey. I know; what a task. I hope we don't find anything too creepy or weird. I'm sure it will be fine." Brooke climbed out of her car and tried to calm Lindsey's nerves.

Lindsey asked agitatedly, "Maybe John was a secret weirdo, and hid it from me all these years." Lindsey voice was on edge, nervously wavering as she spoke.

"I'm sure we won't find anything bizarre, but you never know."

Lindsey knew Brooke was right; how well do you really know anyone? She hoped that John didn't have a strange, dark side to him. Lindsey tried to focus on what they were there to do, "Let's go in and see if we find anything that implicates someone besides me for John's murder." Lindsey and Brooke went up to the double wooden door and Lindsey plugged in the code to the alarm system.

Before they opened the door Brooke spoke. "If we find anything too bizarre that doesn't relate to the case, let's throw it away and we'll erase it from our memories. Who needs that added to an already difficult situation?"

Lindsey nodded her head up and down, as she opened the door and replied, "I hear you. Let's go in and see what we find, the house looks abandoned already."

Lindsey looked around.

The door opened into a tiled foyer and everyone entering was met with a sparkling grand crystal chandelier; past the foyer was a living room with hardwood floors and an elegant fireplace. On the fireplace mantle were pictures of the kids and John on various ski trips, Wisconsin Dells trips and trips to New York. On the walls were Chinese symbols of good fortune, harmony, longevity and peace. Hopefully the house was all that and more for John, except the longevity part; that will hopefully rub off on Leo and Lilly, poor John.

After a moment of looking around, Brooke said, "Everything is so clean. I bet the police took his computer and barely looked at anything else. Everything is so neat and in order, one glance at everything and you can see what he has." Brooke opened up a closet, "Look at his shoes lined up in this closet, one pair in each cubby. There's nothing else in here besides shoes, his motorcycle helmet and jacket. This search might be easier than I thought." Brooke and Lindsey were looking into the door of the front hall closet.

If Lindsey's house were only half as orderly and clean, she might cut down on half the time it usually took her to find things. Lindsey closed the closet door. The two women looked around the opulent house, looking for anything that was out of place. The kitchen, dining room, John's bedroom, the kids' bedrooms, living room, recreation room and bathrooms were spotless.

Brooke exclaimed, "There's nothing here, Lindsey. John was so organized, everything is lined up perfectly, hung up perfectly; everything is in its place. There's nothing, no lewd pictures or sex toys, no crazy letters, videos, drugs, puppets, magazines, clown faces, nothing!! Everything is way too neat, there isn't even any dust and everything is displayed so nicely." Brooke and Lindsey had met back in the kitchen and were leaning on John's counter, looking out the windows to the back yard.

Lindley replied, "I know, it's disgusting isn't it. Seriously, I'm disappointed. We're not getting anywhere here. Let's go into his study, it's the cockpit of his house. Let's hope there's something in there, maybe we will find a smoking gun, a lead." Lindsey started walking towards the study.

"I really thought we'd find something wrong, something scandalous. Could it be that underneath his charismatic, charming personality John was anal and boring?" Brooke asked.

Lindsey replied, "John was John. He was definitely not boring in the sense of being a fun person. However, he did live cleanly, no drugs etc. Thank God. That's something I wouldn't have been able to tolerate."

Brooke shot back, "Well, somebody had something against him."

Lindsey looked inquisitively at Brooke, "I know, let's go into the study."

The women had left the kitchen and opened the glass French doors to John's study. The computer had been taken off the desk, which is what Lindsey expected. She looked around and didn't see anything unusual.

"Hey, come look over here Lindsey," said Brooke. Brooke was standing next to a book shelf with more pictures on it. "Do you see what I see?" Lindsey looked but didn't spot anything.

"No, you're going to have to spell it out for me; I'm not good at guessing games." Lindsey didn't know what Brooke was getting at.

"Look, right here, there was a picture and it's gone. You can see the faint dust marks." Lindsey looked and realized that Brooke was right. There was a picture missing.

"It could be something, or it could be that John's parents took a picture or the police have taken the picture for some reason." Lindsey wasn't too excited about Brooke's discovery.

Brooke contemplated Lindsey's response and shrugged her shoulders, "Oh yeah, I guess you're right."

They kept looking around the office and after a brief delay Lindsey said, "But I'll ask them, maybe someone other than John's parents or the police took the picture. Maybe the killer didn't want their picture up on the shelf and took it....... or maybe not. Let's keep looking in here, there's got to be something, an old business receipt, a copy of a check or bank account, something!"

Lindsey loved old detective movies, the kind where the detective always found a cigarette butt, or a matchbook, a ripped letter, or a ripped picture with half of the face gone, or a button left by the murderer. Here at John's house there was no such red herring, just neatness and one picture gone, which may or may not be a clue. Lindsey and Brooke continued to search around the office.

"There's nothing here, Lindsey. Let's look in the garage. Maybe there's something in the garage."

Lindsey was losing hope, "I doubt it. How are we supposed to solve this crime without any real evidence?"

Not liking Lindsey's defeatist tone Brooke reminded Lindsey, "Remember, this is where John was his 'family man' personality. We'll probably have much better luck at his condo."

"That could be true, but I'm beginning to wonder."

Just then the doorbell rang." Ahhhhhhhh," Lindsey screamed as she heard the bell vibrate throughout the house.

"My god, Lindsey, it's just the doorbell."

"I know, but it scared me. I guess I'm jumpy. Who would be ringing the doorbell?" Lindsey had her hand on her heart.

"I don't know and there's only one way to find out. Let's go answer the door." Lindsey and Brooke left the office and walked to the front door. Lindsey looked out the window before opening the door.

"Hi Rita," Rita was one of Lindsey's realtor friends.

Rita smiled, "How are you?" Rita took off her sunglasses and walked into the foyer, "I hope I'm not interrupting anything. I saw your car and thought I'd stop and see if I could help with anything. You haven't been in the office and I've been meaning to call and tell you how sorry I am. How are you doing?" She had a pouty expression on her face.

As she talked to Lindsey she looked all around assessing John's house. Lindsey wanted to tell her meddling puffy faced friend how she really felt....... *Well, let me see, my ex-husband is dead and they think I killed him*', but she said the polite words that Rita expected to hear, "Oh I'm fine. I'm going through John's house with my friend Brooke, seeing if anything needs to be taken out to the garbage or cleaned." Lindsey put on her best fake smile. Rita wasn't all bad, but Lindsey thought she was more concerned about putting the house up on the market for Lindsey then actually concerned about her welfare or how she was doing.

Rita turned her gaze on Brooke, "Oh, hi." Rita extended her arm out to Brooke, "I'm Rita, nice to meet you. Have I seen you with John before? Are you one of John's girls? I know I met one of John's girlfriends at the mall, was it you? I thought you had long blond hair though, have you recently dyed it?"

There was something about Rita that made Brooke feel uneasy. One of 'John's girls'? The whole connotation made Brooke want to vomit.

She replied curtly, "We might have met, I'm an optometrist at the mall and John's office is close by. He and I may have bumped into one another but I don't remember being introduced to you, sorry. You must be confusing me with someone else." Brooke was polite, but Rita had a way of being extremely nosey and insinuated things by the tone of her voice. Rita gave Brooke an icy stare, but Brooke held her ground and stared Rita down.

An awkward pause followed; Lindsey filled the awkward pause, "Well, we've got to get back to work, going through John's things and cleaning. Thanks for stopping by, Rita. In case you're wondering I'm not ready to put John's house on the market. I'll let you know when I list it." Lindsey opened John's front door to let Rita out.

Rita said, "Of course, if you need me let me know. I'm always willing to help." I'm sure you are, thought Lindsey.

Lindsey half-smiled and said, "Okay, great. Bye now." Lindsey wanted Rita to leave.

Rita waved, "Bye." As soon as Lindsey shut the door they burst out laughing.

Lindsey spoke, "What a busy body. Could she be less subtle? And what was that about you and John? It sounded like she was implying you two were together."

"I know. Some people have nothing better to do than spread gossip and rumors." With a shrug, Brooke said, "Let's go into the garage for a look around. Maybe we'll find something in there."

They went through the living room, past the formal dining room, through the kitchen and went through the kitchen door out to the garage. John's Lincoln Aviator was parked in the parking space. Brooke pointed, "Let's look in his car." Brooke and Lindsey opened up the door and got in. They searched the glove compartment and the storage compartment between the seats. They looked under the seats and went to the back of the truck.

"What do we have here?" Lindsey held up a package of cigarettes and a packet of matches that she found in the compartment between the seats. She commented, "Look, just like in the old time movies. John hated smoking; these have to be someone else's. They're Marlboros, that's a women's brand. I don't smoke but that's what I've been told. Maybe it belongs to one of John's girlfriends. Maybe it's the murderer's." She held the cigarettes up and shook them in front of Brooke's face.

"Lindsey, you're imagination is running wild, those cigarettes may or may not mean anything. Maybe they belong to the murderer, and maybe they don't." Brooke was looking through the glove compartment. "Now look at what I found, a purple rubber and some photos." Brooke rifled through the pictures. "They're pictures of one of John's lake parties. Look at this one of the guys mooning the camera. That is too funny." Brooke handed the picture to Lindsey.

"Looks like it was a fun time, but……..,no pun intended, it doesn't look like it will help us." Lindsey took a look at the rest of the photos in the pile.

On the back of one of the pictures was the phone number that she had repeatedly seen in John's cell phone. On the front of the photo was a woman in a bathing suit, but the photo only showed her body. Whoever took the photo didn't have very good aim or had way too much to drink, or was aiming to get only the woman's body in the film. Lindsey put the group of photos in her purse. Nothing was making sense right now, but maybe the picture would be the link to some other facts.

She held up the photo of the woman in the bikini for Brooke, "Now this is a clue. That's the same number that was in John's cell phone. If we find out who it belongs to we might have our murderer." Lindsey's 6th sense was kicking in and she felt that the picture was significant, but didn't know why.

She turned to Brooke, "Let's go, Brooke. I'm starved and I've got to go pick up Leo and Lilly from my mom's. It's already 5:30." They were sitting in John's truck, taking one last look around. "Thanks for coming over here with me. John was so predictable; I knew everything was going to be in its place." They looked around the neat and orderly garage. She conveniently forgot that they were both worried about finding something strange, dark, or a peculiar sinister item from John's house. Lindsey continued, "Let's get out of his truck. We'll have to go back through the house to lock up."

The two women got out of the car and went back through the house. They looked around one last time but nothing seemed out of place. After closing the front door Lindsey activated the alarm system that locked up the house. The two women walked to their cars, Brooke turned to Lindsey, "Lindsey, take care of yourself, let me know what else I can do to help you out. If I don't talk to you tomorrow I'll see you tomorrow night." Brooke got in her car.

"Bye Brooke, thanks for helping, I'll see you tomorrow night." Lindsey got in her car and they both drove off thinking about John and wondering who could have committed such a heinous crime against another person.

*Why wasn't Lindsey arrested? Everything was taking too long. Lindsey should have been arrested and her possessions taken away. Why was she allowed to go into John's house and search for evidence? The police are so inept. What do I have to do to make things right? What do I have to do to make sure that all leads point to Lindsey? I'm going crazy, waiting and waiting. If she could see in my head the way that I can see in to everyone else's head she would realize that my actions have saved a lot of people from suffering. Why was this gift given to me? Why can I see how things should be but no one else can? If Lindsey had my gift she would see that my act was going to bring fresh life to everyone.*

# CHAPTER 14
## Traci's numbers: Wednesday

John's house hadn't turned up any outstanding criminal evidence. Lindsey had the pictures and the purple rubber in her purse. Why purple; she never knew John to be a big Prince fan? The only item she felt could be associated with the murder was the picture with the phone number on the back, and that was pure speculation. She didn't even know who the number belonged to.

After exploring John's house, Lindsey had picked up Leo and Lilly from her parents. She had been exhausted. The emotional turmoil she felt was taking its toll; she was trying to solve this murder before getting arrested and things were coming to a head. Somehow she had managed to make sure that Leo and Lilly had their homework finished so they would be prepared for school the following day. Once they were in bed she had opened a bottle of wine and sat in her bedroom with the TV on and tried to relax.

As she was sitting on her bed, with Merlin by her side, she was startled by the phone ringing. It was only 10:00, but it seemed too late to receive a phone call. She answered it and was pleasantly surprised to hear Heather's voice on the other end. Heather had called to tell her that the police had performed the autopsy on John and had given details about his murder that had shocked her.

She knew from the papers that John had been strangulated with dental floss; Heather told her it was dental floss, wrapped around his throat 10 or so times and tightened around the neck using a toothbrush. Heather also told her that something had been done to John's teeth. Poor John, how was she going to make sense out of that? Lindsey's heart pounded harder and her mouth went dry when Heather told her that her fingerprints and blood were found on one of the murder weapons. How could that be when she had nothing to do with the murder?

No wonder the police were always driving by her house. She wasn't sure if anyone had been following her, but with what Heather was saying she felt almost positive that her instincts were right and that she had a tail on her during the day. Lindsey felt this case was a trail without a clear path, like being in a forest and trying to get out to clear land. But instead of getting anywhere you kept on walking in circles, passing the same tree without getting to where you needed to go and becoming more frustrated with each new turn. Which way should she precede?

After talking to Heather, Lindsey nervously made her rounds, making sure all the doors were locked and the windows were secure. Who knows what could happen? After locking up, Lindsey had sat down on the couch, wading through the evidence in her mind. Unexpectedly she had fallen asleep on the couch; too exhausted to move back to her bed. Leo woke her up, promptly at 7:00am the next morning.

"Mom, wake up, it's 7:00." Leo found Lindsey sleeping on the couch.

"I'm up, Leo." Lindsey looked out onto the cold fall day, wondering what the day would bring, hoping it wouldn't be her arrest. "Come here, Leo and give me a hug." Lindsey sat up and opened her arms up so that she could give Leo a big hug.

"Mooooom." Leo came and gave Lindsey a hug even with the exaggerated moan. "Why are you sleeping on the couch?" Leo asked.

Lindsey tiredly replied, "I was so tired last night; I fell asleep without even making it to my bedroom. That's the only reason, Leo, nothing except that your mom was tired last night."

Leo listened and nodded his head up and down. "Okay, mom, as long as you're okay." He was talking and walking to the kitchen absorbed with his next thought of getting some breakfast.

"I'm fine," Lindsey shouted so that Leo could hear her. That was all he had to say on the matter, which was good. Lindsey didn't want the kids to worry about anything, except being kids and having fun at school, working to get good grades and hanging out with their friends. Their father's death was enough to deal with; she didn't need them worrying about her too.

After her and the kids' morning routine, Lindsey dropped the kids off at school, and drove home. She was eager to start the day and investigate by making phone calls, looking at more of John's text in his cell phone, and taking notes. She wanted to try and relax too; she was still tired from the anxiety-producing search of John's office and his home and her phone conversation with Heather.

Back at home she made herself a strong pot of coffee and poured some in her favorite mug before settling down on the couch to look at John's text messages. A lot of the messages were from Jess, all negative and accusatory. The nemesis number also had scathing text messages. Lindsey would have to find out whom that number belonged too. She had already written it down and decided to call the phone company to see who belonged to the number, or if that didn't work, ask Tom for some police help. She was still unsure of how he would react to her delving into his territory. And given what Heather had told her, she was too apprehensive to call him and let him know what she knew.

Would Tom help, or would he turn on her and corner her. Would he try to convict her of the murder? Now she knew the bitter truth about the evidence, and without a doubt, Tom knew too. His temperament from the other night might change from a cozy warm feeling towards her to a cold and distant feeling where he would try to stay as far away from her as possible. She wasn't sure. As she was contemplating Tom and her feelings for him and his feelings for her, the phone rang startling her out of her reverie. Looking at the caller ID, she saw it was from Tom and was excited but skeptical, "Hello, this is Lindsey."

Tom's sincere sounding voice was at the other end, "Hi, it's Tom, from the police department."

As if she didn't know, she was only thinking about him constantly. Lindsey's reply was anxious, "Hi, Tom, what is it that you want?" The question was asked abruptly, maybe too abruptly but what if he wanted to interrogate her again. She wanted to know right away.

Tom's voice was serious, tinged with concern, "I was wondering how you were doing? I was also hoping you could meet me out for lunch today. I wanted to ask you some questions. I don't want you to have to go down to the police department again. Would you be able to make it out for lunch today at Jetski's on Capital Drive?" Tom waited for the reply.

He wasn't officially going to ask Lindsey about the case or tell Lindsey details surrounding John's murder. His superior had advised him to watch Lindsey and interview her again at the station. He was sticking his neck out for her. It wasn't standard police procedure to call the main suspect and take them out to lunch and tell them details about the case that could exonerate them. Usually the purpose of taking a suspect out was to ask them questions under the pretense of helping them, but the real motivation was to get them to trip up, stumble on their own words. That wasn't Tom's motivation with Lindsey. Too many things were bothering Tom about the forensic evidence incriminating Lindsey.

He had to admit that his romantic feelings for Lindsey were getting him in trouble too, gnawing away at his resolve to stay away from her and keep their relationship impersonal. His practical side lost out and he called her. He was bending the rules for her, not breaking them. If his hunch was wrong he could end up without a job, or possibly end up six feet under.

Lindsey remembered what her friends had told her about Tom. Against the advice of her friends Lindsey responded, "Yes, I can make it today. You're not bringing any handcuffs, are you?" Lindsey loved playing with Tom, but was only half joking when she asked.

Tom's reply was serious, but he played along too, "Of course not, this lunch is off the record, just between me and you. I'd like to share some details about John's case with you. You knew John well, and I also want to see you." Why did he have to tag that on the end? He was flirting and he knew it. He waited for her reply.

Lindsey thought about his comment, Hmmmmm? He wanted to see her. The dreamy part of Lindsey's personality jumped on that phrase. She wanted to see him too. "Okay, I can meet you out there. What time?"

"1:00, I'm finishing up some work at the precinct and then I'll see you at Jetski's?"

"Okay, 1:00 is fine with me. I'll see you there, bye." Lindsey replied in a flirtations tone.

"Bye, Lindsey."

Lindsey hung up the phone wondering if she had conjured him up while she was on the couch thinking about his keen mind and what she perceived as his caring personality. Lindsey placed the phone in the receiver and focused on John's cell phone again. She hadn't seen any new numbers that piqued her interest so she decided to call Traci and find out if she had called any of the numbers yet from her list and if she had spoken to any of them.

"Hello." Traci picked up her cell phone after the fourth ring.

"Hi Traci, its Lindsey. I've been sitting around all morning looking at John's cell phone and text messages and I was wondering if you had connected with any of the people from the list I gave you Monday?" Lindsey hoped she was going to hear some good news, like that Traci had gotten in touch with one of the numbers and they had confessed. If only this case could be that simple.

"Lindsey, I'm so glad you called. I've been meaning to get in touch with you. I called the numbers. The numbers proved to belong to people who knew John extremely well. Three of the numbers that I called belonged to his inventor friends who all said that they were tremendously shocked and saddened by John's murder. All of them professed to liking John and honestly they each told the same story. They could have been clones."

Lindsey wasn't surprised by Traci's perception of John's inventor buddies; she agreed, "Really? They were that predictable? Actually, I've met John's inventor buddies before, and frankly, I couldn't imagine any one of them committing a murder. The men I met were all slightly balding and pudgy, very interested in writing code, book smart but not adventurous. Writing code was their entire life. Truthfully, I found them to be boring."

Traci had talked to them by phone, but thought the same thing. She continued, "They seemed very boring, which isn't to say that that is a bad thing. They didn't even go to John's birthday party. Each one was home with their families. They are all from Brookfield and work in the Farley building and live practically in the same neighborhood as John's. That Saturday night Derek was at his sons wrestling match and then he and his wife went home. Dan was playing racquetball at the health club in Brookfield with some guy named Pete and then he went home to his family. Randy was at home all night, he said he ordered pizzas for his family and they watched a movie." Lindsey listened and wrote down the names and the alibis on a sheet of paper. It wasn't probable that the three men were involved with John's murder, but she wanted to keep notes just in case there was a discrepancy later on in the investigation.

She wasn't counting anyone out just yet. Lindsey stopped writing and responded, "I didn't think that John's inventor friends would have a reason to murder John. For one thing they have absolutely no flare for that sordid kind of life, which is a good thing. I really need to find someone who is boring and predictable." Lindsey blurted that out, not meaning to talk about men and relationships, but Traci caught on.

"Lindsey, are you obsessing about someone? I can't believe that you're thinking about any guy with what just happened to John." Traci read Lindsey like a book and knew Lindsey had her mind on romance even with a murder rap attached to her body like a shadow on a sunny day.

Lindsey carefully said, "I know, there is something definitely wrong with me. I'm going out to lunch today with Tom and I keep thinking about him and how I'd like to wake up with him next to me some morning."

Traci emphatically said, "Lindsey you are crazy. He's out to pin a murder on you, not nail you."

Lindsey rolled her eyes, "Ha, ha, very funny Traci. I know he's trying to pin a murder on me, but for some reason he calms me down when he's around. I've got to get over it. I don't need a detective in my life. I need a boring guy, not the devil in disguise, but I like talking to him and hearing his voice."

With exasperation Traci answered Lindsey, "Lindsey, you haven't liked anyone in six years. See, this is what you do. Anytime a guy is completely unavailable you like him."

Lindsey laughed, "I know. Why do you think I've been single for six years? It's a bad trait of mine. Okay, back to business. What about the other two numbers?"

Traci looked down at her notepad and told Lindsey the information, "Well, one number belonged to a patient who had veneers put on and John was trying to get in touch with her for a follow up appointment, but she didn't want to go in again because she was too busy. She also didn't attend the party and was at home with her five- year- old daughter and husband. She didn't know John in a personal way. He was recommended to her by a friend. She said she liked her veneers and didn't want another appointment. She was quite friendly about everything and said she was sad when she heard of John's death. There was nothing suspicious about her." Lindsey wrote down the number and the women's name.

Traci continued talking, "I've saved the best for last. The last number belonged to John's new girlfriend Tara and what a nut case she was. When I was talking to her she heaved and huffed with exaggerated sobs. I wanted to hang up on her. I ended up holding the phone away from my ear because she was so loud. She went on and on for five minutes. She spouted out stories about her dreams for her and John to live a long and glowing life; free of obligation. She felt they had a shared soul." Traci paused and took a breath. "I listened to her endless babbling, which seemed to last for an hour or more. It might have been 40 minutes; she can talk. I asked if she would meet me on the premise of finding out who murdered John. She stopped crying for a minute and changed her voice. In a squeaky, quiet voice she agreed to meet me. It was weird. I can't wait to meet her. She seemed to be playing a part out of a movie, like she was acting."

Lindsey reflected on Traci's impressions of Tara, "Wow, I think they were only dating for three months. It sounds like she thought they were serious and were a monogamous couple. I'm not sure John felt the same; he recently told me he went to a Packer game with a woman named Peg. It doesn't mean that John and Peg were dating, but you never know. Don't bring it up to Tara though, she might go ballistic. When are you going to meet with Tara?"

Traci responded, "I asked if she could meet me for coffee at Starbucks on Moreland tomorrow at 8:00. Can you make it?"

Lindsey would have to be late for that meeting, because she needed to drop Leo and Lilly off at school, "I could be there by 8:30. I can't wait to meet her, I haven't heard much about her. John never told me too much about his girlfriends, but because we talked the conversation would lead to who he was dating or who I was dating. Thanks for calling those numbers Traci. Are you coming over tonight?"

"Of course, have I ever not come?" Traci laughed.

Light-heartedly Lindsey said, "Okay, I'll see you tonight." Traci said, "Bye."

Lindsey hung up the phone thinking about Tara, even the name sounded theatric. That meeting should be interesting.

Lindsey looked up at the clock, 12:00 already. She got in the shower, dried off with a fluffy towel and got ready with extra care. She headed out to meet Tom at Jetski's restaurant, ready to play ball, or maybe go surfing.

# CHAPTER 15
## Lunch with Tom: Wednesday afternoon

Lindsey had been to Jetski's several times before and enjoyed the upscale fast-food restaurant. The food was good, not the greatest, but it was priced fair and it was fast. She parked her car in the lot and noted that Tom's black Pissat was already there. Bummer, she liked to arrive first so she could watch him as he walked in. Now he would be waiting for her. She looked around as she opened the door to the restaurant, and walked through the tables until she found Tom.

Could he look even cuter than last time she saw him? Tom was wearing regular blue jeans and a dark blue, long sleeved cotton shirt that was snug but not tight. Lindsey caught herself looking at his biceps and broad shoulders before making eye contact and saying hi. She remained standing, smiled and was eager to find out what he had to tell her, "Hi Tom, I hope you have some pleasant news for me; as pleasant as it can be considering the circumstances. You said something on the phone about this being off the record?"

Tom smiled up at Lindsey and gestured for her to sit down in the booth. He had anticipated the meeting but his heart lurched forward anyway. "Hi Lindsey, I'm glad you could meet me. Have a seat." Lindsey slid into the booth and took off her coat, laid it on the bench next to her and looked across the table at Tom.

Tom asked, "Do you want to order anything? The menu's on the board up front, wave burgers or high tide fish tacos? Have you ever been here before?"

"Yes, I like this place; it has a 1950's vibe to it." Did she just say vibe out loud? What a dork I am, thought Lindsey. She let Tom know what she wanted, "Um, a cheeseburger would be perfect, no ketchup, no mustard but onion, tomato and lettuce would be great."

Tom stood up, "Okay, do you want some fries?"

"Of course," said Lindsey. "Who doesn't eat fries with a burger?" He walked away to order their food. Tom went up to order for Lindsey and in less than five minutes was back with her food and a cup for a soda.

"I thought you would want a drink, the fountain is right over there," Tom said, as he glanced with his eyes at the soda fountain, placed the tray of food on the table and sat down at the booth.

"Great, you thought right. I'll be back in a flash." Lindsey went to fill up the cup with diet coke and then came back to the booth, 'back in a flash' what was she saying! She brought back her drink and said, "Okay, now I'm set. Why are we here Detective Tom?" Lindsey smiled, settled into the booth and then took a bite of the cheeseburger.

Tom began telling her the reason for the meeting, "Well, this is an unofficial meeting. I've got to tell you that the evidence against you is damaging." Tom looked right at her and she could only think to respond with a question.

"What do you mean?" Lindsey's brow was furrowed and she put down the sandwich.

"I shouldn't be telling you this, but I'm going to anyway. There is some forensic evidence that has been analyzed and that points to you as the murderer," Tom let that sentence hang in the air, and took a bite of his fish tacos.

Lindsey looked at him, but didn't let him know that she already knew about the forensics from Heather; it didn't come as a surprise to her. She didn't let on that she already had heard about her fingerprints and blood found on one of the murder weapons. She was more surprised that Tom was sitting across from her and talking about the case with her. Was he trying to get something out of her or did he really care about her and wanted to warn her. Her verdict was still out.

Lindsey answered as best she could with a wary eye on Tom. "I didn't do it, if that's what you're wondering. I don't know who did it. I don't know why there's evidence at the crime scene that's linking me directly to the murder. What is it that they have? How could it directly implicate me?" Lindsey thought she knew what Tom was going to tell her but didn't want to let on that she knew.

Tom obviously had more to say. "Lindsey, off the record, they have your prints on the knife that was used to murder John. They also found your finger prints on the package of dental floss that was left on the floor of the car after the dental floss was used to strangle John, and your blood was also found at the scene. It doesn't look good. It's enough to get a warrant for your arrest and a warrant to search your house. Both warrants are on hold, but it won't be long before they're issued." Tom looked at Lindsey for her reaction.

He was breaking the rules now; he shouldn't be telling her that warrants were issued for her arrest. She could take that information and start packing a suitcase to the Caribbean. He was basically taking his job and kissing it goodbye if he was wrong. It was Lindsey's turn to confess.

She looked down at her food as she talked to Tom, not wanting to look directly into his eyes, "I know, I found about the DNA from a friend. I can't understand how it happened; I had no part in his murder." She looked up at him. "Somehow, I'm being set up. Someone planned this against John, someone who knew him really well. Tom, I know you know I didn't do it." She was emphatic, "You would have already secured the warrants if you truly believed I did it." Lindsey leaned in to where Tom was sitting, looking directly into his eyes, waiting for his response.

Somberly Tom said, "I know. That's why I'm here."

Lindsey sat back with relief, Tom was on her side and she was almost certain she could trust him. She didn't know if his influence was enough to keep her out of jail but she knew she had an ally.

"Why haven't they issued the arrest warrant yet?" Lindsey asked. There had to be more than Tom being on her side for the police and judge not to issue the warrant.

Tom was slow to respond, "We haven't made the warrant for your arrest yet because we're still trying to tie up some loose ends. John was a big man and someone was able to convince him to be handcuffed to the steering wheel. It seems like John thought whoever he was with would be fulfilling a fantasy with him, and it doesn't' make sense that the person he was with would be you. I'm basing that off the assumption that you two were strictly parents and past that stage of your relationship." He looked at her for some affirmation.

Tom didn't know how true those words were, she couldn't even imagine wanting to be with John in a romantic way. The only reason they talked or were in the same place together was because of Leo and Lilly.

She answered Tom agreeing with his assumption, "We were never alone together. We would meet out for a coffee or lunch sometimes if we needed to discuss the kids' schedules or money, but it never was a problem. We were very cordial to each other and very friendly, but that was it."

Lindsey spoke the words that Tom wanted to hear. He believed every word she said even though a twinge of suspicion lingered in a distant part of his mind. He thumbed that up to past experiences and his training.

Tom added to his explanation, "Lindsey, John struggled with whoever he was with. Another reason that they haven't arrested you was because John had skin under his fingernails and it didn't match your DNA. There's reason to believe that whoever did it is the same person whose DNA will match the skin samples from under his fingernails. We haven't been able to determine who it belongs to. We've interviewed a lot of potential suspects and taken a lot of DNA samples, but so far we haven't had any luck. The higher ups are getting hungry to make an arrest and discount the DNA found under his nails. They're willing to chalk it up to someone who was at the party and who John hugged. It's total bullshit. I'm telling you all of this because I believe you're innocent and I know you've been working at finding out who did it." With that statement he reached over and grabbed Lindsey hands. "I'm going to find out who did it, don't worry."

Lindsey didn't know what to do or say. Wow, here he was, telling her about the case, the cat helping the mouse. She always loved the *Tom and Jerry* episodes when they were friends. She knew if he didn't find the murderer she would, but his help could be invaluable. She was stunned but collected her thoughts. Here he was touching her and she could hardly stay grounded in her seat. She was nervous around Tom, he affected her that way.

Breathing deeply she composed herself. "Tom, I didn't do it. So far I know that John was strangled with dental floss and that there was something done to his teeth? What is that all about?"

Tom was impressed, Lindsey was certainly resourceful. "Yeah, it was strange. Whoever murdered John had pulled out his teeth and tied up the teeth with the dental floss. They knotted the dental floss around the teeth, like you would with a bead on a necklace and strung the teeth around the rear view mirror. The teeth were dangling there, like you would see with dice or a cross or other items that people hang up on their rear view mirrors. It was a message, but we're not certain what it means."

Tom put his hand over his mouth and stroked his whiskers on his chin and moustache. "The crime scene was something out of a horror movie, created by an angry assailant and definitely premeditated. I don't see why your fingerprints would be on the murder weapon but not on the handcuffs or the door knobs. So why would you, if you were the murderer, leave your prints on the weapon and the dental floss? Too many things don't add up, as far as convicting you of this murder."

Tom's mouth went up in a half smile; he was trying to put Lindsey at ease.

She could see it in his face, she looked at him and quietly spoke, "That's because I didn't do it. If I tell you something....... it's off the record right?" Lindsey thought everything they were saying was but needed some reassurance. She didn't want the tables to turn on her.

He nodded his head up and down, "Lindsey, everything we discuss here is off the record. I'm going out on a limb, hoping that you might have a piece of evidence or some insight about John or that night that could help us solve the case before we arrest you. I believe you're innocent, but not everyone on the force does. My being here today with you and telling you the things I've told you could get me in trouble."

Lindsey didn't like the sound of that but knew he was right. She drew a deep breath in and then let out information that she had learned from her own investigation. "I've got a phone number that I found in John's cell phone. Brooke and I went through his office and found it in his drawer; he must have used this cell phone as a backup in his office when his other one was charging. There was a number on it that has been disconnected. The person called and called and left some pretty horrific text messages. I called the number to figure out who it belonged to but it had been disconnected. Could you find out who the number belonged to? I really believe that the person who left all the messages might be the guy, or girl." She watched his face as he assimilated the information.

He was so serious and in a low, reasonable voice answered. "I'll try; sometimes it's hard to track down cell phone numbers. People can get accounts all the time and use any name or pay on the prepaid cards and not have an account. I'll see what I can do. I will be able to determine where they were calling from by looking at the satellite stations that were used to relay the calls. That might help cross check some of the other suspects on our list. Unfortunately, the DNA under John's fingernails doesn't match any of our other suspects."

"Did you get some from Dave?" Lindsey asked.

"No, we were concentrating on women. Why?" Tom asked, wanting to know why Lindsey would suspect Dave.

"I've been doing my own snooping, as you know. When we were in John's office we found some folders. One of the folders was the insurance folder for John's business. Dave had a lot to gain. He would get a large amount of insurance money and also profit by signing up John's patients. When we searched Dave's office, we found a couple of high heeled shoes, some wigs, make-up in the closet and several dresses that looked like they would fit him. It doesn't mean he did it or anything, but it's odd don't you think?" Lindsey asked and Tom was surprised.

"We never thought of Dave as a suspect because he's a man and this looked like it was a crime committed by a woman. The crime scene would indicate that it was committed by a woman who wanted to get back at John. I'll talk to Dave and get his DNA. It sounds like he will profit from John's death more than we had assumed."

Lindsey was excited. If he only knew, thought Lindsey; she was sure it was Dave now. If it wasn't him, than who else could it be?

"Are you doing anything else with your investigation?" Tom asked Lindsey.

She was but she decided to hold some things back. She didn't want to endure a lecture about being careful and letting the police do the rest of the sleuthing. "Oh, I'm doing a little bit of asking around and keeping my eyes and ears open. I'm not doing anything risky or too dangerous." She smiled at Tom, hoping he would believe her.

Tom looked at Lindsey's smiling, beautiful face and knew she was investigating more than he would have liked, but didn't say anything to her. "Okay, whatever you do, be careful. And both of us have to pretend like we never had this conversation. Here's my private cell phone number. If you need me, or find something out, call me on this line. I always answer." He wanted to ask her out for dinner, see a movie, and cuddle with her.

Lindsey took the card and put it in her purse. "Thanks Tom, I can't tell you how much it means to me to have you looking out for me. We'll find out who did it." *And I think I could love you.* She couldn't help but feel there was something, some chemistry between them. When it happened it just happened and this was definitely happening.

"Take care, Lindsey. I'll be in touch." Tom stood up and started to leave.

"Bye Tom, and thanks for lunch." Tom left and Lindsey sat idly looking around and thinking about Tom and their conversation. How strange, he told her so much. He trusted her, just like that. Would he continue to be on her side if they arrested her? Would he find out who did it? She could only sit there and wonder what would happen to her, to Leo and to Lilly. The race was on to find the killer.

*How did Lindsey and Tom become so close in such a short amount of time? What were they talking about? Are they conspiring against me? The lead detective in John's case shouldn't be romancing the main suspect. Do they suspect me? I'm going to have to get rid of Tom; he's too infatuated with Lindsey. He's on her side, but not really. He's a faker, a player, just like all of them.*

The women were seated around Lindsey's oval table in her kitchen, drinking wine, eating crackers and writing down the clues that they had uncovered so far. In a smiling voice Lindsey started the conversation, "We are doing really well you guys, for not having a 'clue' as to what or how to investigate; we've uncovered a lot."

Lindsey rallied the ladies around the table and congratulated them on their hard work. To get everyone up to speed she recapped her and Brooke's morning, sleuthing for clues at John's Brookfield house. Everyone got a laugh about Rita's perfect timing and her allusion to the fact that she had seen Brooke and John together at the mall. Rita was a piece of work; she could be such a bitch. Lindsey showed the ladies the photo of the mystery woman and the purple rubber. They also got a laugh over that. John was still up to having a good time but at least he was being careful, if not weird.

Traci told them that she had called the numbers from John's cell phone and was meeting with John's new girlfriend, Tara. Traci had found out Tara was an actress and she gave quite a performance for Traci over the phone. Traci had relayed to the group that Tara was sobbing and hysterical on the phone, so much so that she had to hang up and compose herself before she could continue with their conversation. Tara had given Traci a lot of information; she didn't act outwardly angry. She acted as if she had lost a husband and best friend that she had known her whole life. Traci thought it was too acted out and planned, as if she were up on stage. Later in the conversation Tara had revealed that she felt John was getting ready to commit to a long-term exclusive relationship with her. Unfortunately for her she had found out that John had been fooling around on her with another woman. Tara was adamant that it was a one-time fling and that John was going to marry her. She had no reason to murder him.

The women speculated that when Tara found out that John had no intention of being only with her, she lost control and planned her best acting role yet; conning John out to his car to murder him. John had the reputation of being a womanizer. How come these women thought he would change for them? John was John and you got what you got with him. He never pretended to want to be with one woman and get married. Lindsey felt that these women were either naive or very delusional when it came to John.

In addition to the regular members of their case crackers and wine club, Lindsey had invited Lori, John's office assistant. Lori was an asset to the club. She knew the ins and outs of the office and had contacted John's lawyer. She was also spying on Dave. Dave was drumming up a lot of business from John's death. She had contacted many of John's patients and they had decided to use Dave as their dentist. Lori was certain that Dave murdered John because he wanted to run the business and make more money.

Lori let everyone in on her suspicions, "It has to be Dave. I've been watching him since Monday and he's been a machine. He's had me call all of John's patients and sign them up for his practice. He's also been ordering a lot of equipment that John never would have agreed too. I've heard them argue in the past about getting inhalation sedation N20-02, in other words laughing gas. He wanted it for patients who were afraid of the needle or who preferred the gas as an anesthetic. John never would have agreed to order another gas apparatus at half a million dollars. The one we have right now barely gets used. John was always afraid of the side effects that the N20 had on the patients. Dave thinks it's the way to drum up more business and he has total control of the office now. He's only been a dentist for two years; this is such a coup for him. Think about it. He hasn't had to struggle a bit and now he's got a thriving practice."

Lindsey couldn't agree more. She remembered John struggling the first years after dental school. She looked at the other women and then at Lori. "You're so right. He had everything to gain from John's death. John built up that business from scratch and ran it like a tight ship. Dave could step right in and at a relatively young age, own the practice and become mega rich. John's life insurance covers his income which goes straight to Dave for a whole year. No wonder why he's spending all of that money." Lindsey could picture Dave with big white fake veneers on his teeth and a gold chain around his neck with two playboy bunnies at his side or maybe too playgirl bunnies, or maybe both.

Lori continued with briefing the ladies on Dave's odd behavior. "Dave is always holed up in his office between patients, he is ultra-reclusive. One night he thought I had gone home but I was still in the office trying to catch up on all the paperwork that needs to be changed because of John's death. I needed to ask Dave about one of the patient's procedures and grabbed the folder to take to Dave's office. I had the folder in my hand, walked over to his door and turned the knob with my free hand. Without knocking I opened the door; that's when I saw him busy primping himself with lipstick and nail polish. He tried to hide it but I saw it, lipstick can't be washed away that fast." She slapped her table with the palm of her hand and then said, "He told me to knock from now on before entering and he said it in a low, whispery evil voice. It was frightening. It worked on me; I've been knocking ever since. I've been thinking about the three dresses hung up in the back of his closet and the blond long-haired wig. He could have used those items as a disguise at the party! The guy is so guilty. We've got to go to the police now." Lori checked her notes and was waiting for the other women to respond. Her eyes were lit up and she wanted to take action now. Urgency was in her voice.

It was Lindsey's turn to fess up and tell them about her meeting with Tom. She wasn't going to divulge all of the information because that would put Tom in a precarious position. She also didn't want Heather to feel that her cousin's information was compromised or for her to feel threatened by her talking with Tom about the forensic evidence. Tom was no dull nail and probably with a little digging could figure out who gave Lindsey the forensic information. Lindsey let the women know that she had met with Tom.

After a sip of wine and a nibble on a cracker, she looked at all the women and told them about her lunch date with Tom. "I've met with Tom. He was the one who contacted me because of the forensic evidence against me. He doesn't believe it was me, but he wanted me to be aware that I might be arrested based on certain DNA evidence. He couldn't tell me about it but you all know what it is. A weapon at the crime scene had my fingerprints on it and some blood of mine was also found at the crime scene.

John was murdered with dental floss; the case that was left on the floor of John's car also had my fingerprints on it. How stupid would I be though to leave my fingerprints on a weapon that was used in a crime that was obviously premeditated? Tom's not buying it and he, in not so many words, told me that the case against me had a lot of holes. Which I would hope it would! I told him about Dave and what we found in his office. He already knew we were there from following me that day. He said that he had tested some people from the party for DNA but not everyone. Guess who's going to have their DNA tested soon?"

"Could it be Dave?" Lori answered.

"You guessed it," said Lindsey. "Tom is going to bring in Dave for questioning and get a sample. They've got some unidentified DNA from under John's fingernails and how much do you want to bet its Dave's? It has to be and then I'll be off the hook and Dave will be in jail right where he belongs. He's not going to get away with it." Lindsey's eyes were on fire and so were Lori's. The room was quiet as each of the women contemplated Dave as the guilty party.

Lori continued to talk about Dave, "I could see him being guilty. No one knows Dave that well. I've worked with him for two years and don't know much about him except that he went to Marquette. He's a loner and an introvert; he always hides in his office between patients. He barely has social calls at work and he never talks about himself. I asked him to go out to lunch with me but so far he has made excuses, too busy, too tired, brought his lunch that day. I can't pin him down for one ½ hour lunch. He's the psychopath for sure."

Julia raised her wine glass and was nodding her head up and down before she took a sip of her wine. It was her turn to share what she had uncovered. "And speaking of psychopaths, I did get a hold of Jess and she and I are going to meet for a happy hour drink tomorrow. We were going to meet for lunch today but she called me and asked if we could meet later. She was too busy at work." She nodded at Lindsey and added, "I sent you an email about it, Lindsey."

Lindsey sat up straighter and nodded her head up and down, "Thanks, Julia. I did get the email this morning. And I'll definitely go with you tomorrow. That should be eye-opening!"

Julia continued talking about Jess, "She can talk a mile a minute and it's all about her. She laced her conversation with stories about John's misbehavior and peppered the story with details of how he was a control freak and a womanizer the entire length of their relationship. I never got a word in. When she came up for air I told her that it would work out for me to meet out for a drink on Thursday after work to talk about things. She agreed. I think she's crazy, a real psycho. I'll get more of a feel for her after we talk over tomorrow's drink.

Julia paused and then said, "From the way she sounded on the phone, I wouldn't put murder past her. The phone was scorching my hand after I talked with her as if little sharp daggers were sticking out of it. I swear; she is one angry lady. I can imagine her luring John to his car for a sex romp and then throwing all of her anger and accusations at him. From the way she was talking on the phone she would have relished seeing him take his last breath, especially without satisfying any of his sexual urges. According to her that would be what he deserved. I don't know about Dave or Tara; I might put my money on Jess. Did Tom say he took a sample of her DNA?" Julia turned and looked at Lindsey.

"Actually, no, he couldn't tell me who he had taken samples of, but if I see him again I'll mention her name. I'm not sure who or why they've picked certain people from the party or John's life to do the DNA testing on. Lindsey took another sip of wine before getting up to get out another bottle of red wine for the women.

Lindsey uncorked the bottle and set it on the table for any one of the women to refill their glasses. They had done an admirable job with what little experience they had. Lindsey was holding her refilled glass of wine up, "I can't thank you all enough. The meeting with Tom today was encouraging and scary. Some things just don't add up. We have a challenge to complete and we're going to do get to the bottom of this!

"We all could be CSI investigators from *CSI Milwaukee*," Heather raised her glass in a toast. "Here's to Lindsey and us, the Case Crackers, plus a little Wine Club," They all raised their glasses and drank. The meeting had gone well. Then Lindsey heard Lilly yelling.

"MOM!" Lilly called from the family room. Lindsey left for a minute to see what Lilly wanted. "I have to do a science experiment. I need some copper, clay, a jar and vinegar."

Where had this come from? It was the first time Lindsey had heard of this.

"Why didn't you tell me earlier? When do you need the supplies?" Lindsey didn't like it when these projects for school sprung up on her.

Lilly nonchalantly replied, "I need to do the experiment tonight. Oh yeah, and the copper can't be a penny."

In exasperation Lindsey said, "You should have told me when you got home. We'll have to search the garage for a copper tube and I hope we have some vinegar on hand. Lilly, what am I going to do with you?"

Lilly shrugged her shoulders and smiled.

"I'll help you as soon as my friends leave." Lindsey gave Lilly a hug then looked over to see what Leo was up to. "Are you finished with all of your homework, Leo?"

Leo could barely turn his head from the computer. "Yes, mom; I'm finished"

"You better be, I don't want to hear about any missing assignments or late assignments."

"I've got everything done mom," was Leo's short reply.

"Okay." Lindsey gave Leo a hug too and went back into the kitchen to join her friends.

Lindsey and the women continued to chat about the case and other aspects of their lives.

Julia was off and on again with Charlie, but none of the women were surprised with that bit of information.

Heather had loving stories about Isabella. She told the group how she continued to cause baby destruction in her house. Isabella would constantly open and close cabinets and take everything out, grab on to any string she could and pull on it and put everything she could find into her mouth. The stories were so funny and cute; the women forgot for a moment about all of their problems.

Brooke had been on a date with a 'nice' man, but she didn't feel like it would lead anywhere. The women asked if maybe there was at least a little bubble of attraction, even a burp. Brooke could be so hard on any man she dated. Brooke nodded her head back and forth, claiming there was nothing there and smiled.

Traci talked about her job, happy that she was still enjoying the work. She hadn't tried to date anyone serious after her last romance. She had several casual dates but none that lead anywhere. She had been with Scott for two years, but that ended when she found he had asked another woman out. That was just too depressing for any of the women to bring up. Traci had weathered it well, but the women knew that it would take a long time for her to recover from the blow of another man in her life leaving her.

After the women had shared their present day lives and all of the information about the case, they left wondering what else they would uncover tomorrow with Tara and Jess. How vindictive and jealous were these two women?

# CHAPTER 17
## Tara Thursday

Is everything set up for the funeral on Saturday?" Lindsey was talking with John's mother about Saturday's service for John. John's parents, John, Lindsey and their children had been a member of an ecumenical church since the 70's. The church was set on a high hill in Brookfield and was built in the 1950's.

Allison's, John's mother, was commenting about the service, "Everything is set up. Could you meet us tomorrow at church so we can go through the funeral details with the pastor? We're meeting him around 11:00. I've been working at getting his best friends to talk about him at the service. I don't think me or Roger will be able to get up and say anything. It's too heartbreaking. The priest will be speaking and three of John's closest friends from high school and dental school. I've picked out several songs that I knew John enjoyed singing at church. I can't believe he's dead. The casket will be closed so a recent picture of him smiling and laughing at Leo's birthday party will be displayed. How are you and the kids doing?" John's mother was a powerhouse of energy and strength.

Lindsey felt guilty for not helping out more with the funeral arrangements. She replied, "Of course I'll help tomorrow and meet you at the church at 11:00. I'm sorry I haven't helped you out more. As far as the kids and myself go, we're doing fairly well.

The kids have a lot of questions and they've had their sad moments of crying and hugging me. Lilly has been especially clingy to me when she's home. They're young enough to separate their school life and friends from their dad's death. They're not overanalyzing everything and so they're still enjoying school. As far as I go, I've been surrounded with my girl friends non-stop since John's death and have been so busy that his death hasn't been processed yet. I'll miss him but I can't think about that right now." Lindsey fought back the urge to cry; she wanted to continue to talk with Allison about Saturday's funeral and didn't want Alison to cry.

In a quiet, purposeful voice, Allison said, "I've been doing a lot of crying and wondering who did this to John. The papers said the killer used dental floss to strangle John. What a queer thing to use to murder someone with. I'm sure the police disclosed that so that everyone wouldn't worry about a serial killer on the loose. The use of dental floss had to be directly related to John and his dental practice. Have the police talked to you?" Allison asked.

"Yes, they've been talking to me. Have they been talking to you?" Lindsey was curious if the police were actually looking at other people.

"They actually thought of me and Roger as suspects. I have no idea why they would ever think that, but they said it was standard procedure to look at all family members first. They even took a DNA sample of us to rule us out. I was glad to do it and impressed that they had started right away on the investigation. I hope they find the bastard that did this to John." Allison didn't swear much but when she was overly emotional certain expletive's started flying out.

Lindsey replied gravely, "Allison, they suspect me too. I loved John, I'd never hurt him because it would be hurting my children too much. I gave them a sample of my DNA too. They think I had something to do with the murder but I didn't. I'd never kill anyone. I'm determined to find out who did kill John and I need to before they put me away and throw away the key." Lindsey realized she was holding her breath. It wasn't fun disclosing this information to Allison. Allison and Lindsey had always gotten along but with the evidence against Lindsey she wasn't sure if Alison would believe her.

There was sincerity in Allison's voice as she replied, "Lindsey, I know you would never harm John. We knew John loved you but that you two couldn't live together. John was hard to live with, he wanted everything his way and hadn't had any brothers or sisters to share things with or learn the fine art of compromise. I wasn't blind to my son's selfishness; I just didn't know how to change him."

Alison was such a kind woman; Lindsey could see how John could get his way on almost every matter when he was growing up. "Allison, thank you for saying that; it means a lot to me. I will see you tomorrow at the church."

"After the funeral on Saturday, bring the kids to my house. We're having a family get together with Roger's sister and brother from California and John's cousins. Your mother and father are also invited and sisters and brothers."

"Okay, we'll see you tomorrow. Thank you Allison, you've been a terrific mother- in- law and ex- mother- in- law."

"Lindsey, we love you too. See you tomorrow." Allison hung up the phone. Lindsey held the receiver in her hand for a long second before placing it back on the holder. Her ex-in- laws had always been kind to her. She wondered how they would feel once they heard that the police found her prints and blood at the crime scene.

Traci had moved the coffee date with Tara to 10:00 so Lindsey could make it on time. She had called Lindsey that morning to confirm their meeting with Tara at 10:00. Lindsey put on her jeans and pink sweater and some low boots. It was only the end of September but the air was chilly enough for a sweater and boots.

She grabbed her keys and drove to Java World, a coffee house on the second floor of a boutique overlooking state street in downtown Milwaukee. Java World was full of young energetic twenty to thirty-somethings buzzing around, high on coffee and laughter. Lindsey arrived at Java World at 9:45 and met up with Traci. After Lindsey had bought her coffee she went over to where Traci was sitting. "Hey Traci; no sign of Tara yet?" Lindsey stated the obvious.

"No, I talked with her last night after I left your house and she still planned on meeting us here. I'm not sure what we'll be able to find out from her but at least we will get a sense of who she is."

Lindsey sat down at the little round table. "I think I know what she looks like; I remember John showing me all the pictures he had on a digital photo frame from previous parties. John carried his digital camera everywhere he went. I wonder if the police have the camera. He probably had that camera on him the night of the party and the person who killed him has the camera."

Traci looked up at Lindsey and said, "You know what Lindsey, you are so right. Whoever has that camera, is the murderer. Now how do we find the camera?" Lindsey wasn't able to respond, she saw Tara entering the coffee house.

Traci waved Tara over to their table, Traci smiled, "Hi Tara. This is Lindsey and I'm Traci. We've been talking on the phone."

Tara pinched up her mouth and narrowed her eyes as she looked over Lindsey and Traci. She said in a serious, quiet voice, "Hi, nice to meet both of you. I just want you both to know before we start discussing John's life that I'm not the murderer. I wouldn't have come down here if I was; I thought I would come here because I might be able to help. I loved John; even though we were only beginning our romance we were so into each other. He and I had such a connection, it was as if the sun was touching me when he was around and I felt warm and fulfilled. He was my sun and I was his flower."

Oh brother, Lindsey thought she might puke and hoped her expression didn't give her thoughts away. Lindsey wanted to roll her eyes or laugh at Tara but she said, in a calm voice, "We know you didn't do it. That's not why we wanted to talk with you. Since you were so close to John we thought you might know who killed him. Or at least have some idea about who did it and why. Go grab yourself a coffee and then sit down and join us."

Tara stood in line to get her coffee and then came back to the table and sat down next to Lindsey and across from Traci. Tara leaned into the table and spoke in a confidential manner. "Oh, I've got an idea all right. I have a pretty good idea of who killed John that night."

Tara paused for dramatic effect and then with her arm raised up and her finger pointing she looked at us and said, "It was Jess. That witch has been stalking me and John from the first day of our romance. She is a jealous hag who couldn't get past the fact that John wasn't in love with her. She has been sending me evil texts and following us. She's come to our table when we've been out to dinner and argued with John about how disgusting he was for sleeping with me when he was with her the previous night. John and I would sit and have to listen to her irrational ranting until she'd leave. Of course, I never believed her, but it certainly worried John and it put some strain on our relationship." Tara took a sip of coffee and waited for one of us to reply.

Traci said, "Did any of the texts threaten his life?"

Tara thought about it for a minute before replying. "Yes, she said he was the scum of the earth and belonged buried in it. She was always telling him things like that. She'd always refer to him as a dead rat and that he should be dead so that the world could breathe again. She said he was lower than shit on the bottom of an outhouse. She had such a sour personality.

She couldn't stand me either. I couldn't believe she showed up at John's party. I didn't think he invited her but he said he felt like she had turned over a new leaf and was trying to make amends with her. He also knew I wasn't going to be there. If I were there he wouldn't have had her come. Of course, he asked me first if it was okay, and I said yes. I am not the jealous type, especially because John reassured me that I was his and that he would only love me forever.

Tara looked around and gave the women a confidential look and spoke, "He told me he loved me after our fifth date. That's how much I affected him, and I knew it too. I had to leave the Thursday before the party for an audition in California. It's only a commercial audition but I've got to start somewhere." Tara stopped took another sip of her drink and crossed her legs.

Tara was quite the actress, she dressed in a somewhat peculiar way but it looked good on her. Her tiny body was covered in black, black tights, a black skirt and a black turtle neck, she paired it with a multi colored striped scarf around her neck and a fleece blue jacket with pink polka dots on it. Tara's hair was shoulder length and the color of an orange leaf in the fall. She had snow white skin, blue eyes and freckles on her face. She must have been 24 years young and every bit as naïve as her years.

Lindsey knew John would never tell her that he loved her and wanted to marry her. He still liked to play, but she kept her opinions to herself and sipped some coffee before she was ready to respond. "Do you know any circumstances of the murder?" asked Lindsey. Maybe Tara would slip up and reveal something that the police hadn't disclosed.

Hesitantly Tara replied. "I know that he was found in his car, at least that's what the papers said. And that he was strangled with dental floss. Other than that I don't know anything."

Traci asked if she knew if John had any other female friends that he was close to during their relationship. "Not anyone that I didn't know about." She responded quite hastily with a tinge of irritability in it, then she steered the conversation back to Jess.

"The only person who could have done it was Jess. Jess is evil and she was possessive. If she couldn't have John, she was going to make sure that no one would. And she was losing him to me; she knew it and she solved the problem by murdering him. There is no doubt in my mind that she did it. I hate her."

Traci and Lindsey looked at each other. "Thanks for your help, Tara. What you've told us will make our investigation easier. I hope you are doing okay after John's death?"

Tara started pouting again, "Well, I'll survive, but I'm mad. Johnny was going to marry me and he was my soul mate. We could have been so happy together." She said this staring off at nothing, then looked at both of the women and added rather flippantly, "Oh well, now it's back to the drawing board. Why are all the men so dull?"

Tara had enough; she switched the topic, "I've got to go; my acting lesson starts in ½ an hour with Nick Stream." Tara's face suddenly brightened up.

Looking at Tara as she talked about her acting class, you would never have guessed that her boyfriend had recently been murdered. Tara continued in an upbeat voice, "Can you believe it? Only the best actors get in with him." She smiled at the two women.

And with that last remark, she picked up her knitted purse, strapped it to her shoulder, stood up and looked directly at the two women. She theatrically said, "Watch out for Jess, she's dangerous." Then she turned around and left with napkins and papers flying off the tables as she walked past the tables and out the door.

Traci's eyebrows were raised, "Wow, she's a trip. Perfect for John, such an extrovert, but not much upstairs. What did you think about her take on Jess?" Traci asked.

Lindsey's face said it all, she looked at Traci with a perplexed stare, "She had nothing nice to say and was quick to accuse Jess of killing John. Maybe too quick, maybe she's the guilty party. Who knows if she really was in California; we'll have to check out her story. People who are angry are capable of following through on devious plans and Tara might be dumb, or she might be smart and a great actress. I'm not ruling her out. She might have had something to do with John's murder. It should be interesting to meet with Jess tonight for drinks and compare stories."

"You got that right, where are you guys meeting?" Traci asked.

"We'll be meeting at Bubbles on Brady Street, not far from here." Lindsey looked around at the rest of the tables.

"What time?" Traci was looking around too.

"Around 5:00 for happy hour." Lindsey looked back at Traci. "Do you want to come?"

"Oh, I can't make it. I've got to meet with a client. Will Julia be with you?" Traci asked, concerned for Lindsey's safety.

"Yeah, she'll be with me. Don't worry. And thanks for getting a hold of Tara and setting up this meeting. It was one less thing for me to worry about."

"It's nothing that you wouldn't do for us. We'll find out who did it. I should probably call her again and ask her where she was in California and verify that she was actually there. Why should we just believe her? She might think that we won't check." Traci looked at her watch, "Well, I've got to get back to work. My next client has anxiety issues so I'll have to listen to her complain about her home renovations taking too long and how she can't wait until everything is finished. I do feel bad for her; I hate it when people are in my house too. I'll catch up with you Saturday at John's funeral. Are you ready?"

"Yes, John's parents made all of the arrangements. I'm going to have to get through it with Leo and Lilly. They're my main concern right now. It's hardest for them and Saturday will be such a final goodbye, I'm afraid they will have a tough time with it. I've been talking about it with them and they're sad, but when they see the casket go into the ground, it's not going to be easy."

"No, I imagine it will be quite trying on you and on them. Let me know if I can do anything. Take care, Lindsey," Traci gave Lindsey a hug before getting up and slowly leaving the coffee house.

Lindsey sat and contemplated Tara. She was so young and silly. Could she really take anything that Tara said seriously? It was hard to get a read on someone who was so theatrical, was she acting or was she sincere? Did she really think that Jess did it or was she trying to use her acting skills to persuade them that it had to be Jess.

Although she and Lori have a good case against Dave, she wondered if Dave would commit a crime against his own partner who gave him all the advantages and who would continue to improve and build their practice. Dave was certainly making enough money that he didn't need John's death to live exceedingly comfortable and was only going to get richer working with John.

Maybe it was Jess who had the need to get rid of John. She couldn't bear to see him with any other woman but herself. Lindsey couldn't wait to meet with Jess, the tall brown-haired, brown-eyed sex siren. Everyone who met Jess thought she was beautiful. It would be interesting to finally meet her. Lindsey went home to ponder the list of suspects before picking up Lilly and Leo from school. She would have to do homework with the children and then get ready for happy hour drinks with Jess. Her story might end up being more entertaining than Tara's. Time would tell.

# CHAPTER 18
## Jess at Bubbles

L indsey left the coffee shop and drove home going over Tara's version of Jess's behavior. Tara knew that John had been with other women, from what Jess had said to Julia about Tara. Could Tara be setting up Jess? Maybe the two of them did it together? John had a lot of drama in his life and both women seemed obsessed to some degree with getting John to marry them.

The first thought that came to Lindsey's mind was, 'Yuck', being married to him was hell, but the second thought she had was would jealousy drive them insane? Did one of them do it? Who was it and why wasn't she picking up any signals about this case. She hoped that Tom had some good news for her. Lindsey kept dreaming about Tom, who she perceived to be strong, reassuring, helpful and damn hot looking too. He looked at her with eyes that were intelligent and honest with just the right amount of intensity and wit.

Lindsey drove home and looked at what clues she had gathered so far and wrote them in a notebook. John's purple rubber, the missing photo from his office in the Brookfield house, the photo of the mystery woman with a mini bikini and her head chopped out of the photo, some matches and cigarettes, John's cell phone, the texts, the mystery phone number, the mystery woman from the mall that Rita mentioned seeing with John, the woman who signed the insurance paper for Dave, Dave and his double life, the inventors, each with their own alibi, Tara and her acting plus her alibi, Jess and her raged- filled texts to John, the knife and dental floss with her fingerprints and blood on it. What did it all mean? What was she missing? She looked at the list over and over again, but couldn't make out any concrete links or evidence that would get her off the hook. There had to be something.

Maybe Tom had taken some samples of Dave's DNA that would implicate him. After looking at the list over and over again the words started to blend together and not make any sense. Lindsey felt like she had had enough for the day and decided to take a warm bath and loosen up her joints before getting Leo and Lilly.

Lindsey felt somewhat relaxed after the bath and wrapped herself in a towel that had been warmed on a warming rack. After drying off, she snuggled into a soft comfortable fleece sweater and a pair of old jeans. She dried her hair, brushed her teeth and headed out the door to pick Leo and Lilly up.

"Hi, you two." Leo and Lilly got in the back seat of the Lexus hybrid SUV and put their seat belts on.

"Hi Mom, did you work today?" Leo asked.

"No, Leo, I went out to coffee with Traci and then did some work around our house."

"Oh, that's great, mom," Leo was so polite. He smiled at Lindsey and sat back in his seat to look out the window as they drove home.

"Mom, turn up the radio, I want to sing along." Lilly had been sitting, listening quietly; more intent on what was on the radio at the moment then having any conversation. Girls Night Out was on the radio from *Hannah Montana* and Lilly started to sing the song at the top of her lungs. Leo just sat back and let her sing and looked out the window until they were parked in the driveway.

"I get the computer first," screamed Lilly as she ran past Leo and headed for the computer.

"Fine; I'm going to go downstairs and play rock band." Leo returned the fire.

"Mom, the internet's not working." Lilly was trying to get on to *Club Penguin*, and the router wasn't cooperating.

Lindsey off-handedly said, "Oh well, Lilly, find something else to do."

Lilly yelled at Leo, "Leo, I want to be the drummer on rock band." Lilly headed to the family room and that was the last she would see of the children for a while. They were busy improving their scores on the guitar and drums with the new rock band cd so Lindsey decided to fix dinner in peace. Her mother would be arriving soon to watch the children while she went out for a drink with Julia and Jess.

At 4:40 Lindsey's mom drove up and walked into the house. "Come on in mom." Lindsey smiled at her mom. "Kids, Grandma's here."

"Hi Grandma!" They both shouted from the family room without missing a beat.

"Thanks for coming over, mom. I've got to meet with John's ex-girlfriend, Jess tonight. The police are trying to pin this murder on me and I'm not taking the rap for it."

"What kind of talk is that, Lindsey? You sound like you're a suspect in an old movie from the 40's, maybe an old *'Thin Man'* movie starring William Powel and Myrna Loy."

"I know, mom. I love those movies and I'm just trying to lighten up the load I feel on my shoulders. I might be headed for the slammer, the big house. I've got to find out somehow who murdered John otherwise I'm going to go to jail." There was a hint of hysteria in Lindsey's voice. She was trying to bring some levity to the situation, but it was hard.

Lindsey's mom looked at her with one eyebrow raised and asked. "You didn't do it?"

"MOM, how could you even ask that? Of course I didn't do it!" Lindsey sometimes thought her mom was crazy; aren't all parents crazy according to their children?

Lindsey gave her mom a pained, dejected look, "I know you didn't mean that Mom. And thanks for watching the kids tonight. I'll be home around 8:00. There's a pizza in the oven and a simple salad in the fridge." Lindsey gave a wave to her mom, shouted good-bye to Leo and Lilly and headed out the door to meet out with Julia and Jess.

Bubbles was a trendy club filled with a young crowd. The women were decked out in tight jeans, high heels and little tops. The men wore any type of jeans or slacks and tight long-sleeved woven sporty-looking shirts or dress shirts. The young, stylish clientele barely looked in Lindsey's direction as she made her way to one of the thick glass bar tables that surrounded the long bar.

The bar stools were classic, sleek looking chrome and plastic frames with black leather backs and faux fur seats. Bubbles could be seen in the center of the thick glass tables and up at the matching glass bar. The wall behind the bar was made of mirrors, glass shelves were attached to the mirrors that held alcohol bottles and a variety of glass-wear made for drinking every type of alcoholic beverage possible. The mirrors made everything bright and dazzling, and sleek, bouncing the light around making it elegant and shimmery.

It was a lively place, with a piano and a piano man singing tunes at one end of the bar. The crowd could sing along with the music and dance on the glass and granite floor that had more tiny blown bubbles in it. The atmosphere was happy and swanky at the same time. It reminded Lindsey of a 1930's pub, with elegance, a sleek feel and a twist of fun.

"Hi Julia," Lindsey waved and raised her voice as she saw Julia enter the bar.

Julia smiled brightly, "Hi Lindsey, I guess Jess hasn't shown up yet."

Lindsey smiled and replied, "Nope; not yet. I'm wondering what she's like. The kids never mentioned her because when John had the kids on his weekend she was never around. I find that to be a bit strange, but whatever." Lindsey shrugged her shoulders.

"Do you think he could have had her around sometimes?" Julia asked interested.

"I'm sure he did, sometimes. You know how kids are, they never say what they're doing and they probably didn't want to say anything to me. Maybe they thought that I would get mad?"

"Why would they think that you would be mad?" Julia gave Lindsey a slightly crooked look. "You always seem calm, even with your kids."

Lindsey gave Julia a slow, soft smile, "Thanks, now remember that when you're up on the stand defending me."

Julia nudged her friend, "It won't come to that." Julia raised her water glass and took a sip as she looked at Lindsey.

A loud voice barged in on their conversation, "Hi, you're Lindsey right?" Jess had snuck up behind them and tapped Lindsey on the shoulder.

She was a stunning woman who was a cross between Liv Tyler and Angelina Jolie. She had a tanned smooth complexion, a beautiful smile and perfect body. Lindsey could see why John was attracted to Jess. Then she thought immediately about Tara, who was the extreme opposite of Jess.

Jess continued talking, barely taking a break to get a response from Lindsey. "I'm Jess. I recognize you from the pictures John had in his house. I'm sorry he's dead, for your kid's sake, I mean, and yours. John and I had our falling out but I still cared about him. I cared about him more than I cared about anyone in my whole life, and what did he do? He didn't care about me; he squashed my heart like it was a mosquito that had landed on his skin and that he couldn't wait to get rid of. And he kept on squashing my heart over and over again. He didn't understand what he meant to me. I wanted him to love me so much; I did everything he asked me to do."

Jess took a breath and then went right on talking, "The romance was great, the trips were great, and our conversations were stimulating and intellectual. How could someone be with another person for three years and then leave them as if they didn't mean anything? God I need a drink. I'm in so much pain. That bastard."

Jess looked around the bar, "I didn't kill him. Don't get me wrong, I wanted to. I wanted to tear out his heart and rip his head off and hurt him. But I would never do it. I loved him too much."

She stopped and looked at the waitress, "Hi, could you get me a vodka tonic?" Jess took a second to place her drink order before starting up the one person conversation.

Lindsey and Julia both ordered their drinks too. Julia splurged and got a malted milk ball martini, something she could never pass by. Lindsey ordered a Cosmo; after listening to Jess rant for five minutes she thought she might need it to survive the rest of the meeting.

As soon as the waitress left and Jess was seated at a bar stool, she continued telling the women her feelings for John. "John and I had something special together. For three years we were in love, we took trips to Bermuda, Washington, New York, Chicago, Las Vegas, California, even Disney World. We traveled together to enjoy each other without the distraction of other people or our jobs. And then just like that, one of my girlfriends started seeing John out with another woman. A tall blond. At first I thought it was you Lindsey, so I didn't think anything of it. John had told me that you and he sometimes had lunch together to talk about Leo and Lilly. Which was cool, I never had any trouble with that or you for that matter. John had said you guys were so finished and I could tell he wasn't interested in you that way at all. No offense, Lindsey," Jess looked at Lindsey.

"None taken," Lindsey responded. Wow, Jess could tie John in the self-absorbed category. How could they have gotten along without fighting for air time?

Jess continued, "Now here is the really bad part. I had sent John scathing emails after I found out the blond bimbo wasn't Lindsey. I still don't know who she was, but John had been seeing her for approximately six months from the time she was first spotted until the time he confessed that he had been with someone else. I was furious. It was so hurtful."

Jess's face had a pained expression, her brows were furrowed and she hastily continued venting, "He denied the fact and insisted that we had been on a break while he and she were first going out. And that might have been true; John and I had a tumultuous relationship. It was a constant sea of high tides, low tides and awesome waves. We were meant for each other and then he had to ruin it by lying, cheating and having sex with this other woman. I'm not the type of person, who can share someone, it's just not right. We had the ultimate package, the all inclusive relationship until that rat bastard screwed the dumb blond. No offense Lindsey."

And then Jess took another sip of her drink, breathed a little and looked around the room again. She said, "So what did you want to ask me today? I didn't have anything to do with the murder. The police already showed me all the emails that I had sent John in the last year and interrogated me for three hours. I couldn't even answer my phone, the jerks. So I sat there and I listened to them barrage me with my emails, but I didn't kill John. I have no idea who did. If I wanted to, I certainly wouldn't have strangled him with dental floss. What a queer thing to use, I would have preferred a silk scarf."

Lindsey thought that was probably true, a silk scarf would be more about Jess and less about John. Lindsey was starting to believe that Jess couldn't have been the murderer, although she certainly exuded a lot of anger.

Slowly and steadily Lindsey explained to Jess why they asked her to meet with them, "We didn't ask you to come out tonight to accuse you of the murder. We were wondering if you had any idea who might have done it. Anything you can remember about the night of the party? Any other women, or boyfriends or business partners that you might know of that had a problem with John?" Lindsey and Julia waited for the tirade.

"I never found out who the blond bombshell was that was reportedly having an affair with John right under my nose, but I do know that his current girlfriend Tara is a whore and a freak with a taste for the darker side of life." A whore? Lindsey didn't get that impression from Tara, but maybe she was a bit of a freak in the eccentric category.

Lindsey listened to more of Jess's assessment of Tara. "Tara has known John for around a year but they recently started dating, at least three months ago. Tara met John at a club down town; I'm not sure which one. I know all this from mutual friends. Tara is only 24 and of course, you know that John was turning 46. I really think Tara is a gold digger, a compulsive liar, and wanted John to finance her acting career." She spoke this in a low, husky voice and then continued rehashing the past, "You might think that she wouldn't have murdered him because she wouldn't get any money, but I know for a fact that John, as you know, was extremely generous. He was such a soft heart, he'd help people in jams and he fell right into her sad sob story, hook, line and sinker. John made provisions for Tara to live in California for a year free and put her on a salary of $2000.00 a month until she made it big, then she was supposedly going to pay him back. My thought is, she got what she needed and without him alive the provision that was stated in their contract will still continue. There wasn't a definitive ending to the $2000.00 a month salary, so the contract will keep on providing for Tara because of insurance money and because there wasn't a specific end date. Tara, the bimbo bitch, is smarter then she looks and she has a boyfriend in California. At least that's what I've been told from my girlfriends who still hung out with John and Tara." Jess looked ready to explode one minute and then seemed to calm down the next moment, revving up, than relaxing over and over again. It was exhausting just listening to her.

Lindsey wanted Jess to continue; so she looked at Jess and said excitedly as if agreeing with her assessment of Tara, "Wow, do the police know about this?"

Jess nodded her head up and down, "I told them the same thing I'm telling you. Tara somehow, someway did it. She's a good actress and had John absolutely fooled, and that is a feat worth an academy award."

Lindsey said with genuine thankfulness, "Jess, I can't tell you how much your input has helped us. The police have already interrogated me too. I didn't do it but I'm their main suspect because of John's insurance policy. I wasn't aware of the contract drawn up between Tara and John. Do you know of the lawyer who drew it up?"

Jess had more information, when she spoke her eyes were on fire, "I do. John used a friend of his for his personal business matters, girlfriends and stuff. His name is Kevin Blunt. We used to have a contract too; he helped me get a start with my finance business."

Jess looked at her watch, her tone was serious, "Hey, I've got to get going. I'll see you Saturday at John's funeral. I'm going out of respect for John, but I'm not looking forward to seeing Tara."

It was time for Lindsey to play a detective role, "One more thing." Lindsey loved using that line from *Colombo* movies. If the cops could use it, so could she. "If you see the blond that had the affair with John and split you two up, will you point her out to me?"

"I'd love to," then Jess left swaying her hips back and forth, tossing her long brown hair around and turning heads as she walked out the door.

"She is something else," said Julia.

"You got that right. Who does she think she is, queen of the hill?" Lindsey took a sip of her Cosmo.

Julia agreed, "I know, how self absorbed. I can't believe John and she lasted for three years without tearing each other's hair out. They both loved to be the center of attention."

Julia had a knack for assessing other people's relationships. But Lindsey didn't feel like Julia was good at assessing her own relationships. Maybe that was harder for everyone. Lindsey replied, "I know. Listen, I've got to get back home to my kids and get some things ready for John's funeral Saturday. You are coming aren't you?" Lindsey took another sip of her Cosmo. With the mood that she was in she could have had another and another but she had to get home. She waited for Julia to respond.

"Of course, I'm bringing Charlie and don't say anything."

Lindsey bit her tongue. "Okay, I'll see you Saturday afternoon. Thanks for setting this up with Jess."

"No problem, let's go." Lindsey and Julia paid their bill, and high tailed it out of bubbles. The funeral was Saturday and Lindsey could only imagine the fireworks that would flare with all of John's exes in one room together.

She would have to spend Friday with Allison and Roger, going over the songs and making sure that the arrangements were to their satisfaction. The case would have to be put on hold until Saturday. The day when she would see all of the facets of her loving ex's, convoluted life.

*Tom, where are you going? He drove to the Eagles' lounge. An old 1970's one story box-shaped building made out of cement block that was an office building turned into a bar, specifically a cop bar. It happened to be a long day, nevertheless the wig had to come out and Simone had to appear. A cop bar, who would suspect any foul play to occur at a cop bar? Actually the thought of putting the vicadin in Tom's drink with other cops around aroused Simone. Simone, you've got to get rid of Tom, cut off his ties to Lindsey. She walked into the club and heads turned, inside she was pleased with the reaction she got from the men and women. The spotlight was on her. She glanced around the room as if looking for someone. The drink bar was situated in the center of the rectangular room in a closed, oval shape. On one side of the bar were three pool tables and some bar height Formica-topped pub tables scattered around each one of the pool tables. On the other side of the bar were more bar tables and arcade games. Big screen TV's were in every corner. Simone saw Tom out of the corner of her eye, sitting at a bar table with another cop, nursing a beer and looking intently at the football game playing on the TV's. Simone ordered a drink from the bar and the bar tender brought over her drink with a basket of popcorn. Simone looked around and realized that mirrors with cameras were placed at intervals overhead in the ceiling. Tom would be spared tonight, Simone wasn't stupid. The cops would use the tapes to get any detail, however small to figure out who Simone was. Simone couldn't risk it, not tonight. It would happen, but it would have to wait.*

# CHAPTER 19
## The Funeral

The day was sunny with high wispy clouds striping the sky. Allison and Roger had enlisted the help of the Douglas Funeral Home to assist with the funeral arrangements for John. Some press had been posted outside the drive to the funeral home, but the funeral attendants were doing a superb job at helping the mourners find parking and escorting them to the viewing, while avoiding the press.

The elaborate white casket had been set up in the parlor of the church. It was a closed casket due to the circumstances of his death, but a picture of John, happy and smiling was displayed. The attendants had set up floral arrangements and helped people sign the register and helped the women and men place their donations to various charities in memory of John.

Lindsey and the kids had been there since 2:00 and were standing by the casket greeting the friends and acquaintances of John. The kids were holding up well, John's parents were standing there stoically as well. Then Lindsey spotted Jess and Tara.

Several of John's friends from high school ran some interference, making sure that Jess and Tara wouldn't get too close to each other. It was somewhat amusing to watch them weave in and out of the crowd and glance at each other every so often. Lindsey hoped they wouldn't cause too big of a scene if they got the chance to speak to each other.

The police looked like they were trying to fit in, but most of them looked too uncomfortable to pass as actual mourners. They needed some acting classes and Tara was doing all she could to get their attention. She was everywhere, walking and talking to anyone that would listen and sashaying with her back as she gestured wildly with her arms. Her only rival was Jess.

Tara was something else, in her black dress that looked like it was made out of two silk scarves pinned together in various places. It was quite interesting and disturbing at the same time. Leave it to Tara to combine it with a black hat with one pink feather in it to gain everyone's attention.

At the opposite spectrum was Jess wearing a black knit dress that a snake couldn't get out of. It was so tight on her that Lindsey could imagine Jess suffocating because of the tightly cinched waist. How was she ever going to sit down in that dress? Jess combined it with heels that must have been at least five inches high showing off her calves which were as taut as a gymnast's. There was no doubt in anyone's mind that Jess was a fitness fanatic, her body was her masterpiece.

Lindsey watched the two women fight over the men's attention at the funeral home; they walked up and down and all around, visiting with mutual acquaintances of John's and causing quite a scene as they meandered here and there and touched the available men's arms and shoulders while they whispered in their ears.

At the end of the viewing Lindsey spotted Dave. He looked extremely serious in a black suit and tie and matching shoes; under his jacket was a white and blue wide striped shirt. He looked handsome in a feminine way. Maybe she was only giving him that characteristic after talking with Lori about his makeup issues. What was going on with Dave? Lindsey looked around the room, observing the interplay of everyone there and wondered which one of the people here was the murderer. With that thought Lindsey's body turned into a million tiny goose bumps. At 4:30 people started to fill the isles of the church and the guests were escorted into the service.

The police stood outside taking pictures; it was necessary but a nuisance so Lindsey tried to ignore them. Her friends were already seated in the church. Lindsey gave a little wave to them as she walked past them and up to the front of the church. On one side of the church pews in the third row was Jess, she had wormed her way up to the front. On the other side of the aisle was Tara, also third row. The two were impossible. Lindsey tried to avoid any eye contact with them as she sat down with Leo and Lilly in the first row to listen to the kind words that the speakers had to say about John.

Lindsey could hardly listen to the speakers because her mind kept wandering to the people that surrounded her. She wished she could have been invisible and float around the room taking pictures just like the police were doing. On and on the service went, she was starting to get bored. Yes, he was a great guy now let's get on with it. John had wanted several songs to be sung, finally they were led into singing, which perked up the funeral goers and everyone sang along to 'Amazing Grace'.

After the singing and several last words it was over. The funeral attendants carried the casket out to the hearse and the immediate family got in the limo that followed. The hearse went through the town and past John's dental practice before ending up at the cemetery. Lindsey, the kids and John's parents rode in one limousine together, no one spoke during the drive and Lindsey couldn't seem to think of anything to say.

Her thoughts drifted to the viewing and the ceremony. She had seen Tom; he had glanced at her and had gone through the greeting line. He looked in her eyes, seemed to want to communicate something other than the expected words of condolences, and then he moved on. She remembered as he grabbed her hand how warm it was and gentle, it melted her heart and eased the tension forming between her eyes. If only he could have held on to her a little longer.

As Lindsey was thinking about Tom, John was being lowered into the ground. She grabbed Leo and Lilly to her and tried to provide as much warmth and comfort as she could. They hadn't said much throughout the service. Lilly had asked if she could call her when they got home. Lindsey didn't know what she was referring to so said she didn't think she could call her. Lilly had looked exasperated at Lindsey and then had said, "MOM, not call her, COLOR. Can I color when we get home?" Of course Lindsey had said yes and that was about all the conversation that her kids had with her today.

Lindsey couldn't wait to get home and have Lilly color and watch Leo do whatever would sooth him, play video games, rock band or be on the computer. There would be time to talk about the day later, no need to rush the kids into conversations they weren't ready for.

The final words were being spoken by the priest. Only family was allowed in the cemetery so Lindsey didn't have to worry about Tara, Dave, or Jess. The kids and John's parents sat back in the limo and rode home as quietly as ever. They were exhausted, all in deep thought. Lindsey knew that her friends were already congregating at her house and she couldn't wait to let loose with them.

The limo drove up to her house, let them out and with a hug and kiss goodbye to John's parents she and the kids got out and began their life without John in it. "Thanks for arranging everything and for inviting us over to your house after the funeral. We'll try to stop by later on, right now I need to get the children in the house to rest and recuperate." Lindsey reached a hand out to Allison and Roger.

Allison was holding up well, but exhaustion lined her face, "It was a nice service, don't you think? John would have been happy. There were so many people who cared for him." Allison was talking slow and was staring out at nothing.

Lindsey replied, "Yes, it was a wonderful service. John would have been happy." She squeezed Allison's hand. "Call me anytime you want to."

Allison replied, "I will, and you do the same."

Lindsey turned around and walked up to her house, depressed now and feeling rather low. Now that the funeral was over it seemed so final, like everything that had to do with his death should also be over. Little did she know that the next week would bring more torment and even more loss.

# CHAPTER 20
## Bitter Cold

A bitter cold northern wind had descended on Wisconsin and the wind burned Lindsey's eyes as she opened the door to grab the Sunday paper. It was Sunday morning and the kids wanted to stay home and watch TV instead of going to church. Lindsey had listened to both kids begging and decided that was what their family needed, a day off.

After the funeral yesterday the women had spent the night talking and quietly rehashing the funeral. Their talk centered on what the speakers said about John, each one had their own personal fun story about John. No one wanted to bring up the fact that he was murdered or that the number one suspect was Lindsey.

Lori had told Lindsey last night that she had some more information about John's business and Lindsey decided to have a brunch on Sunday for her friends to once again go over the past week and discuss the meetings with Tara and Jess. It had been one busy week for all of them and the next week would even be more trying, especially since the police were all over the funeral and Lindsey felt like they were going to arrest her now that John was buried properly. She didn't know when, but she knew it would be soon.

She took out a baking pan and a mixing bowl. Lindsey was going to make baked French toast for her friends. She proceeded to cut up French bread into thick slices before placing them into the pan. She mixed up 8 eggs with milk and poured that over the bread, a sprinkle of sugar, and cinnamon, plus several pats of butter and the dish was ready to be baked. She placed the pan back in the refrigerator so that the flavors would have time to blend together and the eggs had time to soak into the bread.

Lindsey turned on the oven to 350 degrees, opened up the refrigerator again and got out fresh strawberries to accompany the French toast dish. She reached for her favorite paring knife to cut up the strawberries and realized it wasn't in the knife block. Maybe she had put it in the utensil drawer. She couldn't find it so she grabbed a similar knife from her drawer and began cutting the stems off the tops of the strawberries. She proceeded to slice up the strawberries and placed them in a blue ceramic bowl.

Her thoughts went back to yesterday's funeral; it had gone well and she felt some peace after seeing all of the people who had loved John and were there to support John and his family. A bird was outside the kitchen patio door chirping away and singing a song. Lindsey hoped that the song was a good sign, as if she knew anymore or believed anymore in signs, but she wanted to believe that the world was full of nature and good instead of evil and darkness.

The bird seemed to inspire her inner spirit. She started whistling along with the bird. She looked at the one lone bird, when was it going to fly south for the winter? As she was whistling along and thinking about the bird, the oven bell signaled that it had reached 350 degrees. Lindsey placed the pan in the oven to cook for 40 minutes. She felt quite good, knowing that her friends would soon be over to eat her French toast dish and drink loads of strongly brewed coffee.

Lindsey went upstairs to take a shower and get dressed. Her friends were coming at 10:30 that morning and it was only 9:30 so she had plenty of time to get ready. As she got into the shower she thought of the possible suspects and the discussions she had with them. She mentally recalled the conversations hoping that something would pop out at her.

When she got downstairs she found Brooke and the kids in the family room playing rock band. Brooke was the singer, Lilly was on drums and Leo was playing the guitar. They looked like they were having a great time. "Hey stars," said Lindsey. "How are you doing, Brooke? The kids made you a member of their band, isn't that fun?"

"Yeah, this is great. I can't believe how good Leo and Lilly are on the instruments. I could never do that!" Brooke smiled and cheered on the kids. "Hey you two keep playing the fat music and I'll be back later to sing with you." Brooke got up off the couch and followed Lindsey into the kitchen.

Lindsey asked, "Hey Brooke, I'm not quite ready, I've got to add a little more makeup and dry my hair before the rest of the women get here. Can you take out the French toast in 5 minutes if I'm not out here yet?"

Brooke smiled, "Sure, no problem. Where are your hot pads?"

"There hanging on hooks above the stove."

Brooke asked, "Okay, do you want me to make some coffee?"

Lindsey grinned, a twinkle in her eye, ready to give Brooke a hard time, "Yes, but none of that weak coffee, add a lot of beans so we can stay awake today."

"Gotcha." Brooke started to get the coffee maker ready and Lindsey went back to her bedroom to get ready. When she was finished she headed for the kitchen. As she was approaching the kitchen to check on Brooke the doorbell rang. Lindsey expected one of her friends to be on the other side of the door, with a quick stride and an expectation of seeing her friends she got to the door and without checking to see who was on the other side opened it up.

To her surprise she was surrounded by Tom and 3 other officers with uniforms on. They carried an arrest warrant for Lindsey and a search warrant for her home and car. Great, so much for the bird singing as a sign of happiness and peace, it should have been a crow crowing to warn her of the impending trouble that found her that day.

The officers and Tom stood in the front hallway allowing Lindsey to make arrangements with Brooke before taking her down to the station and conducting the search of her home and car. She walked into the kitchen, "Brooke, guess who's here? It's Tom, and he's taking me in." Lindsey whispered to Brooke so she wouldn't disturb the kids in the next room. For a second she was distracted by the smell and look of the French toast, it looked so good and she was extremely hungry. She resigned herself to the task of planning for Leo and Lilly.

It was actually a good thing that the women were all coming over; they could take care of the children and keep their eyes on the police officers rummaging through her house. Lindsey didn't want Leo and Lilly to have to witness the police looking through everything or handcuffing her so she asked Tom if she could say goodbye to her children without handcuffs on and let them know what was happening. She didn't want them to worry. They had been through so much already.

She continued to make arrangements for Leo and Lilly and whispered to Brooke in the kitchen, "I'll let the kids know that I'm going to the police station to talk with the police about the murder. I'll call my mom to let her know what's going on and to tell her that you'll be bringing the kids over to her house. Don't let the police in the family room until the kids are gone. They can start their search in my room. When any of the other women get here, can you take the kids to my parents? I'll let them know that you'll do that. I don't think my parents need to see the police here either." Brooke spoke to Lindsey in a calm, soft voice.

Brooke spoke softly, seriously, "Okay, Lindsey. That sounds like a good plan. Go call your mom. I'll drive them over to your parents' house. Call me to let me know how much money you'll need to bail you out of jail. You're not going to stay there overnight."

"Thanks Brooke. That's a comforting thought. Who knows what would happen to me if I'd have to stay locked up. The thought seems so inhumane."

Lindsey walked into the family room to let the kids know that Brooke was going to take them to their Grandma and Grandpa's as soon as one of her other friends got there. The kids barely looked up, and nodded their heads okay. They were so absorbed in their game.

"Where are you going, mom?" Lilly turned away from the game for a split second.

"I've got to go down to the police station and help the police with your dad's case."

Leo asked, "Oh, when are you going to be back?"

"Hopefully tonight, but if I'm not you'll stay with Grandma and Grandpa. Don't worry; everything will be alright soon enough." Lindsey gave Leo and Lilly a big hug and then left to meet Tom by the front door.

Tom was patiently waiting for her to make arrangements and gave Lindsey plenty of time to collect herself, call her mom, and gather any items she wanted to take with her to the police station. Lindsey looked at Tom's downcast face and thought he would rather be shoveling cow manure at that minute versus taking her down to the precinct. He seemed to be struggling to stay quiet and follow through on the orders that were handed to him by his superiors. He had a job to do and his character demanded him to follow through with them however distasteful he might find them to be.

She looked at him and also remained quiet. Lindsey took a jacket out of the closet and put it on. By the time she was ready, Lori was driving up to the house and Brooke had the kids ready to go to her parents. Lindsey left in Tom's Pissat as if she and he were going on a date. She waved to her kids, got in the car, and as soon as her house was out of sight let the tears cascade down her face.

# CHAPTER 21
## The arrest

Lindsey remembered the 6th precinct well. This time there were several news vans filming her being brought into the police station. Tom had placed handcuffs on her as soon as they parked at the police station due to regulations. She was photographed and overheard some of the copy that the reporters were announcing to their TV audience:

\*\*\*

On September 21rst, Dr. John Wang was murdered and today an arrest has been made. Police have in custody Ms. Lindsey Wang after preliminary forensic evidence linked her to the crime scene. Police aren't commenting on the nature of the forensics at this time. We do know that Mr. Wang was strangled with dental floss, possibly a statement was being made by the murderer. An arrest warrant and a search warrant were handed out by Judge Stickler of the 6th district court yesterday. Chief detective Tom Brady on the case has worked hard at interviewing, securing the crime scene, and going over autopsy and eye witness accounts of Mr. Wang's birthday, the night he was murdered; one week ago on a Sunday morning. The ex Mrs. Wang and the deceased Mr. Wang have two children together. All seemed well with the divorce arrangement and by all accounts people thought that Mr. and Ms. Wang got along exceptionally well. The ex Mrs. Wang was even a member of the guest list for Mr. Wang's birthday. Is this another case of being careful to not judge a book by its cover? What mysteries were behind this couple's demise that led to Ms. Wang potentially murdering her ex in such a violent way? The police are certain that details will surface that will point to and eventually convict Ms. Wang. All eyes will be on this murder trial; Mr. Wang was a well known business man. Ms. Wang is a prominent realtor in the community. Was it unrequited love, greed, custody battles, or revenge? What was the reason behind this brutal murder? We will be right here every minute keeping you posted on the events of this unusual murder and the impending trial. Stay right here with channel 1 for the best news every second every minute, every day—we're here for you.

***

"Ms. Wang, do you have any comment? Did you murder your ex-husband?" Lindsey listened to the pumped up news reporters and looked at the camera with a nod no. Here she was being shouted at by the sharks, in the thick of the media frenzy. For the reporters she had no comment, not yet anyway.

Now things were real, now she needed to keep quiet until she had a lawyer on her side. She couldn't wait to talk to Brooke to see if she had contacted Michelle, a lawyer well respected for her knowledge about the law and her experience with criminal cases.

Tom led her past the reporters and back into the precinct that she had visited before. The same cop was at the window reading the paper; at least this time she wouldn't have to sit on the bench and wait. Tom walked with her through the metal detector and then down a long hallway, past many doors on either side of the hallway until they reached the thick metal door that Lindsey remembered was the door to the basement.

Tom opened the door and as soon as it was closed the darkness seemed to blind her, the air was still and heavy. She went down the stairs, and felt the same coldness seep into her bones from the last time she had been interrogated at the station, only this time her hands were in cuffs in front of her and she couldn't wrap her arms around her or grab her sweater tighter to try and keep warm.

At the bottom of the stairs, Tom turned to her, looked her in the eyes and undid the hand-cuffs. She smiled up at him and grabbed her sweater to warm her body up. Tom had been carrying her purse; he gave it back to Lindsey. Then he continued to lead her down the hall and back into the interrogation room, where he told her to sit and someone would be coming by soon. As soon as she sat down, Tom told her that Brooke had arranged for a lawyer friend of hers to come down right away. Tom gave her this message and then left her to sit in the cold stark room, she was feeling alone and cold and trapped, which is exactly what she was.

Tom had been silent as they walked, was that a good sign or a bad sign? Maybe he was staying tight lipped so he wouldn't get either of them in trouble. Lindsey felt like a drizzling grey cloud was hovering over her head and she wondered if she would ever catch a glimpse of sun or heat again. She looked around the room, got up, sat down, walked around, checked if there was any food in her purse, looked at her receipts, thought about the French toast at home again, counted her money and then sat down again. How long were they going to keep her in this confined room?

She wondered how long the interrogation would take and what amount her bail would be set at. She didn't even know if she needed to have a trial to figure out how much bail was required to let her escape out of here. She had always watched murder mysteries, but couldn't remember the time frame. Did they make you sit in jail for a while before the trial for bail, or did you get to leave right away once a judge had said how much. Lindsey sat there for quite a while before an officer opened the door and let in her attorney, Michelle Plum.

Brooke and Lindsey had discussed who they would retain if Lindsey were to be arrested, and Michelle was their number one choice. Lindsey didn't know that they would need her so soon; I guess the police hadn't found anyone else to arrest for the murder. Lindsey looked up at Michelle and said, "Hi Michelle, here we are. I knew they were going to arrest me, but somehow I hoped or believed it never would really happen. I guess I wasn't totally prepared."

Michelle was upbeat and talked enthusiastically, "Don't worry about anything. The standard procedure will be to have the police book you, fingerprints, pictures that sort of thing. During that time, I'll go down to the judge's chambers and see what he has set as bail for you. They knew you were going to be arrested today so I'm sure some sort of preliminary work has already been done. Don't worry; I'll track him down no matter what. I can't believe they did this on a Sunday, but there's no way you'll have to stay here over night. Sit tight here until they come for you. I can't go with you to be processed, but of course, don't say a thing without me present in the room. They'll go through a whole interrogation with us and disclose more details about the crime. I'll do all the talking and then we'll regroup so that we can start our defense."

Lindsey looked up at Michelle in disbelief. "What do you mean our defense? It can't go that far, I'm innocent. This is just way, so wrong. I don't know what they have on me, but

I didn't do it. I can't help it if I was married to the guy. That was six years ago and I didn't know I would profit so much from his death. Honestly, I'd never hurt John, the kids adored him!" Lindsey knew she was ranting and rambling and heard her voice steadily rise. She tried to relax and catch her breath, but it wasn't easy.

Michelle's voice was soothing, "I know Lindsey. Try to stay calm, you and I know you didn't do it. I'll get the bail set and then we'll go back to your house. I just meant we're going to have to have a strategy. They have enough evidence to arrest you but there are probably gaps in their theory. Don't worry. Now I'm going to go and see what I can find out about your bail. My guess is that they brought you down here on a Sunday to avoid some of the press and to make it harder for you to get out of here. They probably want to question you for a lengthy amount of time and Sundays are somewhat slow so they thought they would be able to focus all their energy on you. They didn't count on me being here so fast. There's no need to worry."

Lindsey took some calming breaths. "Okay, I'll stay calm. I like the idea of not talking too much anyway. I'm too tired."

"Stay strong and I'll be back soon." Michelle got up and walked out of the door.

Lindsey watched her go, but wanted to scream at her to not leave her alone. Okay, just be quiet, how hard could that be? The door opened again and in walked an official looking officer. "Ms Wang, come with me, we need to take photos and take fingerprints."

The officer helped Lindsey off the chair and held onto her arm until they were out into the hallway. He let go and pointed in the direction of the processing room. Lindsey had seen it on her way down to the interrogation room. A computer was set up for fingerprinting and for photos. Lindsey put her hand on the machine and saw her fingerprints light up on the screen, she placed one hand on and then the other. The police officer then directed her to the line and with a digital camera took her photo. A picture of Lindsey came up on the computer screen. Not a bad picture, thought Lindsey.

She was asked to take off her jewelry and give her purse to the officer. Everything inside her purse was taken out and written down and placed in an envelope. After fingerprints and the photo shoot Lindsey was escorted back to the interrogation room and told to sit back in the hard cold chair that she had been occupying before the officer came in. She dutifully sat down and waited and waited and waited.

Lindsey didn't know how long she had waited, but after what seemed like a day and a half, Michelle came waltzing through the door with two other officers. The interrogation was about to begin.

# CHAPTER 22
## The Interrogation

Where were you during the hours of 3:00am and 5:00am the morning of September 16th?

We found the knife that matched your house set and your blood and samples of your blood at the crime scene.

You had the same kind of dental floss that killed John in your bathroom.

How did you feel about your ex-husband?

Did you know that you were his prime beneficiary in his will?

Lindsey, Michelle and the two officers went to a bigger room with a square wooden table and chairs that had padding on them. Lindsey looked around at the new surroundings. The room was quite similar to the one she had just left. It was a stark, cold room with cement blocks painted a dirty pea green. There was nothing hanging on the walls for decoration. It had a two way mirror on one of the walls, but that was the only break from the ugly cement block lit up by a dingy overhead light.

Well, I guess it wasn't supposed to be the Ritz, but why did it have to look so much like a dungeon? At least the chairs had padding on them; that could mean Lindsey and Michelle would be there for a long time, or Michelle had some clout and demanded that we be moved to a different room with some comfortable chairs. Lindsey hoped it was the later of the two reasons.

"Sit down, ladies," said the officer. "We've made the arrest based on some significant findings at the crime scene. What do you have to say about that?"

Was this guy joking, Lindsey wondered. Michelle answered in a much more professional manner. "My client has no idea what you're talking about. Can you be more specific and forthcoming with the evidence you claim you have against my client?" Michelle had her notepad out ready to take notes.

"We found trace samples of Ms. Wang's blood at the crime scene. We also found her fingerprints on the weapon and on the package of dental floss that was used to strangle Mr. Wang."

Michelle spoke up, "My client has no idea how that evidence was produced at the crime scene. This is the first we've heard of any forensic evidence that has linked Ms. Wang to the crime scene and murder. I'm assuming that there is more than that, or you wouldn't have made such an early arrest."

"Yes, we have an eye witness report that said she saw Ms. Wang in the vicinity of the car around 4:00 in the morning. Based on the autopsy, that is the approximate time of Mr. Wang's death."

"My client and I will discuss the time line and her whereabouts during that night. This is the first time we have heard of an eye witness, or any time line. Do you have anything else that my client can answer? She can't respond to these accusations without further consulting with me, and then we'll be able to help you out more."

The official-looking detective spoke in a calm manner. "We understand. Other then the fact that her DNA was found at the crime scene and an eye witness saw her at the scene of the crime during the approximate time of the murder, we have motive. We've looked over Mr. Wang's life insurance policy and last will and testament. Everything that he has goes to

Ms. Wang. She has sole power to manage any trusts that are set up for the children and also for any of the other arrangements set up for his various businesses. Nothing can happen to his money without Ms. Wang's approval and she can revoke set up contracts a year after his death if she thinks it's in the best interest of her and her children and based on what she feels John would have done. We think we have our murderer right here in this room."

His ending sentence was made in a louder voice and his body leaned forward to look at Lindsey. Lindsey shrunk back a little. When she thought about what the police had on her she felt she was a doomed felon, without even having done anything.

Michelle spoke again, "My client is innocent and is not, in any way, involved in Mr. Wang's murder. She has been trying to figure out who murdered John out of loyalty to him. If that's all you have to disclose, then we're ready to leave. My client's bail has been set and paid, please show us the way out now." Michelle stood up, and placed her notepad in her briefcase and waited for the interrogating officer to stand up and lead them out of the police station.

The officer slowly stood up and said to Lindsey and Michelle, "I'm sure you've been warned to not leave the state. The arraignment has been set for next Friday." He turned to Lindsey and handed her his card. "If you have anything you want to tell me, call me."

Lindsey took the card, and held it in her hand, not knowing what to say since Michelle was her attorney and was speaking for her. Michelle turned and said, "She has nothing to say, anything she has to say will be done in front of me after we've spoken together. Now, we'd like to go. Lindsey needs her purse returned to her and any other personal items that were processed during booking."

The officer looked grimly at Michelle. "Follow me," and he led them back to the processing room. Lindsey collected her purse and after everything was accounted for the officer led them up the stairs again and out towards the front of the building.

As soon as they were past the metal detectors Lindsey and Michelle were barraged with the media and microphones were shoved into their faces. Michelle had her car parked in the visitor parking place closest to the building. They shoved and stepped their way to her car, got in and started the car. The media was all over the car but Michelle skillfully and slowly put the car in reverse, edged out of the spot and out of the parking lot.

Great, Lindsey was going to be front page news and the top story on the 10:00 news. The ride to her house was filled with silence. Michelle didn't know how much Lindsey knew and Lindsey didn't know how much she should tell her, especially because she told Tom she wouldn't tell anyone what he told her and she didn't want to jeopardize his job. On the other hand Michelle was her lawyer and couldn't tell anyone their conversations. Lindsey was charged with murder and would need to trust Michelle, but Lindsey was too tired to get into the details of her and her friends investigation so she remained silent and Michelle remained silent too.

There would be enough time tomorrow to sit down and go over the police reports and talk about the clues that Lindsey had uncovered. There was more to this case then what the police were letting on to. Whose DNA was under John's fingernails? John was strong; he would have put up a fight and the police knew it. Why would they arrest her when there was still evidence that led to a different suspect? It was already

8:00pm and Lindsey couldn't wait to get home, close the door and have a drink, her mouth was drier then cotton balls baking in the sun.

Michelle dropped Lindsey off at her door. "Thanks Michelle. I know you worked behind the scenes with the judge and the officers to get me out on bail. I don't know what I would have done without you there." Lindsey was grateful. She didn't know Michelle that well but knew that she had pulled some strings for her.

"That's what I get paid the big bucks for, Lindsey," Michelle smiled back. "Take care of yourself and get some rest. I'll get in touch with you tomorrow. I'm going to do some digging and see if I can find anything out. Now that they've arrested you, they have to disclose anything that incriminates you." Great, thought Lindsey, more evidence that accuses her for something she didn't do, just what she wanted to hear.

Lindsey looked at Michelle, "Ok, I'll talk to you tomorrow and thanks again."

Lindsey got out of Michelle's car and walked up to her house. The house was dark and quiet. Lindsey knew that Leo and Lilly were over at her parents' house being well taken care of but wished that they were home waiting for her, and couldn't wait to get their hugs. She unlocked the door and went in to the kitchen to call her parents and make sure everything was well with them and to tell them their jailbird was home, free on bail.

Lindsey called and talked with her parents and children before heading to her bedroom. She was way too restless to sleep so she put in a yoga tape and did yoga for an hour. She took a warm shower, went around the house to lock the doors, made a cup of decaffeinated tea and snuggled into bed to read her romance novel.

Reading a trashy novel and drinking warm tea felt wonderful. She'd never make it in jail. After reading one chapter she suddenly remembered the French toast. She hadn't eaten anything all day except a roll with butter on it that was provided at the police station. When she realized that, she laughed, thinking about eating a feast of bread and water for the rest of her life. At least she still had a sense of humor.

She thought about getting out of bed and having a piece of the French toast but decided that would have to wait for tomorrow morning. She didn't have the energy to get out of bed. She continued reading and in less than a minute she had fallen asleep. She was dreaming about chasing an unidentified man, she ran through a store trying to see past the next isle of food and he was always one step ahead. She kept getting angrier in her dream. After a slumber of six hours, she was woken up by her friend, the stately bird singing a song, and making Lindsey wonder what was so cheery about the day. Wasn't it time for that bird to fly south?

# CHAPTER 23
## Lunch with Tom

It was time to gather her friends and revisit how they should proceed now that she had been arrested. Michelle had been busy catching up from the women's week of interviewing and searching through John's office and house. Lindsey told her all she could but was still hesitant to tell her what Tom had told her, she kept their meeting a secret because she had promised Tom that she would. Michelle knew everything that Lindsey had been told that afternoon so she didn't feel like she was concealing important details of the case.

Monday and Tuesday went by and Lindsey didn't leave her house. Leo and Lilly were at her parents away from the media frenzy and were going to school and their after school activities as usual. Her parent's brought Leo and Lilly home after their activities and they all ate dinner together. The children knew that Lindsey had been arrested for their Dad's death and were reassured by Lindsey that she didn't do it and that she was on the case. Her children put all their faith in Lindsey and everything rested on her finding out who the real killer was.

Lindsey kept busy making phone calls to all the people she could on John's phone, rehashing the clues she already had and talking to Michelle about the case. It was Wednesday afternoon when the phone rang and to her surprise Tom was on the other end. "Lindsey, it's Tom," he sounded quiet and secretive.

"Hi Tom, what's going on, besides the rush to convict me for a crime I didn't do?" Lindsey couldn't help but snap at Tom even though she knew he didn't deserve it.

"I know. Lindsey, I can't talk over the phone with you and I know you can't leave your house without the news getting wind of it. If it's okay with you I'd like to come over this afternoon and go over some of the findings that the police have. And Lindsey this is off the record, don't invite your lawyer."

Lindsey thought about what Tom was asking her to do, and weighed her options. Tom seemed torn between following the strict procedures of the police force and going out on a limb and helping her prove her innocence. It didn't take her long to answer, "Of course, Tom, come over today. I'll fix us a late lunch. Can you make it over here around 1:00? It would be nice to see you and have your company." Why did she say that? It was true that she would love to see him but what if he read more into her statement than she wanted him to. She sighed on her end of the line, held her breath and turned around as she held the receiver away from her.

She cursed her romantic feelings she shouldn't be having. Why now, why should she feel this way in the midst of her murder conviction? As usual she thought she was a hopeless, impractical romantic, making up a dreamy filled encounter with someone who only wanted to help her because he felt it was the right thing to do.

Tom answered as business-like as he could, but he wanted to tell her he couldn't wait to see her too. "That sounds good Lindsey; I'll be over around 1:00. Thanks for having me over for lunch. You don't have to make anything if you don't want to."

"I know, but I have some food that needs to be eaten and I want to do it. I'll see you at 1:00 for lunch then, okay?" Lindsey couldn't wait to see Tom.

"Yes, I'll be there. I'm looking forward to seeing you and making sure you're okay." Tom's rich voice sent a wave of calmness throughout her body.

Lindsey lightly replied, "Thanks Tom, that means a lot to me."

"See you soon." And Tom hung up the phone.

Wow. Lindsey couldn't wait to hear what Tom had uncovered. A sense of peace surrounded her when she thought about Tom. It was going to be all right. They would find out together who and why John was murdered. So far, everything she uncovered led to nowhere. So much of the information seemed important but there was something missing.

She thought of Dave and Jess and Tara and wondered if the police had interviewed all of them and taken DNA samples. Tom was going to be a huge asset with his knowledge of the crime and his forthrightness with his information to Lindsey.

Michelle had learned that the police didn't have a match for the DNA under John's fingerprints. She wasn't told who had been tested and dismissed as a suspect due to the lack of a match. Michelle had also found out that a toothbrush was used to tighten the dental floss around John's neck, but her prints were not on the toothbrush, or on the handcuffs or steering wheel. That was something that Michelle thought would be valuable if this case went to trial.

Michelle had reviewed the surveillance cameras from the garage, but John's parking space was out of the picture and only two people had walked by the camera at around 4:00 in the morning. One of the individuals was a resident and the other one was a friend of the resident. The surveillance film had been useless. Other than the police interviews of John's neighbors and the party-goers the police didn't have anything that Lindsey didn't have.

Michelle was annoyed with the text messages and emails because they didn't prove anything. Michelle thought that Dave could have done it because of the insurance money but thought he was a weak suspect because his partner, according to the police report, was with him at 4:00 in the morning. They had been at an all night restaurant eating breakfast and had the receipt to prove it. They also had the confirmation from the server that Dave was with Henry, his partner. Still he could have made it to Tom's condo. Why hadn't anyone seen the murderer?

Tara's alibi was that she was out of town during the night of the party. She told Lindsey she had been in California, but Lindsey hadn't been able to prove or disprove her claim. Even If she actually was in California she seemed conniving enough to pay someone to murder John. Lindsey didn't feel like it was Tara, but still thought of her as a suspect.

Jess was the strongest suspect at this point. She had motive, was at the party, couldn't account for her time during the early morning when John was killed and was strong enough and mad enough to do it. Why hadn't the police arrested her? Lindsey would have to ask Tom this afternoon.

Thinking of Tom she went upstairs to put on a nicer outfit then her lounge pants and the t-shirt she had been wearing all week. It would be so nice to see him. She might even go to her Thursday night yoga class tomorrow and brave the media. She needed to get out before she lost her mind. Lindsey decided to wear a pair of tight blue jeans and a light blue sweater, put on some short black boots and checked herself in the mirror. Not bad; being a suspect in a murder case was one way to lose weight. She brushed her hair, applied some makeup and then went back downstairs to make lunch for Tom.

Lindsey had some chicken breasts, corn tortillas, jalapenos and enchilada sauce in her refrigerator and pantry. She grilled the chicken and assembled the enchiladas in a baking pan to place in her oven 30 minutes before Tom's arrival. It was already 12:00 so she didn't have much longer to wait. She decided to go and pay her bills and watch TV before Tom arrived.

At 12:30 she placed the enchilada dish in the oven and started some water to make rice. Her face was hot so she went to check herself in the mirror once more before Tom came. This isn't a date, she reminded herself, but still it couldn't hurt to look good.

Just as she had finished applying more lipstick the doorbell rang, finally Tom was here. Lindsey's bubbly voice answered the door, "Hi, come on in." Lindsey opened the door wider and let Tom in.

He was wearing a brown leather fall coat, cut to fit his body over a white shirt with old faded blue jeans and brown leather boots. She checked him out and her mind drifted. Tom, her handsome cowboy was coming to scoop her up and ride off into the sunset….. that lead, of course, to a fancy five-star hotel resort. Lindsey got back to reality, shut down her imagination and showed Tom into the kitchen.

She turned to look at Tom, "I hope you like spicy food. I've made some enchiladas and rice. Do you want something to drink? Would you care for a diet coke or some water?" Lindsey was nervous and talking too fast.

Tom smiled at Lindsey, "A diet coke would be great." Tom sat down at the table and Lindsey brought over a diet coke.

She continued saying, "The food should be finished, I'll get it out and then we can sit and talk." After putting two plates together Lindsey and Tom sat there and looked at each other, took several bites and began discussing the case.

Tom looked at Lindsey, "These enchiladas taste great. Thanks for making lunch." Then Tom settled down to talk about business. "I came here because I wanted to go over some of the evidence with you."

Lindsey brightened up. "Maybe something will pop out at us."

After finishing a bite of rice Tom replied, "Exactly. That's why I'm here. The police know I'm here, there was no way I could have made it to your house unseen. But I told my superior that we were going to discuss the arraignment on Friday. And I told them that we would be discussing procedural aspects with you and your lawyer. They don't need to know that she's not here. I know I've said it before but whatever we discuss today is off the record. I'm here because I believe you're innocent, but many people think you did it and I've got to follow their orders. Do you know what I mean?"

Of course she did; everyone thought she was guilty except Tom. She loved him for it. "Tom, I trust you too. I'd never tell what we are about to discuss to anyone. Why would I shoot myself in the foot? I need all the friends I can get right now."

Tom spoke seriously to her, "Good, here is what we found out; remember all of this information is between you and me. Michelle will get all of this after the arraignment, but I couldn't wait until then." His eyes stared intently at Lindsey.

Lindsey was nervous, "What is it? What else do the police have on me besides the blood and fingerprints? Michelle was saying that there was an eyewitness?"

Tom calmed her down, "The eyewitness was weak. I wouldn't count on her statement getting to trial. They used her for the purpose of getting an arrest and to try to intimidate you to confess. She said she thought a woman that was your height was in the garage with John in the early morning hours.

She couldn't identify anything except for the woman's height and that the woman had blond hair. Her statement won't hold up in court.

There are some other things though. They found the same type of dental floss that was used for the murder in your bedroom bathroom. Circumstantial evidence, because a lot of people have that type of dental floss. They also took your knife block because the knife that was used in the murder was determined to be from your set."

"What?" Lindsey choked on her bite of lunch. After taking a drink of her diet coke, she recovered but after what Tom told her, she lost her appetite. "What is going on? I didn't do it, but I can see now why they think I did. It's too strange. I can't make any sense of it at all."

Tom confided, "Me either. Now you know why everyone thinks you did it. I still have questions though. Why would your finger prints be on the knife and the dental floss case and other items were wiped down? That doesn't make sense to me."

"Thanks, I was thinking the same thing, but what will other people think?" Lindsey's voice felt hollow.

"Let's not worry about that right now. What did you uncover during your week of investigation?" It was Lindsey's turn to trust Tom and give him everything she knew.

Lindsey tried to talk calmly, she took several breathes and then told Tom everything, "We talked with Tara and Jess. Both of them accuse each other and both of them have a great motive. Tara has a contract with John to help her with her acting career. She was intending to pay him back but now that John is dead she won't have to. Jess is so angry at John for cheating on her that she also could have easily done it. Dave has a duel life and had issues with John about how to run the company. He gets complete control over their practice and has signed up a lot of John's patients, making him a lot more money." Lindsey continued to fill Tom in on what she and her friends had found out over the past week and a half; while Tom listened he finished his lunch.

Tom sat back and reflected on the case but said, "You are a remarkable woman. You've done all that work on your own, you took initiative and I'm really impressed." It wasn't the comment that Lindsey expected and her face started turning hot, she hoped she wasn't red. She could only reply, "Thanks."

Tom looked at her and then he shifted gears again, back to the murder. "I did try to find out who was calling John all the time. It was a cell phone number. We couldn't figure out an account associated with the number since it's no longer in service. It could have been a prepaid phone with cards coming from any store, Target, Wal-Mart, you name it. We did trace where the calls were coming from. The calls were coming from the town of Delafield."

The news didn't sound off any bells for Lindsey. "It seems like we have all these other leads, but the evidence that is most compelling leads right back to me. I get all the insurance money and the concrete evidence points to me."

Tom rubbed his chin in a contemplative manner. "I know. There has got to be something that we're missing. What was so unusual about the crime scene was John's teeth were pulled out and strung to the mirror. It's so odd; I can't imagine you doing that."

Lindsey's face said it all, "I can't imagine anyone doing that. Did the killer pull out all of his teeth while he was still alive, to torture him?"

Tom speculated, "They probably did pull out his teeth to torture him while he was still alive. The even stranger part of that scene was that they only pulled out his eye teeth. It was torture, a ruthless act, something I hope I never have to see again."

Lindsey contemplated this new piece of information. "Wow, someone is really insane. The only one I could think of that was angry enough at Tom to want to torture him was Jess. Did you take a sample of her DNA?"

"Yes, it didn't match the DNA under John's fingernails. We've taken approximately 75 samples of DNA from people and not one has been a match. There were some long strands of blond hair too, but they came from a wig and therefore we couldn't get any DNA from it."

Lindsey looked at Tom and noticed how tired he looked and how tired she felt. At that moment she wished they were merely an old couple and were happily eating lunch together before taking a walk or going shopping together for a dishwasher; something domestic and normal.

Snap out of it, and get back to reality. Lindsey got up and put the dishes in the sink. Once the dishes were cleared Lindsey sat down again at the table. "I don't know what to do, Tom. I feel like I'm being cornered and there's no way out."

Tom continued to stare at Lindsey with intensity. He placed his hand on her thigh. "Don't worry, Lindsey, I'm not going to stop searching for who did this. What we discussed today put more light on which way I'm going to proceed. I'm going to look more intensely at Jess, Tara and Dave. Try not to worry. The police have interviewed all three of them but there might be something that we're missing." Lindsey didn't hear a word he was saying; she only felt the pressure of his hand on her thigh.

Tom knew he shouldn't have touched Lindsey, he knew it was a bad move. He couldn't resist the temptation of her. He wanted to feel her and let her know that he liked her without saying it to her. He only had two days before the arraignment and didn't know if that would be enough time to find out who murdered Johnny Wang.

Tom took his hand off Lindsey's thigh before he did something he'd regret. He cleared his throat. "I better get going," he said this half-heartedly. He wanted desperately to stay.

"Of course, you have to go." Lindsey recovered from the unexpected warm touch of Tom. Lindsey led Tom out the door. She wanted him to hug her and kiss her goodbye.

Instead Tom said, "I'll be in touch. Thanks for lunch, it was great."

"Thanks Tom, let me know if you find anything more and thanks for coming over today." She gave a little smile, she wanted to say so much more but all she could do was close the door and watch Tom walk away.

Her heart was heavy and she felt drained. Once again, alone in her house, she started to feel dread. It began in her toes and worked itself up until it was in every cell of body.

# CHAPTER 24
## Yoga Class

It was 3:10 and time to pick up the kids from school and take them to their after school activities. Lindsey had called her mom and told her that she was ready to get out of the house and brave the media. She looked out the drive and was relieved to see that the media was gone; they gave up on her after a couple of days so she escaped out of her drive and to the kids' schools.

She dropped the kids off at their practices and decided to go to the 4:30 yoga class at the Milwaukee spa. She really needed to stretch and focus on nothing but the stances and try to free her mind of all the negative thoughts that kept continuously popping up.

When she arrived at the spa she parked and looked around. She noticed that Brooke's Mercedes and Traci's old beat up jeep were also parked in the lot and was hoping they would be at the yoga class too. She hadn't been talking with them the past week as much as she would have liked to. With all of the preparations that Michelle was making, she didn't have time.

Michelle could talk and talk and talk, sometimes they were on the phone for four or five hours. It was hard for Lindsey to even follow what Michelle was saying and she found herself nodding on the other end of the phone as if Michelle could see her. Michelle never seemed to mind the long silence on the other end and always continued to talk and tell Lindsey about what she had found out and how they were going to present her defense. For the arraignment they were going to ask to have the trial as soon as possible, because right now the prosecutor's case had many holes that could be poked at. Lindsey got out of her car and decided to try and not think about the arraignment and the trial.

She walked to the locker room but didn't see Brooke or Traci anywhere. When she had finished changing her clothes, she started to feel calmer and was ready to commit her mind to the yoga class. She entered the room and was surrounded by the calming tones of the yoga music, and her shoulders started to move away from her ears. She was glad she had decided to get out.

"Hey, Lindsey, over here," Brooke was waving her over to where she and Traci had already placed their mats and blocks.

"Hi, I'm glad you two are here. I missed you guys this week. I have been going crazy at home, all alone except for Merlin. He's been great staying by my side wherever I go, but he's not much of a conversationalist."

Brooke smiled, "It's so great that you're here. I've missed you too, but knew how busy you were with Michelle. How do you like her?" Brooke was the one who recommended Michelle to Lindsey.

"She's great, really smart and thorough. Sometimes, too thorough. I feel like I'm in really good hands. I'll tell you more later; right now I just want to focus on the class. Where's Marci?" Marci was the yoga instructor.

Traci answered, "I don't know, I haven't seen her yet, but we still have five minutes," Traci was on her mat stretching her hamstrings.

Traci added, "You look good, Lindsey; I think I'd be a complete wreck if I were in your shoes." Traci continued stretching as she talked with Lindsey.

"I know. I mean, not that I think I look great or anything, but I'm okay. Somehow I know that the real murderer will be found, and Michelle has been very reassuring to me this week. She has a great case for it being someone other than me, there's a lot of room for doubt in the case. And Tom came over to see me." She said the last sentence with a twinkle in her eye.

Just then Marci walked in and started the class, Traci whispered, "He did? What did he have to say?"

Lindsey whispered back, "Do you want to go into the Jacuzzi after yoga? I'll tell you then."

"Okay, sounds good," Traci replied.

All three of the women concentrated on what Marci was telling them. 'Sit back on your heels, raise your arms shoulder height and reach for the walls, now lift your arms over your head and lace your fingers together. Stretch your arms to the ceiling as you sit down on your heels.'

Lindsey listened and was absorbed with feeling how her body moved and was soothed by the simple movements. At the end of class she didn't want to get up off her mat and face the reality of what her life had become. Marci gently told the class to open their eyes and slowly turn to one side before sitting up. Lindsey felt terrific; she could have stayed there all night.

"Let's go, Lindsey, get out of your trance," Brooke prodded Lindsey back into the present.

"Oh, I don't want to get up and go home yet. This was so relaxing."

Traci said, "Let's go to the Jacuzzi now, that will be relaxing too, and then you can fill me in on Tom's visit." Traci was getting up off her mat and started rolling it up.

"Okay, I guess I can get up for that reason." Lindsey got up and rolled up her mat and the three women headed for the locker room to change into their swimsuits.

After changing they entered the Jacuzzi room which was warm and soothing. Somehow the Milwaukee Spa had found a way to have a Jacuzzi that didn't overpower the user's eyes or nose with the smell and burning sensation of chlorine. Instead there was a faint hint of vanilla in the room from the candles that burned on a side table that held soft terry cloth towels in baskets. The candles and the smell of vanilla along with the hot jets were just what the women needed.

Brooke's eyes were closed as she said, "This is great. I haven't been in here since last fall and the rain today is making my bones hurt." Brooke was sitting on one side of Lindsey and Traci was on the other side of her.

Lindsey replied to Brooke, "I know what you mean. My mom has a steel rod in her neck. She had it placed in her neck after it was broken when she was in a car accident. We were just commenting this morning how the cold, damp weather was making our bodies hurt. I feel really bad for her; she can't even move her neck from side to side it's so sore. I'll have to remember to invite her to come for a soak sometime. I never think to ask my mom to come along and she has helped me out so much with the kids and has been so supportive. I'll have to make a mental note of it. It might sooth her neck." Lindsey sat back and enjoyed the jets pulsating over her aching shoulders.

The women were sitting in the Jacuzzi with their eyes closed and with their heads resting on the back of the Jacuzzi side.

Traci replied, "A steel rod, how terrible. I was in a car accident too, about four years ago and my mom helped me through it. She stayed by my side at the hospital day and night. That's when I had to have cosmetic surgery on my mouth. John did the repair work; he fixed me right up. I was such a mess.

My teeth were smashed right through my tongue and I had to have both eye teeth pulled. It was the only way to save the rest of my teeth and make my smile as beautiful as it is now."

Lindsey opened her eyes as Traci smiled and for the first time Lindsey realized that Traci didn't have any eye teeth; that's why her smile was different. Then she remembered what Tom had told her about the crime scene. The murderer had pulled out John's eye teeth and had strung them up on the rear view mirror.

Lindsey looked right at Traci and a cold shiver slowly crept all over her body. Lindsey tried not to react to how she was feeling. But had the expression on her face given her away? Did Traci guess what she was thinking? Lindsey closed her eyes again and luckily Brooke started talking, but Lindsey didn't hear a word of it.

She wanted to get out of there before she started shaking and she wanted to call Tom as soon as she could. Thoughts were making her head spin......the eye teeth from the crime scene. She could barely breathe as the hot tub started to feel as if it were a hundred degrees too hot, making her struggle for every breath. Meanwhile, the inside of her heart felt like a frozen lake, barely able to beat.

Lindsey couldn't take it anymore and abruptly got out of the tub. "Hey you guys, I'm not feeling so well right now. I don't know if the hot water got to me or if I'm dehydrated. I haven't had any water today and am starting to get dizzy." Lindsey grabbed a towel. She could barely look at Traci but she made a concerted effort to steady her voice and stare directly at her and then at Brooke. She didn't want Traci to guess that she knew about the eye teeth from the murder scene.

Traci looked concerned. "Do you want me to walk with you to the locker room?"

Lindsey looked at Traci and eased her mouth into a smile. "No, no I'll be okay. Just finish up here. I'm going to go drink some water and then head home. Don't worry." Lindsey wanted to run out of there, but she wrapped the towel around her and slowly walked to the door, "Bye you guys. I'll call you tonight or tomorrow."

"Okay, Bye," Brooke waved and then put her head back against the side of the Jacuzzi and closed her eyes.

"Bye," Traci watched her leave and somehow Lindsey thought Traci knew she had been found out.

Lindsey felt Traci's eyes on her, watching Lindsey go until she couldn't see her anymore.

Shit, thought Lindsey. It can't be one of her best friends. But as she got out of her suit and into her clothes she put all the pieces together.

The knife, the dental floss, the blond woman that Rita had seen with John, a woman that John would go to his car with, the cell phone with the calls made from Traci's neighborhood in Delafield.

Lindsey shivered and practically ran to her car. She called her mom after she was in the car with the doors locked. "Mom, could you pick up Leo and Lilly from their practices? I've got to meet with Tom. Something important has happened and I've got to see him tonight."

"What is it, Lindsey? Are you in more trouble?" There was anxiety in Lindsey's mother's voice.

Worry resounded in Lindsey's voice, "Mom, no, I can't talk about it right now. I'm not sure but I think I may know who murdered John."

"Who?"

"I'm not sure yet, mom, but I've got to go. Can you get the kids?"

"Of course I can. And Lindsey, be careful."

Hurriedly Lindsey said, "Of course I will, mom. That's why I've got to get a hold of Tom. He'll be able to help me. I'll talk to you later tonight and fill you in, after I talk to Tom about it."

"Okay Lindsey."

"Bye Mom."

"Bye." Lindsey raced home. She got in her house and locked all the doors.

She went to her office and got Tom's private home number. It was 7:00, hopefully he was home. The phone rang and rang and then an answering machine picked up. After listening to the message Lindsey left a rushed, frantic message. "Tom, I think I know who murdered John. Come over to my house as soon as you can. I'll be waiting here for you. Please hurry, I need your help."

Next Lindsey called Tom's cell phone, again there was no answer. Where was he? She went to the kitchen to pour herself a glass of wine and to try to piece everything together. She was shaking. Why would her good friend do it? What had gone on between John and Traci?

Lindsey was terrified at the prospect of learning the why and could only sit and wait for Tom to get back to her. She sat down in her living room and turned on the TV, with her wine in one hand and the phone clenched in her white knuckled hand she sat and stared at the TV while hoping Tom would call. At 8:00 the doorbell rang.

# CHAPTER 25
## A Confession

Lindsey was watching a home decorating show when she heard the doorbell ring. Finally, she thought, what had taken Tom so long to get back to her? And why hadn't he called first? She got up off the couch and went to answer the door. "Tom?" She opened up the door and before she knew it, the door was being pushed open by a tall, blond woman with a gun in her hand and wearing leather gloves.

"No, it's not Tom." It was Traci made up in a wig looking disheveled and crazy. She was wielding a gun and had it pointed directly at Lindsey. Lindsey didn't know what to do, she took a step back and then another until she couldn't move back anymore. The wall supported her as she watched Traci pace around her living room, with the gun in her hand and talking a mile a minute.

Her pupils were pinpoints that darted around the room not settling on anything. Her blond wig looked like it was hastily put on and hair strands were tangled around each other. Lindsey thought Traci looked insane, and by what Traci was telling her Lindsey knew she was looking at an extremely agitated sick person.

Aggravation was evident in Traci's words as she spoke to Lindsey in a hostile, excited tone. "Lindsey, why did you have to do such a good job investigating John's murder? You should have left it alone. There's no way that a court would have found you guilty. You dug yourself into your grave now. I have no choice but to get rid of you. I love you, but there's no way I'm going to go to jail for John's murder. He deserved to die and you deserved to be free from him. We all deserved to be free from him."

Traci's voice got even louder, "He was no good, Lindsey. Every relationship he was in was tainted by sleeping around with other women, probably three or four at a time. I couldn't stand it. He was the reason my husband cheated on me and left me."

Traci waved her gun around, "My ex-husband always looked up to John. When he saw what John was doing after he divorced you, he thought that was the lifestyle of the rich and famous. He wanted to be just like John. Your John was the reason why Mark left me, and my life has been shit ever since. I've never forgiven John. I had to do it, don't you see? I'm sure Mark will stop his womanizing now too and come back to me. John was never going to stop; he kept up his two-timing, three-timing, devious ways no matter who he was with. I murdered him for the sake of all women, but especially for you and for me!"

The words came out in a tirade of angry emotion and sincere conviction. Traci believed every word she said. Lindsey couldn't believe what she was hearing. She didn't realize her friend was so ill and had such a distorted view of reality.

She said the only thing she could think of that might save her life and get Traci to calm down. "Traci, you're right, we suffered because of John. We don't need to suffer anymore. It's over. You don't need to go to jail." Lindsey thought but didn't say what she really felt. Maybe Traci shouldn't go to jail, but definitely she should be put in an insane asylum.

Traci wasn't buying what Lindsey was saying. With a total disregard of what Lindsey said Traci shouted, "I won't go to jail because you're not going to be able to tell anyone that I murdered John. Everyone is looking for a tall, blond woman and they'll never suspect one of your best friends. Lindsey, this murder is going to go unsolved. No one saw me come up here and I know your kids are over at your parents' house. I called over there and talked to your mom on the pretense of asking her how she's been holding up. Your mom always liked me. You and I are going to take a nice little walk to the end of your yard; a little fall from the bluff into Lake Michigan should do the trick. I'm sorry for you, Lindsey. But I want my husband back and I'm not going to jail." Traci was shaking, her eyes were deranged.

Lindsey could only plead with Traci and try to buy more time to think of a way out of the situation. "Traci, don't do this. I won't tell anyone, you'll get Mark back and my mouth will stay closed. I'll tell them I did it so they don't investigate anymore," Lindsey wasn't really going to do that and Traci guessed as much.

"Yeah right; if I were you I'd say the same thing. Let's go." Traci waved the gun and Lindsey didn't have a choice but to start walking through the house, past the family room and through the French doors that led to the terrace and back yard.

She couldn't believe Traci was the murderer and was here to kill her. Somehow she would have to overpower Traci. It was too bad she hadn't been taking Tai Kwon Do, she didn't think her yoga training would do the trick.

Just as she was headed out the French doors and trying to think of a plan out of her predicament the doorbell rang. She screamed and kicked Traci in the shin. "TOM, HELP!"

Tom came rushing through the house and found Lindsey and Traci in the family room fighting over control of the gun. Lindsey wanted to get the gun away from Traci before it went off and killed one of them. Tom stood with his gun drawn, but couldn't shoot. The women were entangled in a game of twister.

With an all out effort Lindsey grabbed Traci's arm and turned it back until she had to let go of the gun. It dropped to the ground and Lindsey kicked it to Tom.

The two women sat and looked at each other, contemplating their next move. Lindsey stood up to go over to Tom. Tom kept his gun trained on Traci who seemed to be in a trance. He spoke firmly and with authority, "Stand up slowly Traci, and put your arms up in front of you."

In a slow whispery voice Traci said, "I had to do it." She was staring off.

Tom repeated the command, "Stand up slowly and put your arms in front of you over your head," Traci did as she was told. She stood up, but as soon as she was standing she ran out the French doors.

"Tom, go get her, she's headed for the bluff. She's going to jump!" Lindsey was screaming. Tom took two big strides and was out the French doors after Traci. Lindsey could only watch as Tom chased Traci. "Hurry Tom!" She couldn't stomach the thought of her friend lying broken at the bottom of the bluff. Tom ran as fast as he could, but Traci was fast too. He barely reached her in time but was able to tackle her and save her life. He placed the handcuffs on her and read her the *Miranda* rights before bringing her back into Lindsey's house.

Traci was sobbing; she looked angry and sad, upset that she had been caught but not for what she had done. She said, "I can't believe this is happening. I try to do something nice for you and it backfires."

Traci was so twisted she didn't even realize what she had done. Lindsey didn't know what to do, she looked at Traci. "Traci, you need help."

She looked at Tom. "What do we do now?"

Tom had called for backup and police sirens could be heard in the distance. Tom needed to go down to the station and file a report. He would be up all night. "I've got to go down to the station. This is over." A hint of a smile played at Tom's mouth.

Lindsey spoke next, "Tom, call me when you get the chance. I'm glad you showed up when you did." She wanted to hug Tom and collapse in his arms. She wanted to be comforted by his warmth.

Tom replied, "I'll call you as soon as I can. As soon as the police are here I'll take Traci down to the police station. You'll need to give a statement to the police. I'll let them know to take it from here. You've had enough of the station. Are you going to be alright here by yourself?"

Lindsey smiled at Tom, "I'll be fine. It's over. This nightmare is over." Lindsey's life would never be the same. She was too shocked to understand all of Traci's motives, but she was relieved that the murderer had been caught.

Tom looked at Lindsey; he wanted to say so much more but he said, "Okay. Stay here tonight; call your mom to come over with your children. I'll call you later tonight to see how you're doing." He had kept a firm hold of Traci's arm while they were talking. Tom left with Traci in handcuffs.

Traci didn't look at Lindsey as she left. Her eyes were looking down at nothing. Lindsey's friend was led away looking small, frail and misplaced. After the police left, Lindsey locked the door behind her and then called to talk with her parents and Leo and Lilly.

# CHAPTER 26
## The End. Case Crackers, Meeting three

It had been a week since Traci had come over to Lindsey's house and confessed to the murder. The women gathered at Lindsey's breakfast nook table, drinking wine and eating cheese and crackers.

Julia said, "I can't believe that Traci killed John because she thought he was the reason for her and Mark's divorce. Poor Traci, she went completely insane." Julia started the conversation and it took off.

The women pieced together all of the clues that they had uncovered from the past month.

Lindsey spoke in a 'matter of fact' voice, but sadly too, "She took that knife that I cut my finger on the night we went to John's party. I was cutting limes for our drinks and she must have pretended to put it in the sink. She probably hadn't intended to even have the knife, but when I cut myself she seized the opportunity. She also took the dental floss from my kids' room from their bathroom. They had the thick type of dental floss that was used by Traci in the murder. Funny, that dental floss was given to them by John."

Lindsey took a sip of wine, "To make sure that the police found the dental floss in my bathroom, she must have come in that one night and put it in my bathroom. That was the night that Tom came over and because of that night I had all the locks changed. I can't believe she was so psychotic, so delusional. I hope she gets help." Lindsey was sipping wine and staring out the patio doors.

Julia looked with concern at her friend, "You're awfully forgiving of her. She did kill your ex-husband."

Lindsey answered quietly, "I know, and I'm angry more than you know, and sad for Leo and Lilly. But I don't think that Traci knew the reality of what she was doing. She blames John for her divorce and that's crazy. She was fixated on John. She followed him everywhere, called him endlessly. She told him that she was going to give the insurance papers to me and then went to the attorney as me and signed them. I can't believe how sneaky she was, it's freaky really. It's downright scary and makes you wonder how well you know your best friends. I wonder if she had my driver's license too." Lindsey's voice had gotten louder.

Lindsey shook her head, remembering the time when she and John had a delicious lunch together. She added, "I hope you guys aren't planning anything weird. If you are, can you let me know so that I can get you some help and get the hell out of your way?"

Julia was eyeing Lindsey with one eyebrow raised, worried about Lindsey's state of mind. She wanted to reassure Lindsey that what happened with Traci was an anomaly, nothing that would happen again.

Julia responded, "Traci was obviously depressed since her divorce and never let us know how she was feeling. We could have helped her if we would have known. That's what secrets do, they make you go crazy. She could have come to any one of us for help and we would have listened."

Brooke added to Julia's explanation. "We would have helped if we would have known. She married Mark and that's all she wanted. She didn't have anything else; well, she had us but I guess she felt like she didn't have anyone once he was gone."

Lindsey thought that she knew her friends and was almost certain that each one of them could stand on their own feet. She didn't know Traci had such low self esteem. She said, "Traci hid her insecurities and jealousy well. I got caught up in her insane life quite by accident. And poor John, he's dead. It's strange; he never said anything to me about Traci."

Brooke tried to make sense out of the situation, "He probably didn't want to upset you. He obviously, after some point in time, didn't want a relationship with her and she wouldn't take no for an answer. She was spying on him. John was smart and knew she wasn't after him for the right reasons. Remember all of the phone calls on John's phone. He never called her back. They were all missed calls without any messages and none of the 'recent calls' were to her number. She was absolutely determined to carry out her plan."

Heather tilted her head to one side and asked, "Okay, what about Dave, Jess and Tara? I was certain it was one of them."

Brooke agreed, "Me too. They all acted odd. Well, now we know that Dave is gay….not that it matters. He is strange but I think it's because we don't know him that well."

"I'm sure I'm to blame for that one." Lori was now part of their group. She had helped out during their investigation and the women had bonded with her. Lori thought it was Dave, and followed his movements like a hawk. "Anything he did I thought was suspicious. Now that we know that he's not a quiet, serial killer, I guess half the things were 'normal' and half was because he was trying to hide the fact that he was gay. I guess he thought we'd care or the patients would care." She gave a little half laugh remembering how she hounded Dave.

Heather asked, "What about Jess and Tara?"

"They're both weird but harmless." Brooke took a sip of wine before bringing the conversation back to Traci. "Now we can forget about Lindsey going to trial but what are we going to do about Traci?"

Julia had a heart of gold and understood a lot about mental illness. "She'll get help. She'll be okay. We'll have to help her even though she was deceptive and murdered John. We are her friends, but we have to consider your feelings Lindsey. What are you thinking?"

Lindsey grabbed her wine glass a little bit too hard as she looked at her friends and wondered how she would feel if she were Traci, then she answered. "Of course we should support her and help her. I probably won't see her until she is more stable. The look in her eyes when she was here was like a possessed tiger. I'll listen to her after she has help, but she needs to realize that what she did was wrong before I'll see her." Lindsey let that hang in the air and then switched subjects. The room fell quiet for a minute.

Lindsey decided to let her friends know about her feelings for Tom. In an excited voice she let out, "Okay, my next news has nothing to do with the murder. Well, it's related but not really." Lindsey strung the rest of the woman in the room along with a slow grin and a pause.

Finally Heather asked impatiently, "What is it Lindsey?"

"It's Tom. I've got a date with him tomorrow night. He's taking me to the Milwaukee Rep."

The women raised their glasses, gave a little cheer and laughed together. They were all smiling at Lindsey's news. Who knew what tomorrow would bring but on this Wednesday night, things were as 'back to normal' as they could be.

The five women sitting at the table were enjoying each others' company, commiserating with each other and sharing their present lives while dreaming about the future and the possibilities to come.

Made in the USA